Ed Dawson should have known better
than to get involved with his boss's
daughter, but with a girl like Helen
Chalmers it was difficult – if not
impossible – to refuse her anything.
So when Helen suggested a holiday
together in a lonely Italian villa, Ed
found himself agreeing – even though
it meant risking his promotion and
his job.
But there was a lot more at stake
than even Ed realized, for when he
arrived at the villa he found Helen
lying at the bottom of a cliff – dead...

YOU FIND HIM – I'LL FIX HIM

Also by James Hadley Chase

AN ACE UP MY SLEEVE
JUST ANOTHER SUCKER
I WOULD RATHER STAY POOR
LAY HER AMONG THE LILIES
DOUBLE SHUFFLE
THE SOFT CENTRE

and published by Corgi Books

James Hadley Chase

You Find Him –
I'll Fix Him

CORGI BOOKS
A DIVISION OF TRANSWORLD PUBLISHERS LTD

YOU FIND HIM – I'LL FIX HIM

A CORGI BOOK 0 552 09603 2

Originally published in Great Britain
by Robert Hale Limited

PRINTING HISTORY
Robert Hale edition published 1956
Corgi edition published 1974

This book is set in 10pt Times

Corgi Books are published by
Transworld Publishers Ltd.,
Cavendish House, 57–59 Uxbridge Road,
Ealing, London W.5.

Made and printed in Great Britain by
Cox & Wyman Ltd., London, Reading and Fakenham

You Find Him – I'll Fix Him

PART I

I

On a hot July afternoon I was dozing in my office, being offensive to no one and with nothing important to do, when the telephone bell brought me awake with a start.

I picked up the receiver.

'Yes, Gina?'

'It's Mr. Sherwin Chalmers on the line,' Gina said breathlessly.

I became breathless too.

'Chalmers? For Pete's sake! He's not here in Rome?'

'He's calling from New York.'

I got back some of my breath, but not all of it.

'Okay, put him through,' I said, and sat forward, no calmer than a spinster who has found a man under her bed.

For four years I had been in charge of the Rome office of the *New York Western Telegram*, and this was my first contact with Chalmers who owned the paper.

He was a multi-millionaire, a dictator in his own particular field and a brilliant newspaper man. To have Sherwin Chalmers call you on the telephone was like having the President ask you to tea at the White House.

I put the receiver to my ear and waited. There were the usual clicks and pops, then a cool female voice said, 'Is that Mr. Dawson?'

I said it was.

'Will you hold on for Mr. Chalmers, please?'

I said I would, and wondered how she would have reacted if I had told her I wouldn't.

There were more clicks and pops, then a voice that sounded like a hammer beating on an anvil barked, 'Dawson?'

'Yes, Mr. Chalmers.'

There was a pause and I wondered what the kick was going to be. It had to be a kick. I couldn't imagine the great man would be calling unless something had displeased him.

What came next surprised me.

'Look, Dawson,' he said, 'my daughter will be arriving in Rome to-morrow on the eleven-fifty plane. I want you to meet her and take her to the Excelsior Hotel. My secretary has fixed a reservation for her. Will you do that?'

This was the first time I had heard he had a daughter. I knew he had been married four times, but a daughter was news to me.

'She'll be studying at the university,' he went on, words tumbling out of his mouth as if he were bored with the subject and wanted to get done with it as quickly as possible. 'If she wants anything, I've told her to call on you. I don't want you to give her any money. That is important. She's getting sixty dollars a week from me, and that is quite enough for a young girl. She has a job of work to do, and if she does it the way I want her to do it, she won't need much money. But I'd like to know someone is at hand in case she needs anything or gets ill or something.'

'She hasn't anyone here then?' I asked, not liking the sound of this. As a nurse-maid, I don't rate myself very high.

'I've given her some introductions, and she'll be at the university, so she'll get to know people,' Chalmers said. I could hear the impatience in his voice.

'Okay, Mr. Chalmers. I'll meet her, and if she wants anything, I'll fix it.'

'That's what I want.' There was a pause, then he said, 'Things all right at your end?' He didn't sound particularly interested.

I said they were a little slow.

There was another long pause, and I could hear him breathing heavily. I had a vision of a short, fat man with a chin like Mussolini's, eyes like the points of an ice-pick and a mouth like a bear trap.

'Hammerstock was talking to me about you last week,' he said abruptly. 'He seems to think he should get you back here.'

I drew in a long, slow breath. I had been aching to hear this news for the past ten months.

'Well, I'd certainly like that if it could be arranged.'

'I'll think about it.'

The click in my ear told me he had hung up. I replaced the receiver, pushed back my chair to give me a little breathing space and stared at the opposite wall while I thought how nice it would be to get home after four years in Italy. Not that I disliked Rome, but I knew, so long as I was holding down this job, I wouldn't get an increase in pay nor a chance of promotion. If I were going to get somewhere I would only get there in New York.

After a few minutes of intensive brooding that got me nowhere, I went into Gina's office.

Gina Valetti, dark, pretty, gay and twenty-three, had been my secretary and general factotum since I had taken over the Rome office. It had always baffled me that a girl with her looks and shape could have been so smart.

She paused in her typing and looked inquiringly at me. I told her about Chalmer's daughter.

'Sounds terrific, doesn't it?' I said, sitting on the edge of her desk. 'Some bouncing, fat undergrad needing my advice and attention: the things I do for *Western Telegram*!'

'She could be beautiful,' Gina said, her voice cool. 'Many American girls are beautiful and attractive. You could fall in love with her. If you married her you would be in a very happy position.'

'You've got marriage on the brain,' I said. 'All you Italian girls are the same. You haven't seen Chalmers—I have. She couldn't possibly be beautiful coming from his stable. Besides, he wouldn't want me for a son-in-law. He would have a lot bigger ideas for his daughter than me.'

She gave me a long, slow stare from under curled, black eyelashes, then lifted her pretty shoulders.

'Wait 'til you see her,' she said.

For once Gina was wrong, but then so was I. Helen Chalmers didn't appear to be beautiful, but neither was she fat and bouncing. She seemed to me to be completely negative. She was blonde, and she wore horn-rimmed spectacles, sloppy clothes and flat-heeled shoes. Her hair was screwed back off her face. She seemed as dull as only a very serious-minded college girl can be dull.

I met her at the airport and took her to the Excelsior Hotel. I said the usual polite things one says to a stranger, and she answered as politely. By the time I had got her to

9

the hotel I was so bored with her that I couldn't get away fast enough. I told her to call me at the office if she wanted anything, gave her my telephone number and bowed myself out. I was pretty sure she wouldn't call me. There was a touch of efficiency about her that convinced me that she could handle any situation that might crop up without my help or advice.

Gina sent flowers to the hotel in my name. She also had composed a cable to Chalmers to say the girl had arrived safely.

I felt there wasn't much else for me to do, and, as a couple of good stories broke around this time, I put Miss Chalmers out of my mind and forgot about her.

About ten days later, Gina suggested that I should call the girl and find out how she was getting on. This I did, but the hotel told me she had left six days ago, and they had no forwarding address.

Gina said I should find out where she was in case Chalmers wanted to know.

'Okay, you find out,' I said. 'I'm busy.'

Gina got her information from police headquarters. It seemed Miss Chalmers had taken a three-room furnished apartment off Via Cavour. Gina got the telephone number and I called her.

She sounded surprised when she came on the line, and I had to repeat my name twice before the nickel dropped. It seemed she had forgotten me as completely as I had forgotten her, and, oddly enough, this irritated me. She said everything was under control, and she was getting along fine, thank you. There was a hint of impatience in her voice that suggested she resented me inquiring about her, and also, she used that polite tone of voice that daughters of very rich men use when talking to their father's employees, and that infuriated me.

I cut the conversation short, reminded her again that if there was anything I could do I would do it, and hung up.

Gina who had got the set-up from my expression said tactfully, 'After all, she is the daughter of a millionaire.'

'Yeah, I know,' I said. 'From now on she can look after herself. She practically gave me the brush-off.'

We left it at that.

I heard no more of her for the next four weeks. I had a lot to do in the office as I was going on vacation in a couple

of months' time, and I wanted everything ship-shape for
Jack Maxwell who was coming out from New York to
relieve me.

I had planned to spend a week in Venice, and then go
south for three weeks to Ischia. This was my first long
vacation in four years, and I was looking forward to it. I
planned to travel alone. I like a little solitude when I can get
it, and I also like to be able to change my mind where to stay
and how long I would stay, and if I had a companion, I
wouldn't have this freedom of movement.

Four weeks and two days after I had spoken to Helen
Chalmers on the telephone, I had a call from Giuseppe
Frenzi, a good friend of mine who worked on *L'Italia del
Popolo*. He asked me to go with him to a party the film
producer, Guido Luccino, was throwing in honour of some
film star who had made a big hit at the Venice festival.

I like Italian parties. They are gracious and amusing, and
the food is always exciting. I said I would pick him up around
eight o'clock.

Luccino had a big apartment near Porta Pinciana. When
we got there, the carriage-way was packed with Cadillacs,
Rolls-Royces and Bugattis that made my 1954 Buick flinch
as I edged it into the last of the parking spaces.

It was a good party. I knew most of the people there.
Fifty per cent of them were Americans, and Luccino, who
cultivated Americans, had plenty of hard liquor circulating.
Around ten o'clock, and after a flock of straight whiskies, I
went on to the patio to admire the moon and to cool
off.

On the patio, alone, was a girl in a white evening gown.
Her naked back and shoulders looked like porcelain in the
moonlight. She was resting her hands on the balustrade, her
head tilted back while she stared up at the moon. The moonlight made her blonde hair look like spun glass. I wandered
over to her and paused by her side. I stared up at the moon
too.

'Pretty nice after the jungle inside,' I said.

'Yes.'

She didn't turn to look at me. I sneaked a look at her.

She was beautiful. Her features were small, her lips were
a glistening red; the moonlight sparkled in her eyes.

'I thought I knew everyone in Rome,' I said. 'How is it
I don't know you?'

She turned her head and looked at me. Then she smiled.

'You should know me, Mr. Dawson,' she said. 'Have I changed so much that you don't recognize me?'

I stared at her, and I felt a sudden thumping of my pulse and a tight feeling across my chest.

'I don't recognize you,' I said, thinking she was the loveliest woman I had seen in Rome, and how young and desirable she was.

She laughed.

'Are you so sure? I am Helen Chalmers.'

II

My first reaction when I heard who she was was to tell her how she had changed, how surprised I was to find her so beautiful, and stuff like that, but after looking into her moonlit eyes I had other ideas. I knew it would be a mistake to say the obvious.

I spent half an hour with her out on the patio. This unexpected meeting threw me off balance. I was sharply aware that she was my boss's daughter. She was cagey, too, but she wasn't dull. We kept the conversation on an impersonal plane. We talked about the party, who was who, and wasn't the band good and what a lovely night it was.

I was attracted to her the way a pin is attracted to a magnet. I couldn't keep my eyes off her. I couldn't believe this lovely creature was the same girl I had met at the airport: it just didn't seem possible.

Suddenly, from out of the stilted conversation we were making, she said, 'Have you a car here?'

Why, yes. It's in the carriage-way.'

'Will you take me back to my apartment?'

'What—now?' I was disappointed. 'The party will warm up in a little while. Wouldn't you like to dance?'

She stared at me. Her blue eyes were disconcertingly searching.

'I'm sorry. I didn't mean to drag you away. Don't bother; I can get a taxi.'

'You're not dragging me away. If you really want to go, I'll be happy to drive you home. I thought you were enjoying yourself here.'

She lifted her shoulders and smiled.

'Where is your car?'

'At the end of the line—a black Buick.'

'I'll meet you at the car then.'

She moved away, and as I made to accompany her, she lifted her hand in an unmistakable gesture. She was telling me we shouldn't be seen together.

I let her go on ahead while I lit a cigarette. This had suddenly become a conspiracy. I noticed my hands were unsteady. I gave her a couple of minutes, then I went back into the vast lounge that was packed with people, looked for Luccino, but couldn't see him and decided I'd let my thanks drift until to-morrow morning.

I walked out of the apartment, down the flight of stairs and down the long drive.

I found her sitting in the Buick. I got in beside her.

'It is just off Via Cavour.'

I drove away down Via Vittorio Veneto. At this hour the usual heavy traffic had thinned a little, and it only took me ten minutes to reach the street in which she lived. During the drive, neither of us said anything.

'Please stop here,' she said.

I pulled up and got out of the car. I went around and opened the off-side door for her. She got out and looked up and down the deserted street.

'You'll come up? I'm sure we have a lot to talk about,' she said.

I remembered again that she was my boss's daughter.

'I'd like to, but perhaps I'd better not,' I said. 'It's getting late. I don't want to disturb anyone.'

'You won't do that.'

She started off down the street, so I turned off the car's lights and went after her.

I am explaining this in detail because I don't want to give the wrong impression about my first relations with Helen. It may be difficult to believe, but if I had known there was no one in her apartment—no girlfriend, no servant, no nobody—wild horses wouldn't have dragged me inside. I didn't know. I thought there would at least be a servant.

All the same I was uneasy about going into her apartment at that time of night. I kept wondering what Sherwin Chalmers would think if someone told him I had been seen entering his daughter's apartment at ten forty-five at night.

My future and all that it meant to me was in Chalmers' hands. A word from him and I would be out of the news-paper racket for good. Fooling around with his daughter could be as dangerous as fooling around with a rattlesnake.

Thinking about it later, I realized that Helen also wasn't taking any chances. She had prevented me from accompanying her from Luccino's apartment, and she had fixed it that I had parked my car two hundred yards from the entrance to her apartment block so if one of my bright friends happened to see the car he wouldn't put two and two together.

We rode up in the automatic elevator, meeting no one in the lobby. We got inside her apartment without anyone seeing us.

When she had shut the front door and had taken me into a large pleasant lounge, lit by shaded lamps and decorated with bowls of flowers, I suddenly got the impression that we were the only two in the apartment.

She dropped her wrap on a chair and went over to an elaborate cocktail cabinet.

'Will you have rye or gin?'

'You aren't alone here, are you?' I asked.

She turned and stared at me. In the shaded lights she looked stunning.

'Why, yes—is that a crime?'

I felt my palms turn moist.

'I can't stay. You should know that.'

She continued to stare at me, her eyebrows lifting.

'Are you so frightened of my father then?'

'It's not a matter of being frightened of your father,' I said, angry that she had so shrewdly put her finger right on the point. 'I can't stay here alone with you, and you must know it.'

'Oh, don't be stupid,' she said impatiently. 'Can't you act like an adult? Just because a man and a woman are alone together in an apartment, do they have to misbehave themselves?'

'That's not the point. It's what other people will think.'

'What other people?'

She had me there. I knew no one had seen us enter the apartment.

'I could be seen leaving. Besides, it's the principle of the thing. . . .'

14

She suddenly burst out laughing.

'Oh, for heaven's sake! Stop acting like a Victorian and sit down.'

I should have grabbed my hat and walked out. If I had done that I would have saved myself a lot of trouble, and that's an understatement. But I have a reckless, irresponsible streak in me that occasionally swamps my usual cautious judgment, and that's what it did at this moment.

So I sat down and took a stiff rye and crushed ice she gave me and watched her while she fixed a gin and tonic.

I've kicked around Rome for four years now and I haven't led an entirely celibate life. Italian women are good and exciting. I have had my big moments with them, but as I sat there, looking at Helen in her white dress, I knew this could be the biggest moment of all my moments: this was something special, something that made me short of breath and a little crazy in the head.

She went over to the fireplace and leaned against the overmantel while she regarded me with a half-smile.

Because I knew this was dangerous, and I wouldn't need much encouragement to walk right into trouble, I said, 'Well, how are you making out at the university?'

'Oh, that was just a gag,' she said carelessly. 'I had to tell my father some story or he wouldn't have let me come here alone.'

'You mean you don't go to the university?'

'Of course I don't.'

'But won't he find out?'

'Why should he? He's too busy to bother about me,' she returned and I caught the bitterness in her voice. 'He's only really interested in himself and his latest woman. I was in the way, so I told him I wanted to study architecture at the university at Rome. As Rome is miles away from New York, and once here, I couldn't suddenly walk into his room where he might be trying to convince some little gold digger that he is much younger than he looks, he fell over himself to send me here.'

'So the horn specs, the flat-heeled shoes and the scraped-back hair were part of the gag, too?' I said, realizing by telling me this she was making me an accessory, and if Chalmers found out, the chopper might come down on my neck as well as hers.

'Of course. When I'm at home I always dress like that.

15

It convinces my father that I am a serious-minded student. If he saw me as I am now, he would have hired some respectable old lady to chaperone me.'

'You're pretty cold-blooded about it, aren't you?'

'Why not?' She moved over and dropped into a lounging chair. 'My mother died when I was ten. My father has had three other wives: two of them were only two years older than I am now, and the other was younger. I was as welcome to all of them as an outbreak of polio. I like being on my own: I have lots of fun.'

Looking at her, I could believe she did have lots of fun: probably more than was good for her.

'You're just a kid, and this is no way for you to live,' I said.

She laughed.

'I'm twenty-four and I'm no kid, and this is the way I want to live.'

'Why tell me all this? What's to stop me sending a frantic cable to your father, telling him what's going on?'

She shook her head.

'You won't do that. I've talked to Giuseppe Frenzi about you. He gives you a very good reference. I wouldn't have brought you up here if I wasn't sure of you.'

'Just why did you bring me up here?'

She stared at me: the expression in her eyes made me suddenly breathless. There was no mistaking that expression: she was giving me an invitation to go ahead and make love to her.

'I like the look of you,' she said. 'One can get very tired of Italian men. They're so intense and so direct. I asked Giuseppe to bring you to the party, and here we are.'

Don't imagine I wasn't tempted. I knew all I had to do was to get up and take her in my arms and there would be no opposition. But it was all a little too blatant; too cold-blooded, and this attitude of hers shocked me. There was also the question of my job. I was more interested in holding on to that than fooling around with her. I got to my feet.

'I see. Well, it's getting late. I've got some work to do before I turn in. I'll be moving along.'

She stared up at me, her mouth tightening.

'But you can't go now. You've only just come.'

'I'm sorry. I've got to go.'

'You mean, you don't want to stay?'

16

'It's not what I want to do: it's what I'm going to do.'

She lifted her arms and ran her fingers through her hair. That is perhaps the most provocative gesture a woman can make. If she has the right shape, there is no more telling move she can make than to raise her arms and look at a man as she was looking at me. I nearly fell for it, but not quite.

'I want you to stay.'

I shook my head.

'I really have to go.'

She studied me for a long moment, her eyes expressionless. Then she shrugged, lowered her arms and stood up.

'All right, if that's the way you feel.' She crossed to the door, opened it and went out into the hall. I went after her and picked up my hat that I had left on the hall chair. She opened the front door, glanced out into the corridor and then stood aside.

I was reluctant to go. I had to force myself out into the corridor.

'Maybe you might like to have dinner with me one night or take in a movie.'

'That would be very nice,' she said politely. 'Good night.'

She gave me a distant smile and shut the door in my face.

III

Of course it didn't remain like that. I wish it had, but a relationship between a man like myself and a girl like Helen is certain sooner or later to become complicated.

I tried to put her out of my mind, but I didn't succeed. I kept seeing the expression in her eyes when I had left her, and that did things to me. I knew I was inviting trouble, and yet there was this fascination about her that made any trouble seem unreal. In my saner moments, I told myself that as far as I was concerned she was rank poison, but in my less saner moments I told myself—who cares?

For the next five or six days she was constantly in my mind. I didn't tell Gina that I had met Helen at the party, but Gina has an awkward knack of being able to know to some extent what is going on in my mind, and I caught her looking at me several times with a puzzled, inquiring expression.

By the sixth day I was more or less a dead duck. I had got this blonde, lovely girl so much on my mind that I found I wasn't concentrating on my job. I decided to ease the strain, and when I returned to my apartment, I called her.

There was no answer. I called three times during the evening. At the fourth try, around two o'clock in the morning, I heard the receiver lift and her voice said, 'Hello?'

'This is Ed Dawson,' I said.

'Who?'

I grinned into the receiver. That was a little too obvious. That told me she was as interested in me as I was in her.

'Let me jog your memory. I'm the guy who runs the Rome office of the *Western Telegram*.'

She laughed then.

'Hello, Ed.'

That was better.

'I'm lonely,' I said. 'Is there any chance of you coming out with me to-morrow night? I thought if you hadn't anything better to do, we might have dinner at Alfredo's.'

'Will you hold on a moment? I must look in my little book.'

I held on, knowing I was being given the treatment and not caring. After a two-minute pause, she came back on the line.

'I can't manage to-morrow night. I have a date.'

I should have said it was too bad and hung up, but I was too far gone for that.

'Then when can you fix it?'

'Well, I'm free on Friday.'

That was three days ahead.

'Okay, let's make it Friday night.'

'I'd rather not go to Alfredo's. Isn't there somewhere else quieter?'

That brought me up short. If I wasn't thinking about the danger of us being seen together, she was.

'Yeah, that's right. How about the little restaurant opposite the Trevi fountain?'

'I'd like that. Yes, that would be lovely.'

'I'll meet you there. What time?'

'Half-past eight.'

'Okay: good-bye for now.'

Life didn't mean much to me until Friday. I could see Gina was worried about me. For the first time in four years I was short-tempered with her. I couldn't concentrate, nor could I work up any enthusiasm for the job on hand. I had Helen on my mind.

We had dinner at the little restaurant. It wasn't a bad dinner, but I can't say I remember what we ate. I found talking difficult. All I wanted to do was look at her. She was cool, distant, but at the same time, provocative. If she had invited me up to her apartment I would have gone and to hell with Sherwin Chalmers, but she didn't. She said she would take a taxi home. When I hinted I would go with her, she handed me a beautiful brush-off. I stood outside the restaurant, watching the taxi edge its way up the narrow street until I lost sight of it. Then I walked home, my mind seething. The meeting hadn't helped: in fact it had made things worse.

Three days later I called her again.

'I'm pretty busy,' she said, when I asked her to come to a movie. 'I don't think I can manage it.'

'I was hoping you could. I'm going on vacation in a couple of weeks' time. I won't be seeing you then for a month.'

'Are you going away for a month?'

Her voice had sharpened as if I had caught her interest.

'Yes. I'm going to Venice and then on to Ischia. I plan to stay there for about three weeks'

'Who are you going with?'

'I'm going alone. But never mind that: how about this movie?'

'Well, I might. I don't know. I'll call you. I have to go now. There's someone at the door,' and she hung up.

She didn't call me for five days. Then, just as I was about to call her, she rang my apartment number.

'I've been meaning to telephone you,' she said as soon as I came on the line, 'but I haven't had a moment up to now. Are you doing anything particular right now?'

The time was twenty minutes past midnight. I was about to go to bed.

'You mean *right* now?'

'Yes.'

'Well, no. I was going to bed.'

'Will you come to my place? Don't leave your car outside.'

I didn't hesitate.

'Sure, I'll be right over.'

I entered her apartment block like a sneak thief, taking elaborate care no one would see me. Her front door was ajar, and all I had to do was to step across the corridor from the elevator into her hall.

I found her in the lounge, sorting through a stack of Long Play records. She was wearing a white silk wrap and her blonde hair was about her shoulders. She looked good, and she knew it.

'So you found your way up?' she said, putting the records aside and smiling at me.

'It wasn't so hard.' I closed the door. 'You know, we shouldn't be doing this: this is the way to start real trouble.'

She shrugged her shoulders.

'You don't have to stay.'

I went over to her.

'I don't intend to stay. Why did you ask me over?'

'For heaven's sake, Ed!' she exclaimed impatiently. 'Can't you relax for a moment?'

Now I was alone with her, my caution asserted itself. It was one thing to imagine being alone with her, but with my job hanging to the consequences of being found out, actually being with her was something else besides. I was sorry now I had come.

'I can relax,' I said. 'Look, I've got to think of my job. If your father ever found out I was fooling around with you, I'd be through. I mean that. He would see I never got another newspaper job as long as I live.'

'Are you fooling around with me?' she asked, opening her eyes very wide and looking surprised.

'You know what I mean.'

'He won't find out—why should he?'

'He could find out. If I were seen coming here or leaving he could hear of it.'

'Then you must be careful not to be seen. It shouldn't be difficult.'

'This job means everything to me, Helen. It's my life.'

'You're not what I would call a romantic type, are you?' she said and laughed. 'My Italian men don't think about their jobs, they think about me.'

'I'm not talking about your Italian men.'

'Oh, Ed, do sit down and relax. You're here now, so why are you getting so worked up?'

So I sat down, telling myself that I was crazy in the head to be here.

She went over to the liquor cabinet.

'Will you have a Scotch or rye?'

'A Scotch, I guess.'

I watched her, wondering just why she had asked me over at this time of night. She wasn't being provocative.

'Oh, Ed, before I forget: would you look at this cine? I bought it yesterday, and the release thing doesn't work. Do you understand cines?'

She waved to where an expensive leather camera case hung from a chair. I got up, opened the case and took from it a 16 mm. Paillard Bolex with a triple lense turret.

'Hey! This is nice,' I said. 'What in the world do you want with an item like this, Helen? It must have cost plenty.'

She laughed.

'It did come high, but I've always wanted to own a cine. A girl should have at least one hobby, don't you think?' She dropped crushed ice into two glasses. 'I want a record of my stay in Rome for my old age.'

I turned the camera over in my hands. It suddenly occurred to me that she must be living well beyond the allowance her father was giving her. He had told me he was giving her sixty dollars a week. He had said he didn't want her to have any more. Knowing the price of apartments in Rome, this one would cost something like forty dollars a week. I looked over at the liquor cabinet that was loaded with every kind of drink. How was she managing to live in this style? Then there was this expensive camera she had suddenly bought.

'Has someone left you a fortune?'

Her eyes flickered, and for a moment she looked confused, but only for a moment.

'I wish they had. Why do you ask?'

'It's not my business, but all this must cost you a lot, doesn't it?' I waved my hand to take in the room.

She shrugged.

'I suppose it does. My father gives me a generous allowance. He likes me to live this way.'

She didn't look at me while she spoke. Even if I hadn't known exactly how much her father was giving her, the lie was pretty obvious. Although I was puzzled, I realized it wasn't my business so I changed the subject.

'What's wrong with the camera then?'

'This release thing won't work.'

Her finger touched the back of my hand as she pointed.

'The safety catch is on,' I said, showing her. 'This thing here. You press it down, and the release then works. They put the safety catch on so the motor won't run accidentally.'

'For heaven's sake! I nearly took it back to the shop to-day. I guess I'd better read the book of instructions.' She took the cine from me. 'I've never been very smart with mechanical things. Look at all the film I've bought.' She pointed to where ten cartons of 16 mm. film stood on the desk.

'You're not going to use all that on Rome, are you?' I said. 'You have enough there to photograph the whole of Italy.'

She gave me an odd look that seemed to me to be a little sly.

'I'm keeping most of it for Sorrento.'

'Sorrento?' I was puzzled. 'Are you going to Sorrento then?'

She smiled.

'You're not the only one who takes vacations. Have you ever been to Sorrento?'

'No. I've never been so far south.'

'I've rented a villa just outside Sorrento. It's lovely and very, very isolated. I flew down to Naples a couple of days ago and arranged everything. I've even got a woman from a nearby village to come in and do for me.'

I had a sudden feeling that she wasn't telling me this without reason. I looked sharply at her.

'Sounds nice,' I said. 'When are you going?'

'The same time as you're going to Ischia.' She put the camera on the table and came over and sat beside me on the settee. 'And, like you—I'm going alone.'

She looked at me. The invitation in her eyes set my heart thumping. She leaned towards me, her full, red lips parting. Before I knew what I was doing, she was in my arms, and I was kissing her.

22

We held that kiss for perhaps twenty seconds, and it really got me going, then I felt her hands on my chest, pushing me back, and that steady, hard pressure brought me to my senses. I let go of her and stood up.

'This is a crazy way to behave,' I said, breathing like an old man who has run up a flight of stairs. I wiped the lipstick off my mouth.

'A crazy way to behave in Rome,' she said, leaning back and smiling up at me, 'but not in Sorrento.'

'Now, look . . .' I began, but she held up her hand, stopping me.

'I know how you feel about me. I'm not a child. I feel the same way about you,' she said. 'Come with me to Sorrento. Everything's arranged. I know how you feel about father and your job, but I promise you it will be perfectly safe. I've rented the villa in the names of Mr. and Mrs. Douglas Sherrard. You'll be Mr. Sherrard, an American business man on vacation. No one knows us down there. Don't you want to spend a month with me—just the two of us?'

'But we can't do it,' I said, knowing there was no reason why we shouldn't do it, and wanting to. 'We can't rush into it like this. . . .'

'Don't be so cautious, darling. We're not rushing into anything. I've planned it most carefully. I'll go down to the villa in my car. You'll come down the next day by train. It's a lovely place. It faces the sea on a high hill. There's no other villa for at least a quarter of a mile.' She jumped to her feet and fetched a large-scale map that was lying on the table. 'I'll show you exactly where it is. Look, it's marked on the map. It's called Bella Vista—isn't that cute? From the terrace you can see the bay and Capri. It has a garden: there are orange and lemon trees and vines. It's completely isolated. You'll love it.'

'I dare say I will, Helen,' I said. 'I admit I'd like to do it. I wouldn't be human if I didn't, but what's going to happen to us after the month's over?'

She laughed.

'If you mean you're scared I shall expect you to marry me, you needn't be. I'm not going to get married for years. This is something I want to get out of my system. I don't even know that I love you, Ed, but I do know I want to be alone with you for a month.'

23

'We can't do it, Helen. It's not right. . . .'

She touched my face with her fingers.

'Will you be a darling and go now?' She patted my face and then moved away from me. 'I've only just got back from Naples, and I am very tired. There's nothing more to talk about. I promise you it will be safe. It now depends whether you want to spend a month with me or not. I promise you there'll be no strings to it. Think about it. Don't let's meet now until the 29th. I'll be at Sorrento station to meet the three-thirty train from Naples. If you're not on the train, I'll understand.'

She crossed to the lobby and opened the front door a few inches.

I joined her.

'Now, wait, Helen. . . .'

'Please, Ed. Don't let's say any more. You'll either be on the train or you won't. That's all there is to it.' Her lips brushed mine. 'Good night, darling.'

I looked at her and she looked at me.

As I stepped out into the corridor, I knew I would be on that train.

PART II

I

I HAD five days ahead of me before I left for Sorrento. During that time I had a lot to do, but I found concentration difficult.

I was like a teenager looking forward to his first date. This irritated me. I had imagined I would be blasé enough to take the situation Helen had engineered in my stride, but I wasn't. The idea of spending a month alone with this exciting girl really got me going. In my saner moments—and they were few—I told myself I was crazy to go ahead with this, but I consoled myself with the knowledge of Helen's efficiency. She had said it would be safe and I believed her. I argued that I would be a fool if I didn't grab the chance of taking what she was offering me.

Two days before I was due to leave, Jack Maxwell arrived in Rome to take over the office in my absence.

I had worked alongside him in New York way back in 1949. He was a sound newspaper man, but he hadn't much talent for anything but news. I didn't care much for him. He was too good-looking, too smooth, too well-dressed and too generally too.

I had an idea that he didn't like me any more than I liked him, but this didn't stop me from giving him a big welcome. After we had spent a couple of hours in the office going over future work, I suggested we should have dinner together.

'Fine,' he said. 'Let's see what this ancient city has to offer. I warn you, Ed, I expect nothing but the best.'

I took him to Alfredo's which is one of the better eating places in Rome, and gave him *porchetta*, which is suckingpig, roasted on a spit, partially boned and stuffed with liver, sausage-meat and herbs: it makes quite a meal.

After we had eaten and had got on to the third bottle of wine, he let his hair down and became friendly.

'You're a lucky guy, Ed,' he said, accepting the cigarette I offered him. 'You may not know it, but you're the white-headed boy back home. Hammerstock thinks a lot of the stuff you've been turning in. I'll tell you something off the record: only not a word to anyone. Hammerstock is having you back in a couple of months' time. The idea is I'm to replace you here, and you're going to get the foreign desk.'

'I don't believe it,' I said, staring at him. 'You're kidding.'

'It's a fact. I wouldn't kid about a thing like that.'

I tried not to show my excitement, but I don't think I succeeded very well. To be given the foreign desk at head-quarters was the top of my ambition. Not only did it mean a whale of a lot more money, but it was also the plum job of all the jobs on *Western Telegram*.

'It'll be official in a couple of days,' Maxwell told me. 'The old man has already okayed it. You're a lucky guy.'

I said I was.

'Will you mind leaving Rome?'

'I'll get used to it,' I said and grinned. 'A job like that is worth the move out of Rome.'

Maxwell shrugged.

'I don't know. I wouldn't want it myself. It's too much like hard work and it would kill me to work so close to the old man.' He sank lower in his chair. 'That pig wasn't half bad. I think I'm going to take to Rome.'

'There's no city in the world to touch it.'

He fed a cigarette into his mouth, scratched a match alight and puffed smoke into my face.

'By the way, how's rampaging Helen getting along?'

The question startled me.

'Who?'

'Helen Chalmers. You're her nurse-maid or something, aren't you?'

The red light went up. Maxwell had a nose for scandal. If he got the faintest suspicion that there was something between Helen and me, he would work at it until he had found out just what it was.

'I was a nurse-maid to her for exactly one day,' I said casually. 'Since then I've scarcely seen her. The old man asked me to meet her at the airport and take her to her hotel. She's working at the university, I believe.'

His eyebrows jerked up.

'She's—what?'

'Working at the university,' I repeated. 'She's on some architecture course here.'

'Helen?' He leaned forward, stared at me, then burst out laughing. 'That's the funniest thing I have ever heard. Helen on an architecture course!' He leaned back in his chair and roared. People turned around to stare at us. He certainly sounded as if he had heard the funniest joke of the century. I didn't find it all that funny. It was as much as I could do not to kick my chair away and plant my fist in his handsome face.

When he got over laughing, he caught my eye. Maybe he saw I wasn't all that amused because he made an effort to control himself and he waved an apologetic hand.

'Sorry, Ed.' He took out his handkerchief and mopped his eyes. 'If you knew Helen like I know Helen . . .' He broke off to laugh again.

'Look, it can't be all that funny,' I said, a rasp in my voice. 'What gives?'

'It *is* funny. Don't tell me she has taken you in too? Up to now, the only guy on the *Telegram* staff who isn't on to her is her old man. Don't tell me you haven't got her taped yet?'

'I'm not following this. What do you mean?'

'Well, you certainly can't have seen much of her. I had an idea she might have gone for you: she seems to fall for big, husky he-men. Don't tell me she showed up in Rome in her flat heels, specs and scraped-back hair-do?'

'I'm still not following you, Jack. What is all this?'

'All this?' He grinned. 'It seems you're luckier than I thought possible, or unlucky, depending how you look at it. All the boys back home know about her. She's notorious. When we heard she was heading for Rome and the old man wanted you to keep an eye on her, we all thought, sooner or later, you'd be a dead duck. She'll make a play at anything in trousers. You mean to tell me she hasn't tried to make a pass at you?'

I felt myself turn hot, then cold.

'This is something new to me,' I said, speaking casually.

'Well, well. She's a menace to men. Okay, I admit she has everything. She has looks, come-on eyes and a shape that

27

would bring a corpse alive, but the trouble she can get a guy into! If Chalmers wasn't the biggest power in newspapers, every paper in New York would be carrying headlines about her at least once a week. She only escapes publicity because no newspaper wants to get on the wrong side of the old man. She gets into pretty near every damm mess there is. It was only because she was involved in the Menotti slaying that she cleared out of New York and came here.'

I sat very still, staring at him. Menotti had been a notorious New York gangster, enormously wealthy, powerful and a one-time killer. He had been hooked up with the Union and vice rackets and had been a bad man to know.

'What had she to do with Menotti?' I asked.

'Rumour had it she was his piece,' Maxwell said. 'She was always going around with him. A little bird told me it was in her apartment that he got knocked off.'

About two months ago Menotti had been brutally murdered in a three-room apartment which he had rented as a love nest. The woman he had been visiting had vanished, and the police hadn't been able to trace her. The killer also had disappeared. It was generally thought that Menotti had been slain on the orders of Frank Setti, a rival gangster, who had been deported as a drug trafficker and was now supposed to be living somewhere in Italy.

'What little bird?' I asked.

'It was Andrews who, as you know, has his ear right to the ground. He usually knows what he is talking about. Maybe he was wrong this time. All I do know is that she used to go around with Menotti. She left for Rome soon after Menotti was killed. The janitor of the apartment block in which Menotti was strangled gave Andrews a pretty good description of the woman in the case: the description fitted Helen Chalmers like a glove. Our people closed the janitor's mouth before the police got to him, so it never came out.'

'I see,' I said.

'Well, if you haven't anything juicy to tell me about her while she's in Rome, it looks as if she has had a scare and is at last behaving herself.' He grinned. 'Frankly, I'm disappointed. To tell the truth when I heard I was going to take your place, I thought I might have a try at her myself. She's really something. As you were told to look after her,

I was hoping to hear by now that you and she were more than old friends.'

'Do you imagine I'd be such a pea brain as to fool around with Chalmers' daughter?' I asked heatedly.

'Why not? She's worth fooling around with, and when she handles this kind of situation, she takes good care the old man will never find out. She's been fooling around with men since she was sixteen, and Chalmers has never found out. If you haven't seen her without her specs and that awful hair-do, you haven't seen anything. She's terrific, and, what's more, I hear she is very, very keen. If she ever makes a play at me I'm not going to stop her.'

Somehow I got him off the subject of Helen and back on to business. After another hour of his company, I took him back to his hotel. He said he would be in the office the following morning to tie up the loose ends and thanked me for entertaining him.

'You really are a lucky guy, Ed,' he said as we were parting. 'The foreign desk is about the best job in the business. There're guys who would give their left arms to have it. Me—I wouldn't want it. It's too much like hard work, but for you . . .' He broke off and grinned. 'A guy who can let a babe like Helen slip through his fingers—well, for heaven's sake! What else could you do except hold down the foreign desk?'

He thought it was a good joke and, slapping me on the back, he went off laughing towards the elevators.

I didn't think the joke was so good. I got into my car and drove through the congested traffic until I reached my apartment. During the drive I did some thinking. The information I had from Maxwell about Helen shocked me. I didn't doubt that what he had told me was true. I knew Andrews was accurate in any story he had to tell. So she had been mixed up with Menotti. I suddenly began to wonder who she was mixed up with here. If she had acquired the taste for dangerous racketeers in New York, she might have continued to cultivate the taste here. Was that the explanation of her high style of living? Was some man financing her?

By the time I had undressed and got into bed, I was asking myself if I were really going to get on that train to Sorrento. Did I want to mix myself up with a girl of this type? If I were really going to get the foreign desk, and I was pretty sure Maxwell wouldn't have broken the news unless he was certain of his facts, I would be crazy to take the slightest risk of the job coming unstuck. As he had said, it was the plum job on the paper. I knew if Chalmers found out that his daughter and I had become lovers that would be that: I'd not only lose this job, but I'd be out of the game for good.

'No,' I said aloud as I turned off the light. 'She can go to Sorrento by herself. I'm not going. She can find some other sucker. I'll go to Ischia.'

But two days later I was on the local train from Naples to Sorrento. I was still telling myself that I was a fool and crazy in the head, but no matter how much I talked to myself, telling myself not to go ahead with this, it made no difference. I was on my way. The train couldn't move fast enough for me.

II

Before I caught the train to Naples, I had looked in at the office around ten o'clock for a final check and to see if there were any personal letters for me.

Maxwell was out, but I found Gina sorting through a stack of cables.

'Anything for me?' I asked, sitting on the edge of her desk.

'No personal letters. Mr. Maxwell can handle all this,' she said, flicking the cables with a carefully manicured finger-nail. 'Shouldn't you be on your way? I thought you wanted to leave early.'

'I've lots of time.'

My train to Naples didn't leave until noon. I had told Gina I was going to Venice and I had had trouble in pre-venting her booking a seat for me on the Rome-Venice express.

The telephone-bell rang at this moment and Gina picked up the receiver. I leaned forward and began to look idly at the cables.

'Who is that speaking?' Gina said. 'Mrs.—who? Will you hold on a moment? I'm not sure if he is in.' She looked at me, frowning and I could see a puzzled expression in her eyes. 'A Mrs. Douglas Sherrard is asking for you.'

I was about to say I had never heard of her and didn't want to speak to her when the slightly familiar sounding name suddenly rang a clear alarm-bell in my mind. Mrs. Douglas Sherrard! That was the name Helen had said she used when renting the villa at Sorrento. Surely this couldn't be Helen on the line? Surely she couldn't be so reckless as to call me here?

Trying not to show my consternation, I reached forward and took the receiver from Gina's hand. Half-turning my back so she couldn't watch my face, I said cautiously, 'Hello? Who is that?'

'Hello, Ed.' It was Helen all right. 'I know I shouldn't be calling you at the office, but I tried your apartment and there was no answer.'

I wanted to tell her she was crazy to call me here. I wanted to hang up, but I knew Gina would wonder what it was all about.

'What is it?' I asked sharply.

'Is there someone listening?'

'Yes.'

To make things more complicated, the office door jerked open and Jack Maxwell breezed in.

'Good grief! You still around?' he exclaimed when he saw me. 'I thought you were on your way to Venice by now.'

I waved him to silence, said into the mouthpiece: 'Is there something I can do?'

'Yes, please. Would you mind bringing me down a Wratten number eight filter for my camera? I find I need it and I can't get it in Sorrento.'

'Sure,' I said. 'I'll do that.'

'Thanks, darling. I'm so impatient for you to get here. The scenery is too marvellous. . . .'

I was afraid her low, clear voice might reach Maxwell's ear. He was obviously listening. I cut in on her.

'I'll fix it. Good-bye for now,' and I hung up.

Maxwell stared inquisitively at me.

'Do you always treat your lady callers like that?' he asked as he glanced through the cables on the desk. 'That was a trifle abrupt, wasn't it?'

31

I tried not to show how rattled I was, but I was aware that Gina was looking at me, puzzled, and as I moved away from the desk, Maxwell was also staring at me.

'I just dropped in to see if there were any personal letters for me,' I said to him, lighting a cigarette in the effort to hide my confusion. 'I guess I'll get off now.'

'You want to learn to relax,' Maxwell said. 'If you weren't such a stolid, well-behaved newspaper man, I'd say from your furtive expression that you were up to some form of mischief. Are you?'

'Oh, don't talk crap!' I said, not being able to restrain the snap in my voice.

'Hey! You're a bit sour this morning, aren't you? I was only kidding.' As I said nothing, he went on, 'Are you taking your car?'

'No. I'm travelling by train.'

'You're not travelling alone?' he asked, looking slyly at me. 'I hope you've got some nice blonde laid on to console you if it rains.'

'I'm travelling alone,' I said, trying not to look as hot as I felt.

'I bet! I know what I'd do if I were going on a month's vacation.'

'Maybe we don't happen to think alike,' I said, going over to Gina. 'Look after this guy,' I said to her. 'Don't let him make too many mistakes, and don't work too hard yourself. Be seeing you on the 29th.'

'Have a good time, Ed,' she said quietly. She didn't smile. This worried me. Something had upset her. 'Don't worry about us. We'll be all right.'

'I'm sure you will.' I turned to Maxwell. 'So long and good hunting.'

'Better hunting to you, brother,' he said, shaking hands.

I left them and, going down in the elevator to the street level, I called a taxi and told the driver to take me to the Barberini. There I bought the photographic filter Helen had asked me for, then I took another taxi back to my apartment. I completed packing, made sure everything was locked up, and took a taxi to the station.

I regretted not having my car, but Helen was taking hers and there was no point in having two cars in Sorrento. I wasn't looking forward to the train journey from Rome to Naples. After I had paid off my taxi, I waved a porter aside who wanted to grab my suitcase, and hurried into the vast station.

I bought a ticket for Naples, checked that the train wasn't in yet, and went over to the newspaper kiosk where I bought a bunch of newspapers and magazines. All the time I was keeping my eyes open for any familiar face.

I was acutely aware that I had too many friends in Rome for my peace of mind. At any moment someone I knew might appear. I didn't want tales to get back to Maxwell that instead of catching the eleven o'clock train to Venice, I had been seen boarding the noon train to Naples.

As I had ten minutes to wait, I went over to one of the benches, away in a corner and sat down. I read a newspaper, sheltering behind its open pages. Those ten minutes were fidgety ones. When I finally made my way to the platform, I hadn't as yet run into anyone I knew. I got a seat on the train with some difficulty, and settled down again behind my newspaper.

It was only when the train moved out of the station that I began to relax.

So far all was going well, I told myself. From now on I could consider myself safely launched on my vacation.

I still felt uneasy. I wished Helen hadn't called up. I wished Gina hadn't heard the name of Mrs. Douglas Sherrard. I wished I was strong-minded enough not to be so infatuated with this blonde, exciting girl. Now I knew a little about her past history, I realized she couldn't be my type. A girl who fooled around with a man like Menotti just couldn't be my type. I told myself this was just a physical thing. I was being a sensual, dumb fool to be infatuated with her.

All this reasoning didn't get me anywhere. I knew if there was one thing I wanted more than anything else in the world, it was to spend a month in her company.

This was just another way of saying as far as Helen was concerned, I was a dead duck.

III

The local train arrived at Sorrento station twenty minutes late. The train was pretty crowded, and it was some minutes before I could work my way past the barrier and out into the station approach where a line of taxis and horse-drawn cabs waited to be hired.

I stood in the hot sunshine, looking around for Helen, but there was no sign of her. I put down my bag, waved away an eager beggar who wanted to conduct me to a taxi, and lit a cigarette.

I was surprised Helen wasn't there to meet me, but, bearing in mind that the train was late, I thought she might have gone to look at the shops to pass the time. So I leaned against the station wall and waited.

The crowd pouring out of the station slowly disappeared. Some were met by friends, some walked away, some hired taxis and carriages until I was the only one left. After perhaps fifteen minutes, and with still no sign of Helen, I began to get impatient.

Maybe she was sitting at some cafe in the piazza, I thought. I picked up my suitcase and carried it to the left luggage office, where I dumped it. Then, relieved of its weight, I wandered down the street to the centre of the town.

I walked around looking for Helen, but I couldn't see her. I visited the car park, but I couldn't see any car that could be Helen's. I went over to one of the cafes, sat down at a table and ordered a café espresso.

From there I could watch the approach to the station and also see any car that arrived in the piazza.

The time was getting on for four-thirty. I drank the espresso, smoked three cigarettes, then, bored with waiting, I asked the waiter if I could use the telephone. I had a little trouble in getting the number of the villa, but after some delay the operator found the number and, after more delay, told me that no one was answering.

This was a let-down.

It was possible that Helen had forgotten the time the train arrived and had only just left the villa and was on her way down to the station. Containing my impatience, I ordered another espresso and sat down to wait, but by ten minutes after five, I was not only irritated, I was uneasy.

What had happened to her? I knew she had moved into the villa. Then why hadn't she come down to meet me as we had arranged?

From the map she had shown me, I knew more or less where the villa was. At a rough guess it was five miles up-hill

34

from Sorrento. I told myself I would be easier in mind doing something, rather than sitting at the café, so I decided to walk towards the villa in the hope that I would meet her as she drove down.

There was only one road to the villa so there was no chance of missing her. All I had to do was to follow the road, and sooner or later we must meet.

Without hurrying, I set off on the long walk towards the villa.

For the first mile I had to make my way through crowds of tourists who were shop-window gazing, waiting for buses and generally cluttering up the landscape, but once free of the town, and on the snake-back road that led eventually to Amalfi, I had only the fast traffic to contend with.

Two miles along this road brought me to the side road that would take me off the main road and up into the hills. The time was now twenty minutes past six, and there was still no sign of Helen.

I lengthened my stride and began the long, tortuous climb into the hills. After I had gone a mile, still without seeing any sign of Helen, I was sweating and anxious.

I saw the villa, perched on a high hill, overlooking the bay of Sorrento, a good half-hour before I reached it. It was as lovely and as exciting as Helen had said it was, but right then I wasn't in the mood to appreciate its beauty. My one thought was to find Helen.

She had been right when she had said the villa was isolated. If anything, isolation was an under-statement. The villa stood in its own grounds, and there was no other house within sight.

I pushed open the wrought-iron gates and walked up the broad drive, bordered on either side by six-foot high dahlias, their heavy heads eight inches across, and of every colour in the book.

The drive opened out on to a tarmac on which stood Helen's Lincoln convertible. Well, at least, I hadn't missed her on the road, I thought, as soon as I saw the car.

I climbed the steps leading to the villa. The front door was ajar and I pushed it open.

'Helen! Are you there?'

The silence that came out of the the house had a depressing effect on me. I walked into a large marble-floored hall.

'Helen!'

I went slowly from room to room. There was a large lounge with a dining-room alcove, a kitchen and a big patio that overlooked the sea, some two hundred feet below. Upstairs there were three bedrooms and two bathrooms. The villa was modern, well furnished and an ideal place for a vacation. I would have been thrilled with it if Helen had been there to greet me. As it was I only took time to assure myself that she wasn't in the villa before going into the garden and beginning to hunt for her there.

No answer came to my repeated calls and, by now, I was getting really rattled.

At the end of one of the garden paths I discovered a gate that stood ajar. Beyond the gate was a narrow path that led upwards to the top of the hill that rose above the villa. Could she have gone that way? I wondered. I decided I wasn't going to sit around in the hope she would turn up. This path appeared to be the only other exit from the villa. I knew I couldn't have missed her on the walk up from Sorrento. There was a chance she had gone for a walk along this path and had either forgotten the time or had met with some kind of an accident.

I hurried back to the villa to leave a note in case she happened to be still in Sorrento and I had somehow missed her. I didn't want her to go rushing back to Sorrento if she returned from there, and not find me at the villa.

I found some headed notepaper in one of the drawers in the desk and scribbled a brief note, which I left on the table of the lounge; then I left the villa and walked fast along the garden path to the gate.

I had walked for perhaps a quarter of a mile and was beginning to think that Helen couldn't have possibly come this way when I saw below me, built into the hill face, a big white villa. It was in the most inaccessible place I have ever seen for a house to be built in. There was only a flight of steep steps leading from the cliff head down to the villa. The only practical way of reaching the place was by sea. I wasn't interested in the villa and I didn't even pause, but I looked at it as I continued my way along the winding path. I could see a big terrace with a table, lounging chairs and a big red umbrella. Down a flight of steps, I could see a harbour in which were moored two powerful motor-boats. As I walked on, I wondered who the millionaire could be who owned such a place. I hadn't walked more than three hundred yards before the villa was completely blotted out of my mind, for lying directly in my path was Helen's camera case.

I recognized it immediately and I stopped short, my heart skipping a beat.

For a long moment I stared at it; then, moving forward, I stooped to pick it up. There was no doubt that it was hers. Apart from the shape and the newness of the pigskin leather, there were her initials on the cover flap in gold. The case was empty.

Holding the case in my hand, I hurried on. Another fifty yards further on the path suddenly twisted at right angles, and cut away inland into a thick wood that covered the last quarter of a mile to the top of the hill.

The right-angle bend in the path brought the path dangerously close to the overhang and, pausing there, I looked down the sheer hillside at the sea that lapped against the massive boulders some two hundred feet below.

I drew in my breath sharply as I caught sight of something white that lay, half-submerged in the sea and was sprawled out like a broken doll on the rocks.

I stood transfixed, peering down, my heart thudding, my mouth dry.

I could see the long blonde hair floating gently in the sea. The full skirt of the white frock billowed out as the sea swirled around the broken body

There was no need to make wild guesses. I knew the dead woman down there was Helen.

PART III

III

SHE had to be dead.

She couldn't have survived that fall nor lie the way she was lying, with the sea covering her head, and not be dead, but I just couldn't believe it.

'Helen!'

There was a cracked note in my voice as I yelled down to her.

'Helen! !'

My voice echoed back to me: a ghostly sound that set me shaking.

She couldn't be dead. I told myself. I had to make sure. I couldn't leave her there. She might be drowning even as I stared down at her.

I threw myself flat and edged forward until my head and shoulders were clear of the overhang. The height made me dizzy. From this point of view the drop was horrifying.

I looked feverishly along and down the chalk face to find some way that would take me down to her, but there was no way. It would be like trying to climb down the face of a monstrous wall. The only way to get down there would be to be lowered by a rope.

My heart was hammering, and there was cold sweat on my face as I edged forward a few more dangerous inches.

From this position I could see her more clearly. I could see that her face and head were completely submerged by the gently lapping sea, and as a shaft of light from the sinking sun lit up the sea, I saw there was a halo of red around her blonde hair.

She was dead all right.

I worked my way back on to the path and squatted on my heels, sick and shaking. I wondered how long she had been lying down there. She might have been dead for hours.

I had to get help. There would be a telephone in the villa. I could call the police from there. If I hurried, they might be able to reach her before it became too dark to find her.

I stood up, took two uncertain, unsteady steps backward and then came to an abrupt stop.

The police!

I suddenly realized what a police investigation would mean to me. It wouldn't take them long to find out that Helen and I had planned to spend a month in the villa. It would only take a little longer for the news to reach Chalmers. Once I called in the police the whole sordid story would come out.

As I stood hesitating, I saw a fishing boat come slowly into the little bay below me. I immediately became aware that I was sharply silhouetted against the sky line. Although the crew down there were too far away to see my features, a wave of panic sent me down on my hands and knees out of sight.

This was it. I was in a hell of a jam. I had known all along at the back of my mind that I was walking into trouble by getting infatuated with Helen, and now I had walked into it.

As I crouched down, I imagined the expression that would come on Sherwin Chalmers's heavy, tough face when he heard the news that his daughter and I had arranged to stay at a villa in Sorrento, and his daughter had fallen over a cliff.

He would be certain we had been lovers. He might even think I had got tired of her and had pushed her off the cliff.

This thought shook me.

There was a possibility that the police might think that too. So far as I knew, no one had seen her fall. I couldn't prove the exact time I had arrived here. I had come out of the crowded train, just one among a hundred other travellers. I had left my suitcase with the station clerk, but he saw different faces every hour of the day, and it wasn't likely he would remember me. There was no one else. I couldn't recall meeting anyone on the long walk up from Sorrento. No one anyway who would be likely to swear to the exact time I had arrived on the cliff head.

A lot depended, of course, on the time when Helen died. If she had fallen within an hour or so of my arrival, and if the police suspected that I had pushed her over the cliff, then I would really be in a bad position.

By now I had worked myself into quite a state of nerves. My one thought was to get as far away from here as I could without being seen. As I turned to make way down the path, I stumbled over Helen's camera case that I had dropped when I had caught sight of her.

I picked it up, hesitated, then made to heave it over the cliff, but stopped in time.

I couldn't afford to make a single mistake now. My fingerprints were on the case.

I took out my handkerchief and wiped the case over carefully. I went over the case four or five times until I was satisfied I hadn't left a trace of any prints. Then I tossed the case over the cliff.

Turning, I moved swiftly back down the path.

By now the light was fading. The sun, a great fiery ball, drenched the sky and sea in a red glow. In another half-hour it would be dark.

I kept on, barely glancing at the lone white villa I had seen on my way up, but noticing that lights were showing at three or four of the windows.

My panic subsided a little as I continued to hurry along the path. I felt bad about leaving Helen, but I was certain she was dead, and I told myself I had to think of myself.

By the time I reached the garden gate, I had got over the first shock of her death and my mind was functioning again.

I knew the right thing to do was to call the police. I told myself that if I made a clean breast of it, admitted I was going to live with the girl for a month, and explained how I had come upon her body, there was no reason why they shouldn't believe me. At least, they couldn't catch me out in a lie. But if I kept quiet, and by some unlucky chance they got on to me, they would be justified in suspecting that I was responsible for her death.

This reasoning would have convinced me if it were not for the new job: I wanted to run the foreign desk more than I wanted anything else in this world. I knew I wouldn't get the job if Chalmers learned the truth. I would be mad to throw away my future by telling the police the truth: that

40

way I had everything to lose. If I kept quiet, and had some luck, there was a good chance I would get away with it.

It wasn't as if there had been anything between us, I told myself. I wasn't even in love with the girl. It had been a stupid, irresponsible impulse. She had been more to blame than I. She had encouraged me. She had arranged everything. According to Maxwell, she was a practised siren. She had a reputation for making trouble for men. I'd be a fool not to try and save myself.

Having got all that off my chest, I calmed down.

Okay, I thought, I've got to make certain no one ever knows I've been here. I've got to establish an alibi for myself.

By now I had reached the gate that led through the garden to the villa. I paused there to look at my watch. The time was half-past eight. Maxwell and Gina believed right now that I was in Venice. There wasn't a hope of getting from here to Venice to-night. My only chance to establish an alibi was to get back to Rome. With any luck, I could get there by about three in the morning. I would go to the office early the following morning, and make out I had changed my mind about going to Venice and, instead, had stayed in Rome to finish a chapter of a novel I was writing.

It wasn't much of an alibi, but it was the best I could think of at the moment. The point was that it would be easy for the police to prove that I hadn't been to Venice, but impossible for them to prove that I hadn't spent all day in my pent house apartment. I had a private stairway to the apartment and no one ever saw me enter or leave.

If only I had brought my car! It would have been simple to get to Rome if I had the car. I didn't dare take the Lincoln convertible which I could see as I rounded the bend in the garden path.

The village woman whom Helen had hired to run the villa was certain to know Helen had brought the car. If it were missing, the police might jump to the conclusion that Helen's death hadn't been accidental.

I would have to walk to Sorrento, and then try for a train to Naples. I had no idea what time the last train left Sorrento for Naples, but I thought it more than likely that by the time I had covered the five long miles on foot, the last train would have gone. I knew there was an eleven-fifteen from Naples to Rome, but I had still to get to Naples. Once again I looked at the Lincoln convertible. I fought down the temptation to take it. Whatever I did, I must not complicate this set-up more than it was already.

As I moved around the car and towards the drive, I looked back at the dark, silent villa and I got a shock.

Had I imagined the flash of light that had appeared from within the lounge?

Moving quickly and silently, my heart hammering, I crouched down behind the car.

I stared at the lounge windows for a long moment, then I saw again the gleam of white light which immediately disappeared.

I waited, breathing hard, as I peered over the hood of the car.

Again the light appeared. This time it remained on longer.

Someone was in the lounge with a flashlight!

Who could it be?

Not the woman from the village. She wouldn't need to creep around like this in the dark. She would have turned on the lights.

I was now really rattled. Keeping low, I moved away from the car, across the tarmac, away from the villa until I reached the comforting cover of a huge hydrangea shrub, I got behind this, then peered back at the villa.

The light was moving around the lounge as if the intruder in there was searching for something.

I wanted to find out who it was. I was tempted to creep in there and surprise whoever it was: probably some sneak thief, but I knew I had to keep out of sight. No one must know I had been to the villa. It galled me to watch the light moving around the room and to know I couldn't do anything about it.

After five minutes or so, the light went out. There was a long pause, then I became aware of a tall figure of a man who came through the front door. He paused for a moment at the head of the steps. It was now far too dark to see more than his shadowy outline.

He moved softly down the steps, went over to the car and peered inside. He turned on his flashlight. His back was turned to me. I could see he was wearing a black slouch hat and the width of his shoulders was impressive. I was glad now that I hadn't gone in there and surprised him. He looked big enough to more than take care of himself.

42

The light went out and he moved away from the car. I crouched down, expecting him to come towards me and make for the exit at the bottom of the drive. Instead, he went swiftly and silently across the lawn, and I just managed to see that he was heading for the path that led to the distant garden gate before he was swallowed up in the darkness.

Puzzled and uneasy, I stared after him, then realizing that time was going, and that I had to get back to Rome, I left my hiding-place and hurried down the drive, through the wrought-iron gates and on to the road.

All the way to Sorrento I puzzled about this intruder. Had he been a sneak thief? Or was he connected in some way with Helen? The question remained unanswered. The only comfort that I could get from this mysterious situation was that I hadn't been seen.

I reached Sorrento at ten minutes past ten. I had run, walked and run again, and I was pretty near bushed as I walked into the station. The last train to Naples had left ten minutes ago.

I had five minutes over the hour to get somehow to Naples. I got my suitcase from the left-luggage office, taking care to keep my head bent so the clerk couldn't get a good look at me, then I went out into the dark station yard where a lone taxi waited. The driver was dozing, and I got into the cab before he woke.

'I'll give you double fare and a five thousand lire tip if you get me to Naples station before eleven fifteen,' I told him.

There is no wilder, madder or more dangerous driver in the world than an Italian. When one gives him a challenge like this, the only thing to do is to sit tight, close your eyes and pray.

The taxi driver didn't even turn around to look at me. He stiffened to attention, sank his thumb into the starter button, threw in his clutch and tore out of the station yard on two wheels.

The road out of Sorrento for twelve miles or so is shaped like a coiled snake. There are hairpin bends, tight corners and only enough room for two buses to pass if they stop, and the drivers lean out of their windows and then take it dead slow.

My driver went along this road as if it were as flat and as straight as a foot rule. He kept his hand on his horn and

43

his headlights gave warning of his coming, but there were moments when I thought my last hour had arrived. It was pure luck that we didn't meet the hourly local bus, otherwise we couldn't have avoided a smash.

Once on the autostrada to Naples it was plain sailing, and I could relax a little. At this hour there wasn't much traffic, and the taxi kept up a roaring, snarling eighty-five miles an hour for a little more than half an hour.

We got into the outskirts of Naples at five minutes to eleven. This was the crucial moment of the drive, for the traffic of Naples at all times is notoriously heavy and slow. It was then that my driver proved to me that he wasn't only a dangerous and mad driver, but he was also completely indifferent to human life and limb.

He cut through the traffic the way a hot knife slices through butter. The fact that other Italian drivers were intimidated underlined his ferocious ruthlessness. No Italian driver will ever give way willingly to another driver, but in this case, they seemed glad to give way, and the whole route to the station was punctuated with the screaming of tortured tyres as cars braked violently, the honking of horns and the yells of fury.

I was surprised the police didn't take action. Maybe it was because the taxi was out of sight before they could get their whistles to their mouths.

We arrived at the station at five minutes after eleven, and as the driver slammed on his brakes and came to a skidding standstill he turned around to grin at me.

I had my hat pulled well down over my eyes and the interior of the cab was dark. I knew he wouldn't recognize me again.

'How's that, signor?' he asked, obviously delighted with himself.

'Terrific,' I said breathlessly, as I shoved a handful of dirty thousand lire notes into his hand. 'Well done, and thanks.'

I grabbed my suitcase, left the taxi and sprinted across the sidewalk into the station. I bought a ticket and legged it along the platform to where the train was waiting.

Four minutes later, alone in a dirty third-class carriage, I watched the lights of Naples fade in the distance.

I was on my way to Rome!

Gina's large blue eyes opened to their fullest extent when she saw me standing in the doorway.

'Why, Ed!'

'Hello.'

I closed the door and came over to sit on the edge of her desk. It was a relief to be back on my home ground. There was a feeling of security in this neat, well-ordered office.

I had spent a horrible six hours sweating it out in my apartment. Being alone with Helen's death on my mind had been bad.

'Is there anything wrong?' she asked sharply.

I wish I could have told her just how wrong things were.

'Why, no: there's nothing wrong,' I said. 'I couldn't get a room in Venice. I called the Travel Association and they said I hadn't a dog's chance of getting in anywhere at short notice, so I decided to let Venice go. Then I thought I might put a little work in on my novel. I got so engrossed with my own cleverness I didn't stop working until three o'clock this morning.'

'But you're supposed to be on vacation,' Gina said. There was a worried, puzzled expression in her eyes that warned me she wasn't sure if I were telling her the truth. 'If you're not going to Venice, where are you going?'

'Don't bully me,' I said. I found it difficult to use a bantering tone and I realized that perhaps it was a mistake to see Gina so soon after Helen's death. I've said before that Gina had a knack of knowing to a certain extent what was going on in my mind. I could see as she stared up at me that she suspected something was badly wrong. 'I thought I might take the car and go to Monte Carlo. You have my passport somewhere, haven't you? I can't find it in the apartment.'

At this moment the door opened and Maxwell came in. He paused in the doorway and gave me a curious stare. His eyes became hostile.

'Why, hello,' he said, then moved into the room, closing the door behind him. 'Can't you keep away from this joint or don't you think I can handle the job?'

I was in no mood to take anything from him.

'You wouldn't be here if I didn't think you could handle it,' I said curtly. 'I've looked in for my passport. I tried to get fixed up in Venice, but all the hotels are full.'

He relaxed a little, but I could see he didn't like my being here.

'You've taken enough time to find that out, haven't you? You want to get organized. What were you up to all day yesterday, for the love of mike?'

'Working on my novel,' I said, lighting a cigarette and smiling at him.

His face hardened.

'Don't tell me you're writing a novel.'

'Certainly, I am. Every newspaper man is supposed to have a good book in him. I'm hoping to make a fortune out of it. You should try: I'm not scared of competition.'

'I've better things to do with my spare time,' he said shortly. 'Well, I've got work to do. Have you got your passport?'

'Which is another way of saying I'm in the way and will I please scram,' I said, smiling at him.

'I've some letters to dictate.'

Gina had gone to the filing-cabinet. She came back with my passport.

'I'll be ready for you in five minutes, Miss Valetti,' Maxwell said, making for his office. 'So long, Ed.'

'So long.'

When he had gone into the inner office and had shut the door, Gina and I exchanged looks. I winked at her.

'I'll be getting along. I'll give you a call when I've found a hotel.'

'All right, Ed.'

'I won't be going for a couple of days. I'll be at my apartment until Thursday morning. If anything blows up, you'll know where to reach me.'

She looked sharply at me.

'But you're on vacation. Nothing will blow up that Mr. Maxwell can't handle.'

I forced a grin.

'I know that, but all the same, should you want me, I'll be at my apartment. So long for now.'

I left her staring blankly after me and went down to my car.

I wasn't sure if it had been wise to have given Gina this hint, but I knew sooner or later the news would break about Helen's death. The police, once they found out who she was, were bound to contact the office, and I was anxious to be in on the investigation from the beginning.

I returned to my apartment.

I wasn't in the mood to work on my novel. Helen's death lay on my mind like a pall. The more I thought about her, the more I realized what a fool I had been. I had been swept off my feet by her physical attractions. I discovered now I hadn't ever been fond of her. Her death, apart from the worry it caused me as to its repercussion on my life, meant little to me. I realized, too, that I shouldn't have run away as I had. I should have had the courage to have called the police and told them the truth. Until the inquest was over and the verdict of accidental death recorded, I knew I wasn't going to have an easy moment.

There was bound to be an inquiry about the mysterious Douglas Sherrard. Helen had said that she had rented the villa in that name. The estate agent was certain to give the police that information. Questions would be asked: who is Douglas Sherrard? Where is he? Maybe the police wouldn't get too curious. They would learn that Helen wasn't Mrs. Douglas Sherrard. They would guess she had arranged an affair with some man and the man hadn't shown up. Would they be content to drop that side of the investigation? Had I covered my tracks well enough to remain undiscovered if they did search for Sherrard?

I sat in my big lounge that overlooked the Roman forum and sweated. When, around four o'clock, the telephone bell rang, I could scarcely force myself out of my chair to answer it.

'Hello?' I said, aware that my voice sounded like the croak of a frog.

'Is that you, Ed?'

I recognized Maxwell's voice.

'Sure, it's me. Who else do you think it is?'

'Will you come over right away?' He sounded excited and flustered. 'My God! I've got a hell of a thing dropped into my lap. The police have just phoned. They say they've found Helen Chalmers . . . she's dead!'

'Dead! What happened?'

'Come over, will you? They're arriving at any moment, and I want you here.'

'I'll be right over,' I said, and hung up.

This was it. It had started a little sooner than I had expected. I crossed the room, poured out two fingers of Scotch and drank it. I noticed my hands were unsteady, and

47

when I looked at myself in the mirror over the liquor cabinet, I saw my face was the colour of tallow and my eyes looked scared.

I left the apartment and went down to the underground garage. By the time I had driven out into the heavy traffic the whisky was beginning to bite. I didn't feel quite so scared. I finally got rid of my shakes as I pulled up outside the *Western Telegram* building.

I found Maxwell and Gina in the outer office. Maxwell looked bad. His face was white as a fresh fall of snow. Gina looked worried too. She gave me an uneasy stare as I came in, and then moved into the background, but I felt she continued to watch me.

'Am I glad to see you!' Maxwell exclaimed. His hostility and smoothness had gone. 'What's the old man going to say when he hears? Who's going to break the news to him?'

'Relax,' I said sharply. 'What happened? Come on! Let's have it!'

'They didn't give me any details. They just said she had been found dead. She fell off a cliff at Sorrento.'

'Fell off a cliff?' I was acting hard now. 'What was she doing in Sorrento?'

'I don't know.' Maxwell nervously lit a cigarette. 'This is just my luck to have a thing happen like this on my first trip out here. Look, Ed, you'll have to tell Chalmers. He'll shoot his top.'

'Take it easy. I'll tell him. What I can't understand is why she was at Sorrento.'

'Maybe the police know. My God! This would happen to me!' He pounded his fist into the palm of his hand. 'You've got to handle it, Ed. You know what Chalmers is like. He'll want an inquiry. He's bound to want an inquiry. He'll expect . . .'

'Oh, pipe down!' I said. 'Stop working yourself up. This isn't your fault. If he wants an inquiry, he can have one.'

He made an effort to pull himself together.

'It's all right for you to talk. You're his white-headed boy. But he hasn't much use for me. . . .'

At this moment the door opened and Lieutenant Itola Carlotti of the Rome Homicide Department came in.

Carlotti was a short, dark man with a tanned, wrinkled face and pale penetrating blue eyes. He was nudging forty-five, but looked thirty. I had known him for two or three

48

years, and we got along well together. I knew him for a smart, conscientious policeman without any genius for his job. He got results by careful, painstaking plodding.

'I thought you were on vacation,' he said, as he shook hands with me.

'I was about to leave when this broke,' I said. 'You know Signorina Valetti? This is Signor Maxwell. He's taking my place while I'm away,'

Carlotti shook hands with Maxwell and bowed to Gina.

'Let's have it,' I said, settling myself on Gina's desk and waving him to a chair. 'Are you sure it's Helen Chalmers?'

'I don't think there's any doubt about that,' he said, planting himself before me and making no move to take the chair I had indicated. 'Three hours ago I had a report from Naples headquarters that the body of a young woman had been found lying at the foot of a cliff, five miles from Sorrento. It was thought she had fallen off a path on the cliff. Half an hour ago, I was told she had been identified as Signorina Helen Chalmers. Apparently she had rented a villa close to where she had fallen. When the villa was searched it became apparent from the contents of her luggage who she was. I want someone from your office to come with me to Sorrento to identify the body.'

I hadn't expected this. The thought of going into the morgue to identify what remained of Helen's loveliness turned me sick.

Maxwell said hurriedly, 'You've met her, Ed. You'll have to go. I've only seen pictures of her.'

Carlotti said, looking at me, 'I'm going down there right away. Can you come with me?'

'I'll come,' I said, and slid off the desk. Turning to Maxwell, I went on, 'Hold everything until I call you. It may not be her. I'll call you as soon as I know. Stick around until you hear from me.'

'What about Chalmers?'

'I'll handle him,' I said; then, turning to Carlotti, I went on, 'Okay, let's go.'

I patted Gina's shoulder as I followed Carlotti out of the office. We didn't say anything until we were driving fast towards the Rome airport, then I said, 'Any idea how it happened?'

He gave me a solid stare.

'I told you: she fell off a cliff.'

'I know what you told me. Is there more to it?'

He lifted his shoulders as only an Italian can lift them.

'I don't know. She rented a villa under the name of Mrs. Douglas Sherrard. She wasn't married, was she?'

'Not as far as I know.'

He lit one of those awful Italian cigarettes and puffed smoke out of the car window.

'There are a few complications,' he said after a long moment of silence. 'Signor Chalmers is an important man. I don't want any trouble.'

'Nor do I. He's not only an important man, but he's also my boss.' I eased myself down in the car seat. 'Apart from calling herself Mrs. Douglas Sherrard—what other complications?'

'Do you know anything about her?' His cold blue eyes searched my face. 'For the moment no one except you and I and the Naples police know about this, but it won't be possible to keep it quiet for long. It looks as if she had a lover.'

I pulled a face.

'Chalmers will love that. You'll have to be careful what you tell the press, Lieutenant.'

He nodded.

'I realize that. From what I hear, she rented the villa in the joint names of Mr. and Mrs. Douglas Sherrard. Do you think she was secretly married?'

'She might have been, but I don't think it likely.'

'I don't think so either. I think she was on an unofficial honeymoon in Sorrento.' Again he lifted his shoulders expressively. 'It happens. Do you know anyone called Douglas Sherrard?'

'No.'

He tapped ash off his cigarette.

'Grandi, who is handling the case, seems satisfied it was an accidental fall. He has only asked me to check with him because il Signor Chalmers is such an important man. It is unfortunate that there is a lover involved. If there was no lover, it would be pretty straightforward.'

'It might not be necessary to mention him,' I said, looking out of the car window.

'That is possible. You wouldn't know for certain if she had a lover '

'I know practically nothing about her.' I felt the palms of my hands turn moist. 'We mustn't jump to conclusions. Until we have seen the body, we don't know for certain it is her.'

'I am afraid it is her all right. All her clothes and her luggage carry her name. There were letters found in her luggage. The description fits. I don't think there's a doubt about it.'

We said nothing further until we were on the plane for Naples, then suddenly he said, 'You will have to explain the position to il Signor Chalmers. The fact that she rented the villa under another name is bound to come out at the inquest. You understand there is nothing we can do to hush it up.'

I could see he was worried about getting tangled with Chalmers.

'Oh, sure,' I said. 'That's not your funeral nor mine.'

He gave me a sidelong look.

'Il Signor Chalmers has a lot of influence.'

'He certainly has, but he should have used some of it with his daughter before she got tied up in a situation like this.'

He lit another of his awful cigarettes, sank further down in his seat and went off in a coma of brooding. I went off into one of my own.

I was surprised he hadn't said any more about Douglas Sherrard. This made me a little uneasy. I knew Carlotti. He moved slowly, but he also moved thoroughly.

We reached Naples around noon. There was a police car waiting. Lieutenant Grandi of the Naples Police was standing by the car, waiting for us.

He was a middle-sized bird with a hatchet face, dark solemn eyes and an olive complexion. He shook hands with me, looking just beyond my right shoulder. I had the impression he wasn't overjoyed to have me in the party. He manoeuvred Carlotti into the back seat and me in the front seat beside the driver. He got in alongside Carlotti.

During the long, fast drive to Sorrento, I could just hear his rapid Italian as he talked continuously, his voice barely above a whisper.

I tried to listen to what he was saying, but the noise of the wind and the roar of the car engine made that impossible. I gave up, lit a cigarette and stared through the wind shield

51

at the unwinding road as it rushed continuously towards us, thinking of the previous night's ride that had been so much quicker and so much more dangerous.

We reached Sorrento. The police driver took us around the back of the railway station to a small brick building that served as the town's morgue.

We got out of the car.

Carlotti said to me, 'This won't be pleasant for you, but it is necessary. She has to be identified.'

'That's all right,' I said.

But it wasn't all right. I was sweating, and I knew I must have lost colour. I didn't have to worry about my appearance. Anyone could have looked the same in such circumstances.

I followed him through the door of the building, down a tiled lined corridor and into a small, bare room.

In the middle of the room stood a trestle table on which lay a body, under a sheet.

We moved forward up to the table. My heart was beating sluggishly. There was a sickness inside me that made me feel faint.

I watched Carlotti reach forward and turn back the sheet.

III

It was Helen all right, and, of course, she was dead.

Although someone with a practised hand had cleaned her up, and had made her as presentable as possible, her face still bore the marks of the awful fall she had taken.

It was pretty unnerving to stand there and look down at the dead, shattered face. I turned away, feeling bad. Grandi, who had come up behind me, put his hand on my arm as Carlotti pulled the sheet back into place.

I jerked away from Grandi and walked out into the corridor. The fresh draught of air coming in through the open doorway did a lot to help me pull myself together.

The two detectives came out silently, and the three of us walked slowly back to the car.

'Yes, it's her,' I said, as we reached the car. 'No doubt about it.'

Carlotti lifted his shoulders.

'I have been hoping that there might be a mistake. This is going to be troublesome. There will be a lot of publicity.'

I could see he was still very worried about Chalmers. He knew Chalmers had enough influence to lift him right out of his job if he put a foot wrong.

'Yeah,' I said. I wasn't sorry for him. I had too much on my mind at that moment to be sorry for anyone except myself. 'I'll have to send him a cable.'

Carlotti lit another of his awful cigarettes. As he flicked away the burning match, he said, 'We'll go to the station now. You can use the telephone there.'

We got in the car: Carlotti and Grandi behind and I with the driver. No one said anything while we drove through the traffic-congested main street to the police station. By the time we got there, I was feeling a little more like my old self, although I was still pretty shaken. They left me in an office while they went off to another office for a conference.

I put a call through to Maxwell.

'There's no doubt about it,' I said, when he came on the line. 'It's Helen all right.'

'Sweet grief! What do we do now?'

'I'm going to send a cable to Chalmers. I'll give him three hours to get over the shock, then I'll call him on long distance.'

I could hear him breathing like an old man with asthma.

'I guess that's all you can do,' he said after a long pause. 'Okay, if there's anything I can do . . .'

'Look after the job,' I said. 'It doesn't mean that because Chalmer's daughter falls off a cliff, the job stands still.'

'I'll look after it if you'll look after Chalmers,' he told me. 'There's no need for me to shove my oar into this, Ed. You're fitted for the job. He likes you. He thinks you're sharp. He hasn't much use for me. I'll take care of the work here: you take care of Chalmers.'

'Okay. Put Miss Valetti on the line, will you?'

'Sure. Hang on a moment.'

The relief in his voice was almost comic.

A moment or so later, Gina's cool voice came on the line.

'She's dead then, Ed?'

'Yes. She's dead all right. Have you got your book? I want to send a cable to Chalmers.'

'Go ahead.'

That's something I have always admired about Gina. No matter how big the emergency is, she never got rattled.

I dictated a cable to Chalmers. I told him his daughter had met with an accident. I regretted that she was dead. I said I would call him at his house at 16.00 hours European time with the details. That gave me three hours in which to get the details and find out how much the police had discovered. It would also give me time to cook up my end of the tale if it seemed necessary to cook up a tale.

Gina said she would get the cable off right away.

'Do that,' I said. 'There's a chance Chalmers will call before I call him. If he does, you don't know a thing—— understand? Don't get tangled up in this, Gina. You don't know a thing. Tell him I'll call him at four o'clock sharp.'

'All right, Ed.'

It was good to hear her calm, matter-of-fact voice. I dropped the receiver on to its cradle and pushed back my chair. As I did so, Carlotti came in.

'I am going to look at the place where she died,' he said. 'Do you want to come?'

I stood up.

'Sure, I'll come.'

As I followed him out of the office, I saw Grandi was waiting in the corridor. Maybe I was suffering from a guilty conscience, but I had an uneasy idea that the look he gave me was full of suspicion.

PART IV

I

THE POLICE LAUNCH rounded the bend of the high cliff.
I was sitting in the stern of the boat by Carlotti. He was
smoking, and he wore blue-tinted sunglasses. It seemed odd
to me that a policeman should wear sunglasses. I felt he
should be above such luxuries.

Grandi and three uniformed policemen were amidships.
Grandi didn't wear sunglasses: whatever he did would
always be official and correct.

As soon as we got around the bend, I recognized the
tiny bay and the massive boulders on which Helen had
fallen.

Carlotti stared up at the cliff head. He made a little face.
I could see he was thinking what it must have felt to have
fallen from such a height. Looking up, I also thought the
same thing. The distant cliff head up there made me feel
like a pigmy.

The boat chugged into the bay. As soon as it drew alongside the rocks, we scrambled out.

Grandi said to Carlotti, 'We haven't touched anything. I
wanted you to see it first. All we did was to remove the
body.'

He and Carlotti began a systematic search of the spot. I
and two of the policemen sat on one of the boulders, out of
the way, and watched them. The third policeman remained
in the boat.

It wasn't long before Grandi found the camera case I had
tossed over the cliff. It was lying half-submerged in water,
between two boulders. He fished it up. Both he and Carlotti
examined it the way a couple of professors would have
examined something that had fallen off Mars.

I noted the careful way Carlotti handled the case, and I was thankful I had got rid of all my prints.

Finally he looked over at me.

'This must be hers. Was she interested in photography?'

I very nearly said she was, but caught myself in time.

'I wouldn't know,' I said. 'Most Americans on a visit to Italy bring a camera.

Carlotti nodded and handed the camera case to one of the policemen who put it carefully into a plastic bag.

They continued their search. After about ten minutes and after they had climbed some distance from where I was sitting, I saw they had made another discovery. Grandi bent and picked something up from between the cliff face and a rock. The two men stood close together, their backs to me while they examined whatever it was they had found.

I waited, smoking, aware that my heart kept thumping and my mouth was dry.

Finally, after what seemed to me a lifetime, Carlotti made his way to where I was sitting. I pushed off from the rock and went to meet him. I saw he was holding what remained of Helen's Paillard Bolex camera. It had obviously hit a rock in its fall down the cliff face. The telephoto lens had snapped off and there was a dent in its side.

'This could explain how the accident happened,' Carlotti said, showing me the camera. 'She was probably taking a picture; holding it like this.' He held up the camera and peered through the viewfinder. 'If she had stood on the edge of the path up there, it would be easy for her to take a false step with this thing obscuring her view.'

I took the camera from him and looked at the little window panel at the back that showed how many feet of film you have run off. It showed twelve feet.

'There's a film in it,' I said. 'From the look of the camera the water hasn't got into it. Get the film processed, and you'll know for sure if she was taking something from the cliff head.'

This seemed to please him.

All the time we had been driving down to the harbour and all the time we had been in the boat, heading towards the place where Helen had died, I knew he had been secretly worrying about the trouble Chalmers might make for him.

'If she hadn't called herself Mrs. Douglas Sherrard,' he said, taking the camera from me, 'this would be a very

56

straightforward affair. We will go to the villa now. I want to talk to the village woman.'

We returned to the harbour of Sorrento, leaving two of the policemen to continue the search for clues. They seemed pretty depressed at being marooned on the rocks. I didn't blame them. It was very hot out there, and there was no shade.

When we reached the harbour, we took the police car and drove out to the villa.

The trip back from the bay and the drive up to the villa took a little over an hour and a half.

We left the police car at the gates and walked up the drive. The Lincoln convertible still stood on the tarmac before the villa.

Carlotti said, 'Did this car belong to her?'

I said I didn't know.

Grandi broke in impatiently to say that he had already checked the registration plates. Helen had bought the car ten weeks ago: soon after she had arrived in Rome.

I wondered where the money had come from. It puzzled me. I told myself that it was possible that she had cabled to her father, and he had sent her the money but, remembering what he had said about her keeping within her allowance, it didn't seem likely the money had come from him.

We trooped into the lounge. Carlotti asked me politely if I would sit down and wait while he examined the villa.

I sat down and waited.

They spent some time in the bedroom. After a while, Carlotti came out carrying a small leather box: the kind of box you buy in Florence when you're hard put to give a friend at home a present.

'You had better take charge of these,' he said, putting the box on the table. 'They must be given to il Signor Chalmers. Perhaps you will give me a receipt?'

He lifted the lid. In the box were some pieces of jewellery. There were two rings: one of them had a large sapphire stone; the other had three diamonds. There was a collar of diamonds and a pair of diamond ear-rings. I don't know much about the value of jewellery, but even I could see that these would be worth quite a lot.

'They are very nice,' Carlotti said. He sounded a little wistful as if he coveted the jewels. 'It is fortunate no one broke in here while the place was unguarded.'

I remembered the tall, broad-shouldered intruder.

'Where did you find them?' I asked.

'They were on her dressing-table for anyone to steal.'

'They're genuine? I mean, they're not paste?'

'Of course they are genuine.' He frowned at me. 'I should say at a rough guess they are worth three million lire.'

While he was scribbling out a receipt for me to sign, I stared at the box and its contents. On her dressing-table for anyone to steal! I felt a little chill of uneasiness crawl up my spine. It didn't seem then that the intruder I had seen had been a sneak thief. Then who had he been? The sound of the telephone bell startled me.

Carlotti answered it.

He said, 'Si ... si ... si.' Listened for a long moment, then grunted something and hung up.

Grandi came into the room. His face wore an expectant expression.

Carlotti lit a cigarette before saying to me, 'They have just had the autopsy report.'

I could see something had upset him. His eyes were uneasy again.

'Well, you know how she died,' I said in an attempt to bridge over the long pause that followed.

'Yes, there is no doubt about that.'

He moved away from the telephone. I could feel his uneasiness the way you feel the touch of a hand in the dark.

'Is there anything else?'

I was aware that my voice had sharpened. I saw Grandi turn to look at me.

'Yes, there is something else.' Carlotti said and grimaced. 'She was pregnant.'

II

It was close on three-thirty by the time Carlotti had completed his examination of the villa and his interrogation of the woman from the village.

I didn't see her.

I could hear the faint sound of their voices as he talked with her in the kitchen. I remained in the lounge, smoking cigarette after cigarette, my mind a squirrel cage of panic.

So Helen had been pregnant.

That would be the final nail in my coffin if they ever found out who Douglas Sherrard was. I knew I was not only innocent of her death, but also of her pregnancy, but if ever the facts came out, no one would believe it.

What a mad, crass stupid fool I had been to have ever got tangled with the girl!

Who had been her lover?

I thought again of the broad-shouldered, mysterious intruder I had seen the previous night. Was he the man? It was possible. It was obvious now that he hadn't been a thief. No thief would have left three million lire's worth of jewellery on the dressing-table.

I went on turning this situation over in my mind, watching the clock on the overmantel, knowing in another half-hour I would have to give Chalmers the details of her death.

The more I thought about it, the more acutely conscious I became that one false step would be my complete finish.

Carlotti came into the lounge as the hands of the clock on the overmantel moved to three forty-four.

'There are complications,' he said gloomily.

'I know. You said that before.'

'Do you think she was the suicide type?'

The question startled me.

'I don't know. I tell you, I don't know anything about her.' I felt compelled to drive this point home so I went on, 'Chalmers asked me to meet her at the airport and take her to her hotel. This was about fourteen weeks ago. Since then I have scarcely seen her. I just don't know anything about her.'

'Grandi thinks it is possible that her lover deserted her,' Carlotti said. I don't think he paid much notice to what I had said. 'He thinks she threw herself off the cliff in despair.'

'American girls don't do that sort of thing. They're too practical. You will have to be careful how you suggest a theory of that kind to Chalmers. He might not like it.'

59

'I'm not suggesting it to il Signor Chalmers, I'm suggesting it to you,' Carlotti said quietly.

Grandi wandered in at this moment and sat down. He stared at me with cold, hostile eyes. For some reason or other, he didn't seem to like me.

'Make all the suggestions you like to me,' I said, looking steadily at Carlotti. 'It won't help you one way or the other, but be careful what you say to Chalmers.'

'Yes,' Carlotti said. 'I understand that. I am relying on you for help. It seems there was a love affair. The woman has told me that the girl came here two days ago. She came alone. She told the woman that she was expecting her husband to join her the following day—that would be yesterday. The woman says there is no doubt that she was expecting him. She was very gay.' He broke off to stare at me. 'I'm telling you what the woman said. Women are very often reliable concerning such matters.'

'Go on,' I said. 'I'm not arguing with you.'

'This man was supposed to be arriving at Sorrento from Naples at three-thirty. La signorina told her she was going to meet the train, and she was to come in at nine in the evening to clear up the dinner things. The woman left the villa at eleven in the morning. Between that time and the time it was necessary for la signorina to leave to meet the train something happened either to prevent her from meeting the train or that made her change her mind about meeting it.'

'What kind of thing?'

He lifted his shoulders.

'She may have received a message. There is no record of her receiving a telephone call. I don't know. I think it is very possible she learned somehow or other that her lover wasn't coming.'

'You're guessing,' I said. 'You'll have to watch out not to guess with Chalmers.'

'By then we may have some facts. I am trying theories.' He moved restlessly. I could see he was perplexed and unhappy with the situation. 'I am seeing if Grandi's theory fits that in a fit of depression she killed herself.

'Does it matter?' I said. 'She's dead. Can't this be put through as an accident? There's no need to broadcast the fact that she was pregnant, is there?'

'The coroner will have the autopsy report. There is no way of keeping it quiet.'

Grandi said impatiently, 'Well, I have things to do. I have got to find this man Sherrard.'

I felt as if someone had touched the back of my neck with a splinter of ice.

'I am going to call il Signor Chalmers,' I said, trying to make my voice casual. 'He will want to know what is happening. What shall I tell him?'

The two men exchanged glances.

'It would be wise to tell him as little as possible at this stage of the investigation,' Carlotti said. 'It would be unwise to mention this man Sherrard, I think. Couldn't you say that she fell off the cliff while using her cine camera, that there will be an inquest and a full investigation and until then . . .'

The telephone interrupted him. Grandi lifted the receiver, listened for a moment, then looked across at me.

'It is for you.'

I took the receiver from him.

'Hello?'

Gina said, 'Mr. Chalmers phoned through ten minutes ago. He said he was flying out right away, and you are to meet him at 18.00 hours at the Naples airport to-morrow.'

I drew in a long, slow breath. This was something I wasn't prepared for.

'How did he sound?'

'He was very curt and sharp,' Gina said. 'He didn't sound like anything except that.'

'Did he ask any questions?'

'No. He just told me the time he would be arriving and asked for you to meet him.'

'Okay, I'll be there.'

'Is there anything I can do?'

'No. Go home, Gina. I won't be needing you now.'

'If you do, I'll be at my apartment all the evening.'

'Okay, but I won't worry you. So long for now,' and I hung up.

Carlotti was watching me, his eyes frowning.

'Chalmers will arrive at Naples at 18.00 hours to-morrow,' I said. 'Between now and then, you'd better get some facts. There'll be no question of telling him as little as possible. He'll have to be told everything, and in detail.'

Carlotti grimaced as he got to his feet.

'We should be able to find this man Sherrard by tomorrow evening,' he said, and looked over at Grandi. 'Leave your man here. He is to remain here until he is relieved. You can drive us down to Sorrento. Don't forget the jewels, Signor Dawson.'

I picked up the leather box and slipped it into my pocket.

As we went down the steps and down the drive to the police car, Carlotti said to Grandi, 'I'll leave you in Sorrento. Try to find out if anyone knows Sherrard and if he was seen in Sorrento. Check up on all American visitors who arrived yesterday; especially on any American travelling alone.'

In spite of the heat, I realized that the sweat on my face felt cold.

III

I got to the Naples airport at a few minutes to six o'clock. They told me the New York plane was on time, and was due in at any moment.

I went to the barrier, lit a cigarette and waited. There were four people waiting; two of them elderly women, the third a fat Frenchman and the fourth was a platinum blonde with a bust on her you only see in the pages of *Esquire*. She was wearing a white sharkskin costume and a small black hat with a diamond cluster ornament that must have cost someone a pile of money.

I looked at her and she turned. Our eyes met.

'Excuse me: are you Mr. Dawson?' she asked.

'That's right,' I said, surprised. I took off my hat.

'I am Mrs. Sherwin Chalmers.'

I stared at her.

'You are? Mr. Chalmers hasn't already arrived, has he?'

'Oh, no. I've been shopping in Paris for the past week,' she said, her deep violet eyes searching my face. She had the hard beauty of a New York show-girl. She couldn't have been more than twenty-three or four, but there was a worldliness about her that made her look older. 'My husband cabled me to meet him. This is dreadful news.'

'Yes.'

I fidgeted with my hat.

'It's a terrible thing . . . she was so young,'

'It's bad,' I said.

There was something in the way she kept looking at me that made me uncomfortable.

'Did you know her well, Mr. Dawson?'

'Hardly at all.'

'I can't understand how she could have fallen like that.'

'The police think she was taking photographs and didn't look where she was going.'

The sound of an approaching aircraft cut this uncomfortable conversation short.

'I think the plane's coming in now,' I said.

We stood side by side, watching the aircraft land. After a few minutes, the passengers began to alight. Chalmers was the first off the plane. He came quickly through the barrier. I drew back and let him greet his wife. They stood talking together for a few moments, then he came over to me and shook hands. He stared hard at me, then said they wanted to get to the hotel as quickly as possible, that he didn't want to discuss Helen at this moment and for me to arrange a meeting with the police at his hotel at seven.

He and his wife got in the back seat of the Rolls I had hired for them and, as I didn't get any encouragement, I got in front with the chauffeur.

At the hotel, Chalmers dismissed me with a curt, 'See you at seven, Dawson,' and they were whisked away in the elevator up to the fourth floor, leaving me feeling a little breathless.

I had seen photographs of Chalmers, but in the flesh he was more than life size. Although he was short, fat and built like a barrel, there was an atmosphere about him that reduced me and the people around him to the size of pigmies. The best description I can give of him is that he reminded me of Mussolini in his heyday. He had the same ruthless, jutting jaw, the same dark complexion and the same ice-pick eyes. It didn't seem possible that he could have been the sire of a girl like Helen whose brittle, uncoarse beauty had been so fatally attractive to me.

When, at seven o'clock, Carlotti, Grandi and I trooped into the lush lounge that the Vesuvius hotel had provided for him, he had changed, obviously shaved and showered, and was now sitting at the head of a big table in the middle of the room, a cigar between his teeth and a glowering, dark expression on his hard face.

Sitting by the window was his wife, June. She had on a sky-blue silk dress that fitted her like a second skin and her long, shapely legs were crossed, showing beautiful knees that attracted Grandi's eyes and made his usually gloomy dark face take on a more animated expression.

I introduced him and Carlotti and we sat down.

For a long moment Chalmers stared fixedly at Carlotti. Then he said in his barking voice, 'Okay, let's have the facts.'

I've know Carlotti pretty intimately for the past three years. Up to this moment, I had never thought much of him as a policeman. I knew he was thorough, and he had a reputation for solving his cases, but he had never struck me as having any great talent for his job. But the way he faced up to Chalmers during the next twenty minutes gave me an entirely different opinion of him.

'The facts, Signor Chalmers,' he said quietly, 'will be painful to you, but since you ask for them, you shall have them.'

Chalmers sat motionless, his freckled, fat hands clasped on the top of the table, his cigar, drifting smoke past his hard face, gripped tightly between his teeth. His small, ice-pick eyes, the colour of rain, stared fixedly at Carlotti.

'Never mind how painful it is,' he said. 'Give me the facts.'

'Ten days ago, your daughter left Rome and flew to Naples. She took the local train from Naples to Sorrento where she paid a visit to an estate agent,' Carlotti said as if he had rehearsed this speech for some time, learning it by heart. 'She introduced herself to the estate agent as Mrs. Douglas Sherrard, the wife of an American business man on vacation in Rome.'

I sneaked a quick look at Chalmers. He sat impassive, his cigar glowing, his hands slack on the table. I looked from him to his platinum blonde wife. She was looking out of the window and she gave no sign that she was listening.

'She wanted a villa for a month,' Carlotti went on in his quiet, excellent English. 'She insisted on a place that was isolated, and the cost was immaterial. It so happened that the agent had such a place. He drove la signorina to this villa and she agreed to take it. She wanted someone to come in and look after the place during their stay. The agent arranged with a woman of a nearby village to do the necessary work. This woman, Maria Candallo, tells me that, on August 28th, she went to the villa where she found la signorina who had arrived a few hours earlier in a Lincoln convertible.'

Chalmers said, 'Was the car registered in her name?'

'Yes,' Carlotti said.

Chalmers touched off the ash on his cigar, nodded, and said, 'Go on.'

'La signorina told Maria that her husband would be arriving the following day. According to the woman, there was no doubt in her mind that la signorina was very much in love with this man, whom she called Douglas Sherrard.'

For the first time Chalmers gave a hint of his feelings. He hunched his broad shoulders and his freckled hands turned into fists.

Carlotti went on, 'Maria came to the villa at eight forty-five on the morning of the 29th. She washed up the breakfast things, dusted and swept. La signorina told her she was going down to Sorrento to meet the three-thirty train from Naples. She said her husband was coming from Rome on that train. Around eleven o'clock Maria left. At that time la signorina was arranging flowers in the lounge. That was the last time, so far as we know, that anyone saw her alive.'

June Chalmers recrossed her legs. She turned her pretty head and stared directly at me. Her worldly, violet eyes went over me thoughtfully: a disconcerting stare that made me look quickly away from her.

'What happened between that time and eight-fifteen in the evening is a matter for conjecture,' Carlotti said. 'It is something probably that we shall never know.'

Chalmers's eyes became hooded. He leaned forward.

'Why eight-fifteen?' he asked.

'That was the time she died,' Carlotti said. 'I don't think there is any doubt about that. Her wrist watch was smashed in the fall. It showed exactly eight-fifteen.'

I had stiffened to attention. This was news to me. It meant that I was in the villa, looking for Helen, when she had fallen. No one, including a judge and jury, would believe I hadn't had something to do with her death if it became known I had been up there at the time.

'I would like to be able to tell you,' Carlotti went on, 'that your daughter's death was due to an unfortunate accident, but at the moment, I can't do it. I admit on the face of it, it would seem to be the solution. There is no doubt that she took a cine camera up on the cliff head. It is possible, when using a camera of this kind, to become so absorbed in what you are taking, that you could get too close to the edge of the path and fall over.'

Chalmers took the cigar out of his mouth and laid it in the ashtray. He stared fixedly at Carlotti.

'Are you trying to tell me that it wasn't an accident?' he said in a voice you could cut a stale loaf on.

June Chalmers stopped staring at me and cocked her head on one side: for the first time she appeared to be interested in what was going on.

'That is for the coroner to decide,' Carlotti said. He was quite unflustered and he met the ice-pick eyes without flinching. 'There are complications. There are a number of details that need explaining. It would seem there are two alternative explanations for your daughter's death: one is that she accidentally stepped off the cliff head while using her camera; the other is that she committed suicide.'

Chalmers hunched his shoulders and his face congested.

'You have reason to say a thing like that?'

He conveyed that Carlotti had damn well better have a reason.

Carlotti let him have it without rubber cushioning.

'Your daughter was eight weeks' pregnant.'

There was a long, heavy silence. I didn't dare look at Chalmers. I stared down at my sweating hands that were gripped between my thighs.

June broke the silence by saying, 'Oh, Sherwin. I can't believe that——'

I sneaked a quick look at Chalmers. His face was murderous: the kind of face you see on the screen of some not-too-good actor playing the role of a cornered gangster.

'Hold your tongue!' he snarled at June in a voice that shook with violence. Then, as she turned to look out of the window, he said to Carlotti, 'Is that what the doctor said?'

'I have a copy of the autopsy,' Carlotti returned. 'You can see it if you wish.'

'Pregnant? Helen?'

He pushed back his chair and got to his feet. He still looked awe-inspiring, tough and ruthless, but somehow he didn't make me feel quite such a pigmy; some of his big-shot atmosphere had gone out of him.

He walked slowly around the lounge while Carlotti, Grandi and I stared down at our feet and June stared out of the window.

'She wouldn't commit suicide,' he said suddenly. 'She had too much strength of character.'

They seemed empty words: unexpected words from a man like Chalmers. I found myself wondering what chance he had ever given himself to find out if Helen had had any character at all.

No one said anything.

He continued to walk around the lounge, his hands in his pockets, his face set and frowning.

After several uncomfortable minutes had ticked by, he paused suddenly and asked the world-old question, 'Who is the man?'

'We don't know,' Carlotti said. 'Your daughter may have purposely misled the estate agent and the village woman by telling them he is an American. There is no American in Italy of that name.'

Chalmers came over and sat down again.

'He's probably not using his own name,' he said.

'That is possible,' Carlotti said, 'We have made inquiries in Sorrento. There was an American, travelling alone, on the three-thirty from Naples.'

I felt my heart contract: it was a horrible feeling. I found difficulty in breathing.

'He left a suitcase at the station,' Carlotti went on. 'Unfortunately the description of him varies. No one particularly noticed him. He was seen walking on the Sorrento-Amalfi road by a passing motorist. All anyone can be certain about is that he wore a light grey suit. The station clerk said he was tall. The motorist thought he was of middle height. A boy from a nearby village said he was short and thick-set. There is no clear description of him. Around ten o'clock in the evening he collected his suitcase and took a taxi to Naples. He was in a great hurry. He offered the driver a five

67

thousand lire tip to get him to the station to catch the eleven-fifteen to Rome.'

Chalmers was sitting forward, his eyes intent. He reminded me of some beast of prey.

'The road to Amalfi is also the road to this villa?'

'Yes. There is a branch road.'

'My daughter died at eight-fifteen?'

'Yes.'

'And this fella took a taxi in a hurry around ten o'clock?'

'Yes.'

'How long would it take to get from this villa to Sorrento?'

'About half an hour by car, or walking, it'd take well over an hour and a half.'

Chalmers brooded for a moment.

I sat there breathing through my half-open mouth and feeling pretty bad. I expected him to come out with some devastating discovery after these questions, but he didn't. Instead, he suddenly hunched his shoulders and said, 'She wouldn't commit suicide. I know that. You can put that theory right out of your mind, Lieutenant. It is obvious: she fell off the cliff while using this camera.'

Carlotti didn't say anything. Grandi moved uneasily and stared hard at his finger-nails.

'That's the verdict I expect to hear,' Chalmers went on, his voice harsh.

Carlotti said smoothly, 'It's my business to give the facts to the coroner, Signor Chalmers. It is his business to find the verdict.'

Chalmers stared at him.

'Yes. Who is the coroner?'

'Il signor Giuseppe Maletti.'

'Here—in Naples?'

'Yes.'

Chalmers nodded.

'Where is my daughter's body?'

'At the Sorrento mortuary.'

'I want to see her.'

'Of course. There will be no difficulty. If you will let me know when, I will take you there.'

'You don't have to do that. I don't like people following me around. Dawson will take me.'

'As you wish, signore.'

'Just fix it with whoever is in charge that I can see her.'

Chalmers took out a new cigar and began to peel off the band. For the first time since I had entered the room, he looked at me. 'Is the Italian press covering this business?'

'Not yet. We've been holding up on it until you came.'

He studied me, then nodded.

'You did right.' Then he turned to Carlotti. 'Thanks for the facts, Lieutenant. If there's anything else I want to know between now and the inquest, I'll get in touch with you.'

Carlotti and Grandi got to their feet.

'I am at your service, signore,' Carlotti said.

When they had gone, Chalmers sat for a moment, staring down at his hands, then he said quietly and savagely, 'God-damn wops.'

I thought this was the time to unload the box of jewels Carlotti had entrusted in my keeping. I put the box on the table in front of Chalmers.

'These belonged to your daughter', I said. 'They were found in the villa.'

He frowned, reached forward, opened the box and stared at the contents. He turned the box upside down, letting the jewels spill out on to the table.

June got to her feet and crossed over to stare over his shoulder.

'You didn't give her those, did you, Sherwin?' she asked.

'Of course not!' he said, poking at the diamond collar with a thick finger. 'I wouldn't give a kid stuff like this.'

She reached over his shoulder and made to pick up the diamond collar, but he roughly pushed her hand away.

'Leave it!' The snap in his voice startled me. 'Go and sit down!'

Slightly shrugging her shoulders, she returned to her seat by the window and sat down.

Chalmers scooped the jewels back into the box and shut the lid. He handled the box as if it were made of egg shells.

He sat motionless for a long time, staring at the box. I watched him, wondering what his next move was to be. I knew he would make a move. He was getting his big-shot atmosphere back. His wife, staring out of the window, and I staring down at my hands, were pigmies again.

'Get this Giuseppe whatever his name is on the telephone,' Chalmers said, without looking at me. 'The coroner fella.'

I turned up Maletti's number in the book and put through the call. While I was waiting for the connection, Chalmers went on, 'Give the news to the press: no details. Tell them Helen, while on vacation, fell off a cliff and was killed.'

'Yes,' I said.

'Be here to-morrow morning at nine o'clock with a car. I want to go to the mortuary.'

A voice said on the line that this was the coroner's office. I asked to be put through to Maletti. When he came on the line, I said to Chalmers, 'The coroner.'

He got up and came over.

'Okay, get busy, Dawson,' he said, as he took the receiver from my hand. 'Mind—no details.'

As I went out of the room, I heard him say, 'This is Sherwin Chalmers talking. . . .'

Somehow he made his name sound more important and more impressive than any other name in the world.

PART V

I

At nine o'clock the following morning I was outside the Vesuvius hotel with the hired Rolls as instructed.

The Italian press had given Helen's death quite a coverage. Every paper carried her picture: showing her as I had first known her with her horn spectacles, her scraped-back hair-do and wearing her intellectual, serious expression.

As soon as I had left Chalmers the previous evening, I had called Maxwell. I gave him instructions to go ahead and break the story.

'Play it down,' I said. 'Make it sound commonplace. The story is she was on vacation in Sorrento, she was using a cine camera, she got absorbed in what she was taking and she fell off the cliff.'

'Who do you imagine is going to swallow a yarn like that?' he demanded, his voice excited. 'They'll want to know what she doing alone, living in a villa that size.'

'I know,' I said, 'but that's the story, Jack, and you're stuck with it. We'll tackle what comes next when it comes. This is the way the old man wants it, and if you want to keep your job, that's the way it's got to be.' I hung up before he could argue further.

I handed it to him when I saw the morning's papers. He had followed out my instructions to the letter. The press carried the story and a photograph, and that was all. No smart alec had an opinion to express. They just stated the facts as known, soberly and without hysterics.

Around nine-ten, Chalmers came out of the hotel and climbed into the back of the Rolls. He had a bunch of newspapers under his arm and a cigar between his teeth. He didn't even nod good morning to me.

I knew where he wanted to go, so I didn't waste time asking him. I got in beside the chauffeur, told him to drive to Sorrento and to snap it up.

I was a little surprised that June Chalmers hadn't come along for the ride. From where I sat I could get a good view of Chalmers in the driving mirror as he read the newspapers. He went through them quickly and searchingly, dropping one after the other on the floor of the car as he finished reading what he wanted to read.

By the time we reached Sorrento he had got through all the papers. He sat smoking his cigar, staring out of the window, communicating with the only god he would ever know—himself.

I directed the chauffeur to the mortuary. When the Rolls pulled up outside the small building, Chalmers got out and, motioning me to remain where I was, he went inside.

I lit a cigarette and tried not to think of what he was going to look at, but Helen's smashed, bruised face was in my mind and had been in my dreams last night, and it haunted me.

He was in there for twenty minutes.

When he came out, he walked just as briskly as when he went in. His cigar, now burned down to an inch and a half, was stilled gripped between his teeth. I decided that to look at your dead daughter with a cigar in your mouth was playing the rôle of 'the iron man' to an ultimate end.

He got into the back seat of the Rolls before I had time to get out and hold the rear door open for him.

'Okay, Dawson, we'll go up to this villa now.'

Nothing was said during the drive up to the villa. When we got there, and I had got out of the car to open the wrought iron gates and got back in again, and we had crawled up the drive, I saw the Lincoln convertible was still standing on the tarmac before the front door.

As Chalmers got out of the Rolls, he said, 'Is this her car?'

I said it was.

He glanced at it and then went on up the steps and into the villa. I went after him.

The chauffeur watched us without interest. As soon as Chalmers's back was turned, he reached for a cigarette.

I kept in the background while Chalmers looked the villa over. He left the bedroom to the last and he spent some time

72

in there. Curious to see what he was up to, I edged to the doorway and looked in.

He was sitting on the bed beside one of Helen's suitcases, his big, fat hands in a mass of her nylon underwear while he stared fixedly out of the window.

There was a look on his face that turned me cold, and I moved silently back until he was out of my sight, then I sat down and lit a cigarette.

The past two days had been the worst I had ever lived through. I felt I was caught in a trap and was waiting for the hunter to come along and finish me off.

The fact that Carlotti had traced me from Sorrento to the villa, that he knew I had been wearing a grey suit, that he knew exactly when Helen had died and that I, as the mysterious man in the grey suit, had been up there at that time, made my flesh creep.

I had lain awake most of the night, worrying and thinking, and as I sat waiting while Chalmers was going through his daughter's things, I still worried.

He came out eventually and walked slowly across the lounge to the window.

I watched him, wondering what was going on in his mind. He remained like that for several minutes, then he turned and came over to sit in a chair near where I was sitting.

'You didn't see much of Helen when she was in Rome?' he asked, staring at me with his rain-coloured eyes.

This question was unexpected and I felt myself stiffen.

'No. I called her twice, but she didn't seem to want me around,' I said. 'I guess she looked on me as her father's employee.'

Chalmers nodded.

'You have no idea who her friends were?'

'I'm afraid not.'

'She obviously got into pretty rotten company.'

I didn't say anything.

'I suppose this guy Sherrard gave her the jewels and the car,' he went on, staring down at his freckled hands. 'It looks as if I made a mistake keeping her so short of money. I should have given her more and sent some woman along with her. When a good-looking punk comes along, well-heeled with money, and is willing to give lavish presents, it doesn't matter how decent a girl is, it's a temptation not to fall for him. I know enough about human nature to know

73

that. I shouldn't have put her in the way of such temptation.'
He produced a cigar and began to peel off its cellophane
wrapping. 'She was a thoroughly decent girl, Dawson,' he
went on. 'She was a student; a serious-minded girl. She
wanted to study architecture. That's why I let her come to
Italy. Rome is the blood and bones of architects!'

I took out my handkerchief and wiped my face. I didn't
say anything.

I have a pretty high opinion of you,' he went on. 'I
wouldn't be giving you the foreign desk if I hadn't. I've
fixed this coroner fella: he's going to bring in a verdict of
accidental death. There's going to be no talk about pregnancy. I've had a word with the police chief. He's agreed
to let the thing lie. The press will toe the line. I've had
a word in that direction too. So now we have a clear field.
I'm going to leave this to you. I have to be in New York
by the day after to-morrow. I haven't the time to dig into
this thing myself, but you have. From now on, Dawson, you
have nothing else to do but to find Sherrard.'

I sat frozen, staring at him.

'Find Sherrard?' I repeated stupidly.

Chalmers nodded.

'That's right. Sherrard seduced my daughter, and now
he's going to damn well pay for it. But we've got to find him
first. That's going to be your job. You can have all the
money you want and all the help too. You can hire a flock
of private detectives. I'll have some sent out from New York
if they're no good here. It won't be easy. It's obvious he
wasn't using his real name, but somewhere along the line he
must have left a clue, and once you find that, you'll find
other clues, then you'll find him.'

'You can rely on me, Mr. Chalmers,' I somehow managed
to get out.

'Let me know how you're going to tackle the job. I want
to be kept informed of every move you make. If I think of
anything, I'll let you know. The thing to do is to find him,
and find him fast.'

'What happens when we do find him?'

I had to ask that question. I had to know.

He looked at me, and there was an expression in his eyes
that turned my mouth dry.

'This is the way I see it,' he said. 'Helen met this punk
soon after she arrived in Rome. It didn't take him long to

seduce her. The doctor says she was eight weeks' pregnant. She arrived in Rome fourteen weeks ago, so he worked pretty fast. She probably told him what had happened, and like all the rats of his type, he started to fade out of the picture. I reckon Helen took this villa in the hope of winning him back.' He turned his head to look around the lounge. 'It's pretty romantic, isn't it? I guess she hoped the surroundings would soften him. From what that wop detective says, Sherrard or whatever he calls himself did come here, but he didn't soften.'

I crossed my legs. I had to do something. I couldn't just sit like a frozen dummy.

'Know what I think?' Chalmers went on, turning the full force of his big-shot personality on to me. 'I think Helen's death was no accident. I think we have two alternatives: she either tried to scare him into marrying her by threatening to commit suicide, and when he told her to go ahead and jump, she jumped or else, to shut her mouth, he shoved her off the cliff.'

'You can't believe that . . . ?' I began. My voice sounded as if it were coming out of a tunnel.

'I don't think she jumped,' he said, leaning forward, his face set and his eyes frightening. 'I think he killed her! He knew she was my daughter. He knew sooner or later I'd hear what he had done to her. He knew if he tangled with me, he wouldn't stand a chance. So he manoeuvred her up on to the cliff top and gave her a push.'

'But that's murder,' I said.

He showed his teeth in a mirthless smile.

'Of course it's murder, but you don't have to worry about that. All you have to do is to find him, then I'll handle it. Let everyone think it's an accident. That suits me. I'm not going to have any publicity on this thing. No one is going to snigger behind my back because she was pregnant. If this guy is arrested and tried for murder, the whole dirty story will come out, and I don't want it to come out, but that doesn't mean I won't make him pay for what he has done. I can kill him in my own particular way, and that's what I intend to do.' His eyes were glaring now. 'Don't think I'm going to murder him. I'm not that crazy, but I can make his life such a hell, in the end he'll be glad to blow his rotten brains out. I've got the power and the money to do it, and that's what I'm going to do. I'll go after the basic things of his life first. I can get him turned out of his house or apartment or wherever he lives. I can prevent him putting a car on the road. I can fix it he can't go into any decent restaurant. Small stuff, you think? Imagine how you'd like it. Then I can get after his money and wipe out his securities. I can make him lose his job, and I can make sure no one else ever employs him. I can hire thugs to beat him up from time to time until he's too damned scared to show himself on the streets at night. I can even fix it that he loses his passport. Then when he begins to think life's bad, I'll really start on him.' He pushed his jaw at me, his face turning a dusky red. 'Every so often I run into odd, tough characters: characters who are a little screwy. I know a guy who would blind this punk for a couple of hundred dollars. He'd tear his goddam eyeballs out, and think nothing of it.' He smiled suddenly, a smile that chilled me. 'I'll make him pay, Dawson, make no mistake about that.' He tapped my knee with a thick finger. 'You find him—I'll fix him.'

II

In the cupboard of the sideboard that stood against one of the walls of the lounge, I found three bottles of whisky and two of gin. I broke open one of the bottles of whisky, found a glass in the kitchen and poured out three fingers of spirit.

I carried the drink out on to the balcony and sat down on the bench seat. I drank the whisky slowly, staring at the magnificent view without seeing it. I was shaking, and my mind was numbed with panic.

It wasn't until I had finished the drink that my eyes began to register again. From where I sat I looked down on the distant snake-back road that led down to Sorrento. I saw the big black Rolls that was taking Chalmers back to Naples, moving fast into the bends.

'It's all yours, Dawson,' he had said as I walked with him to the car. 'Keep in touch with me. Money's no object. Don't waste time writing. Telephone me. As soon as you discover anything, call me; no matter what time it is. I'll fix it from now on my secretary knows where I am all the time. I'll be waiting. I want this punk found fast.'

It was like handing me a razor and telling me to hurry up and cut my throat.

He had gone on to say that I might as well examine the villa in detail while I was up here, and check up on the place where Helen had died.

'Use her car. When you're through with it, sell it and give the money to some charity. Sell all her stuff in there. I don't want it. I'll leave it to you. I've fixed to have her body flown home.' He had shaken my hand, his rain-coloured eyes on my face. 'I want you to find this guy, Dawson.'

'I'll try,' I said.

'Look, you'll do more than try: you'll find him.' His chin pushed out at me. 'I'll hold the foreign desk open for you until you do find him . . . understand?'

Which was just another way of saying if I didn't find him, I wouldn't get the foreign desk.

The whisky did me some good. After the second drink, I was able to shake off my panic and begin to think.

I didn't believe for one moment that Helen had been murdered or that she had committed suicide. Her death had been accidental. I was sure of it.

I hadn't been her lover. It was something I couldn't prove, but at least I knew it. Chalmers had told me to find Sherrard whom he believed was her lover. I was Sherrard, and I wasn't her lover, therefore it followed that there was another man involved. If I were going to save what was left of my future, I had to find this guy and prove he had been her lover.

I lit a cigarette while I let my mind work on this thing.

Was this man I had to look for the intruder I had spotted in the villa? If he wasn't, then who was the intruder? What was he looking for? Certainly not the box of jewels. That had been on the dressing-table and he couldn't have failed to have seen it. Then what had he been looking for?

After thinking around it for five minutes and getting nowhere I decided to shelve it for the moment and try some other angle that might yield dividends.

Helen had lived in Rome for fourteen weeks. During that time she had met this man X who eventually became her lover. Where did she meet him?

I realized then that I knew nothing about Helen's activities in Rome during those weeks. I had taken her out a few times, been to her apartment twice and met her once at a party, but apart from that I had no idea how she had passed her time.

77

She had stayed at the Excelsior hotel, and then had rented an expensive apartment off the Via Cavour. Chalmers probably had paid the hotel bill: giving her a little luxury until she had settled down in Rome. It was probable that after staying at the hotel a few days, she was to move into one of the university hostels. Instead, she had moved into an apartment that must have soaked up nearly all of her sixty dollars a week allowance.

Did this mean that she had met X at the Excelsior, and he had persuaded her to take the apartment, probably paying for it?

The more I thought about it, the plainer it became that I should have to start this hunt for X in Rome. I knew of a firm of private investigators who had a reputation for thoroughness. It wouldn't be possible for me to dig into Helen's past background without help. My first move would be to consult them.

I got to my feet and wandered into Helen's bedroom. I had only glanced into the room previously, but now I examined it in detail.

I looked at the double bed and felt a little qualm. She had planned this for both of us. I must not lose sight of that. It was obvious to me that her affair with X had petered out and, looking for a new lover, she had selected me. Had she been in love with me or had she been looking for a father for her unborn child? The thought was unsettling, but it was something that was a waste of time to brood on. Only Helen could tell me that, and she was dead.

Then another idea dropped into my mind. I remembered what Maxwell had said about Helen. *She makes a play at anything in trousers. The trouble she gets a guy into*! Suppose X had still been in love with her, and she had grown tired of him? Suppose he had found out she had taken this villa and was planning to live here with me? He might have come down to even the score. He might even have thrown her over the cliff.

This would be a sweet theory to lay before Chalmers, who was obviously convinced that Helen was a thoroughly decent girl. I couldn't lay it before him without involving myself.

With this idea nagging at the back of my mind, I spent an hour going through her three suitcases. It was a waste of time, because I knew both Carlotti and Chalmers had been through them and had found nothing. Her clothes carried a faint smell of an expensive perfume that made her memory very alive to me. I was feeling pretty depressed by the time I had completed repacking the suitcases, ready to put in the car when I left.

I looked over the whole villa, but I found nothing that'd tell me what she had done from the time the village woman had left her arranging the flowers to the time she had died.

I carried the suitcases down the steps and loaded them on the back seat of the convertible. I returned to the villa and gave myself another drink.

I told myself that my search must begin in Rome. Here I had found nothing, and as I thought about that, I got another idea. I stood thinking for a moment, then I crossed to the telephone and asked to be connected with Sorrento police headquarters. When I got through, I asked for Lieutenant Grandi.

'This is Dawson,' I said. 'I forgot to ask you: did you have that film processed? The film in Signorina Chalmers's cine camera?'

'There wasn't a film in the camera,' he said curtly.

'No film? Are you sure?'

'I'm sure.'

I stared at the opposite wall.

'If there was no film in the camera, she wasn't using the camera when she died,' I said, speaking my thoughts aloud.

'That doesn't follow. She could have forgotten to put a film in, couldn't she?'

I remembered that the indicator on the camera had shown that twelve feet of film had been run off. I knew a little about these cameras, and I knew that when you put a film in, there is a catch that opens the film gate through which you thread the film, and as the gate opens the indicator is automatically set back to zero.

'I suppose she could,' I said. 'Did Lieutenant Carlotti think anything of it?'

'What's there to think about?' Grandi snapped.

'Well, thanks. Just one other thing: there wasn't anything taken from the villa, was there? Besides the jewels, I mean.'

'We didn't take anything.'

'Have you finished with the camera and the case? I'm collecting la signorina Chalmers's things now. If I drop by, can I have the camera?'

'We don't want it any more.'

'Okay, I'll be along then. So long, Lieutenant,' and I hung up.

The footage indicator on the camera had shown twelve feet. That meant there had been a film in the camera, and it had been removed by someone who wasn't familiar in handling this type of camera. The film had been forcibly removed, ripping the length of the film out of the gate without releasing the gate lock. It meant too that the film had been ruined by taking it out this way, so it followed whoever had taken it out hadn't wished to keep the film. The only purpose for removing the film was to destroy it.

Why?

I gave myself another drink. I was suddenly excited. Could this be the clue Chalmers had said I would find, and having found this one, I'd find another?

Helen wouldn't have ripped the film out of the camera. That was certain. Then who did?

Then the second clue dropped into my mind the way a leaf floats off a tree.

I remembered her showing me ten cartons of cine film when I had called at her Rome apartment. I remembered chaffing her about buying so many, and I remembered she had said she intended to use most of the film in Sorrento.

And yet there wasn't one carton of film in the villa or in her luggage.

There wasn't even a film in her camera. The police hadn't taken the films. Grandi had said they had taken nothing from the villa.

Was this the explanation of the intruder I had seen creeping around in the villa? Had he found and taken them? Had he ripped the film from the camera, and then tossed the camera down the cliff face?

To make absolutely sure, I went over the whole villa again, searching for the cartons of film, but I didn't find them. Satisfied, I locked up the villa, dropped the keys into my pocket, and then, leaving the Lincoln where it was, I walked down the garden path, through the gate and along the path to the cliff head.

By now it was just after midday and the sun blazed down on me as I walked. I passed the inaccessible villa below. This time I paused to look more closely at it.

On the terrace, in the shadow of a table umbrella and lying

on a lounging chair, I could see a woman in a white swim-suit. She appeared to be reading a newspaper. The edge of the umbrella prevented me from seeing much of her. I could just make out her long, tanned shapely legs, part of the swim-suit and a tanned arm and hand that held the newspaper.

I wondered vaguely who she was, but I had too many things on my mind to take any interest in her, and I kept on until I reached the place where Helen had fallen.

Methodically, I searched the path, the rough grass and the surrounding rocks within a thirty-yard radius. I didn't know what I was looking for, but I thought it might pay dividends to do it.

It was hot work, but I kept at it. I found one thing that might or might not mean something. It was a half-smoked Burma cheroot.

As I stood in the hot sunlight, turning the butt over be-tween my fingers, I had a sudden and unmistakable feeling that I was being watched.

I was pretty rattled, but I was careful not to look up. I continued to study the butt, my heart beginning to thump. It was an eerie feeling, being up there on this dangerous path, knowing that someone was close by in hiding and watching me.

I slid the butt into my pocket and straightened, moving away from the edge of the cliff head.

The feeling of being watched persisted. Casually, I looked around. Dense shrubs, and about fifty yards away, the thick wood, showed me that anyone could be hidden and watching me without a hope of my spotting them.

I started back down the path to the villa. All the way back to the garden gate, I felt eyes boring into my back. I had to exert a lot of will power not to look over my shoulder.

It wasn't until I had got into the Lincoln convertible and was driving fast along the snake-back road to Sorrento that I began to relax.

III

My first move when I reached Sorrento was to hand the keys of the villa to the estate agent. I settled the rent that was owing and gave him my Rome address in case any mail came for Helen at the villa. I told him to forward it to me.

He said it was very sad that such a beautiful girl should have such a terrible accident. He said he had written to the owner of the villa advising him to have the path fenced in. I wasn't in the mood for a chit-chat about fences. I made a grunting noise, shook hands with him and went back to the car.

I drove to the police station where I collected the cine camera and its case. Grandi kept me waiting outside his office for a quarter of an hour, then sent a sergeant out with the camera. The sergeant got me to sign a receipt for it.

I left the police station and crossed over to the car, carrying the camera in its case slung over my shoulder. I got into the car, started the engine and drove slowly into the traffic-congested main road.

The experience I had had on the cliff head had made me alert. I noticed in the driving mirror, a dark green Renault pull out from behind another parked car and drift after me.

If I hadn't been certain that someone had been watching me up on the cliff head, I wouldn't have thought anything of this move, but now I was suspicious. The fact that there was a dark blue sun shield covering the windscreen of the Renault, making it impossible to see who was driving, added to my suspicion.

I headed for Naples, driving at a moderate speed, and from time to time glancing in the driving mirror. The Renault kept a respectful hundred yards behind me. I kept going, driving at a steady forty miles an hour, and the Renault kept after me.

It wasn't until I reached the entrance to the autostrada that I decided to see if the Renault was really following me or if it was a coincidence that it hung in my rear.

I eased the speed of the Lincoln up to sixty. The Renault still remained a hundred yards behind me. I pushed the gas pedal down to the floorboards. The Lincoln surged forward. It had plenty of speed and snap, and in a minute or so the speedometer needle was swinging up to eighty-seven miles an hour.

The Renault had fallen back, but it had also increased speed. As I watched it in the driving mirror I saw it was closing the gap again, and I was pretty sure now that I was being followed.

There was no hope of shaking it off on this flat, straight autostrada. The time to try tricks would be when I reached Naples.

I slackened speed to seventy miles an hour, and drove steadily to the end of the autostrada.

The Renault hung on, keeping its hundred yards distance, but as I slowed to hand my ticket to the official at the exit of the autostrada, the Renault, as if the driver realized that once I was in the Naples traffic I would be much more difficult to follow, moved up and closed the gap between us. I took the opportunity to memorize the car's number. As I drove into the thick Naples traffic there were only twenty yards or so between us.

I made one attempt to shake off the Renault, but I wasn't successful. The driver was a lot smarter at manoeuvring in congested traffic than I was, and when I made my bid I only achieved frenzied curses from the drivers of cars either side of me and wild hooting from the on-coming traffic.

I drove to the Vesuvius hotel, swung the Lincoln into the only available space before the hotel, told the porter to keep an eye on it and went quickly into the lobby.

I paused then to look through the revolving doors to see if I could spot the Renault, but there was no sign of it.

I went into the bar, ordered a Scotch and soda and then took the Paillard Bolex camera from its case. I opened the camera. Both the film spool and the take-up spool were missing. When I slid the catch of the film gate release, a strip of torn film about three inches long dropped into my hand.

This confirmed what I had thought had happened. Someone had opened the camera, taken out the two spools with the film wound on to them and yanked the film clear of the gate.

I replaced the strip of film and locked the gate into position. Then I put the camera back into its case.

I lit a cigarette and did some thinking.

It seemed likely that X had ripped out the film. The only reason why he had done so was because Helen had photographed something he didn't want anyone to see. The chances were that he had come on her while she was on the cliff head and, as he approached her, she had turned the camera on him. He had realized the danger of leaving such a record in the camera. After he had disposed of her, he had ripped out the film and destroyed it.

After he had disposed of her.

I realized now that since I had discovered the film was missing from the camera and that the films had been taken from the villa I had known that Helen hadn't died accidentally. It was something I was loath to admit, but now I had to admit it.

Chalmers's wild guess had been right. Helen hadn't died accidentally. She hadn't committed suicide.

I was now in a far worse jam than I had imagined. Helen had been murdered, and if I wasn't careful, the finger of guilt would soon be pointing at me.

PART VI

I

'Iт's Mr. Dawson, isn't it?'

I snapped out of my nightmare, nearly dropping the camera, and looked up.

June Chalmers was standing before me. She had on a grey linen dress, ornamented with a red belt and buttons; red, spike-heeled shoes, and a red skull-cap with a white goose-feather in it.

I got to my feet.

'That's right, Mrs. Chalmers.'

'Were you looking for my husband?'

'I was hoping to catch him before he left.'

'He won't be long.'

She sat down in a lounging chair near to the one I had been sitting in, crossed her legs, and let me see her knees.

'Please sit down, Mr. Dawson, I want to talk to you.'

'Can I get you a drink?'

She shook her head.

'No, thank you. I've only just finished lunch. We are hoping to catch the three-forty plane. Mr. Chalmers is supervising the packing right now. He loves to do that sort of thing himself.'

I sat down and looked at her.

'Mr. Dawson, I haven't much time,' she said. 'Please don't misunderstand me if I seem harsh towards Helen, but I must speak to you about her. My husband is a very ruthless and hard man but, like so many hard men, he has a sentimental side. All his affection and love were lavished on his daughter. It may be difficult for you to believe this, but he worshipped her.'

I moved restlessly. I couldn't see where this was leading to.

I remembered what Helen had said about her father, and how bitter she had been. She had said he had no interest in her, and he only thought of himself and finding a new woman to amuse him. What June Chalmers was telling me didn't add up.

'I've heard that he didn't give that impression,' I said cautiously. 'Most people think he had no time for her.'

'I know. That was the impression he did give, but in actual fact he was ridiculously fond of her. He was anxious not to be thought an indulgent father, and he very stupidly kept her short of money. He thought too much money would spoil her, and he gave her only a small allowance.'

I sank a little lower in my chair. I can't say I was particularly interested in all this.

'I believe you are anxious to return to New York and take up your new appointment: it's the foreign desk, isn't it?' she said abruptly.

That stiffened me to attention.

'Yes.'

'The job means a lot to you?'

'Why, of course. . . .'

'My husband has a very high opinion of you,' she went on. 'He has told me what he wants you to do. I mean about Helen. He is sure she has been murdered. He gets these fixed ideas from time to time, and nothing anyone can say will make him think otherwise. The police and the coroner are satisfied it was an accident. I am sure you think so too.'

She looked inquiringly at me.

For no reason I could think of I felt suddenly uneasy in her presence. Maybe it was because I had an idea that her smiling calmness was phoney. There was a suppressed tension about her I could sense rather than see.

'I don't know,' I said. 'That's something I'm going to investigate.'

'Yes, and that brings me to why I want to talk to you, Mr. Dawson. I want to warn you to be careful how deeply you probe into this business. My husband was crazy about Helen I don't like speaking badly about anyone who can't defend themselves, but in this case I haven't any choice. He thought she was a good, decent, studious girl, but she wasn't. There was nothing she wouldn't do for money: nothing at all. She lived for money. My husband only gave her an allowance

86

of sixty dollars a week. I know for a fact she spent as much as two or three hundred dollars a week when she was living in New York. She had absolutely no scruples how she got money so long as she got it. She was perhaps one of the most worldly, undisciplined, immoral and unpleasant women I have ever met.'

The rasp in her voice as she said this shocked me.

'I know it is a dreadful thing to say,' she went on, 'but it is the truth. If you probe into her past, you will find this out for yourself. She was utterly rotten. This wasn't the first time she was pregnant: a thing like that wouldn't have worried her. She knew what to do and who to go to. The men she went around with were degenerates and criminals. If anyone deserved to be murdered, she did!'

I drew in a long, slow breath.

'And yet you don't think she was murdered?' I said.

'I don't know.' She stared at me. 'All I do know is that the police are satisfied she died accidentally. Why can't you be satisfied?'

'Your husband has told me to make an investigation. That's an order.'

'If you investigate her death as a murder, you are certain to uncover a whole series of unpleasant facts about her. I am sure she behaved in Rome as she has behaved in New York. It will be impossible to conceal these facts from my husband. He is completely convinced that Helen was a decent, clean-living girl. The facts you will have to tell him will shock him. He won't forgive you for shattering his illusions about his daughter, nor is he likely to employ a man in the most important position on his newspaper who has shown him how completely fooled he has been about such a worthless degenerate as his daughter was. Now do you understand why I am asking you not to probe too deeply into this business?'

I reached out, picked up my glass and finished my whisky.

'How is it you know so much about Helen Chalmers?' I asked.

'I'm not blind and I'm not stupid. I've known her for some years. I've seen the men she associated with. Her behaviour was notorious.'

There was more to it than that: I was sure of it, but I didn't say so.

'This puts me on a spot,' I said. 'Mr. Chalmers has told

87

me if I don't uncover the facts, I won't get the job. Now you tell me if I do, I still won't get it. So what do I do?'

'Don't uncover them, Mr. Dawson. Delay things. After a while, my husband will get over the shock of her death. At the moment he is furious and revengeful, but when he gets back to New York and is caught-up once more in his work, he will calm down. In a couple of weeks' time you can safely report progress. I can assure you he will let the matter drop. I can promise you, if you don't start an investigation, you will get the foreign desk, but if you do, I am sure my husband, when he learns the truth about Helen, will never forgive you.'

'So you suggest I sit back and do nothing?'

Just for a moment her fixed smile slipped. Into her eyes jumped a staring fear that startled me. It was there for a split second, then the smile came back, but I had seen her fear all right.

'Of course you will have to make out to my husband that you are doing your best, Mr. Dawson. You will have to send him reports, but no one can blame you if you don't discover any worth-while information.' She leaned forward and put her hand on mine. 'Please don't check up on Helen's life in Rome. I have to live with my husband. I know how he would react if he knew the truth about Helen. It was I who persuaded him to let her go to Rome, and he would blame me, so it's not only for your sake I'm asking you to do this, it's for mine as well.'

I was sitting, facing the reception hall and I saw Chalmers come out of the elevator and go over to the reception desk. I pulled my hand from hers and got to my feet.

'Here's Mr. Chalmers now.'

Her mouth tightened, and she turned to wave to Chalmers who came over. He carried a light overcoat on his arm and a despatch case in his hand.

'Hello, Dawson, did you want to see me?' he asked as he put down his case. 'We haven't much time.'

I had intended to tell him about the missing films and about the Renault that had followed me, but now, having listened to June Chalmers, I decided I needed some time to think over what she had said before I committed myself. I was suddenly stuck to explain what I was doing here.

But June wasn't.

'Mr. Dawson brought Helen's camera,' she said.

For a moment I wondered how she knew the camera was Helen's, but glancing at the case I realized she had spotted Helen's initials on it. All the same this show of quick-wittedness told me she was a lot smarter than I had imagined.

Chalmers scowled at the camera.

'I don't want it. I don't want any of her things,' he said curtly. 'Get rid of it.'

I said I would do that.

'Did you find anything up at the villa?'

I caught June's anxious eyes. I shook my head.

'Nothing helpful.'

He grunted.

'Well, I expect results. We've got to find this punk fast. Get some men on the job. I expect to hear something by the time I get back to New York . . . understand?'

I said I understood.

He took from his pocket a Yale key.

'The police gave me this. It's the key to her apartment in Rome. You'd better arrange to have her things collected and sold. I'll leave it to you. I don't want anything sent back.'

I took the key.

'We should be going, Sherwin,' June said suddenly.

He looked at his strap watch.

'Yeah. Okay. I'll leave this to you, Dawson. Just find this punk and let me know the moment you've found him.'

He nodded, and, picking up his despatch case, he began to move out of the bar towards the reception hall.

June gave me a steady stare as she followed him.

I saw them into the Rolls.

'I want to know what you plan to do,' Chalmers said through the open car window. 'Don't be afraid of spending money. Get as many as you need on this. The quicker you clear it up, the quicker you'll be working at the foreign desk.'

I said I'd do the best I could.

As the Rolls drove away, June Chalmers looked back at me through the rear window. Her eyes were still anxious.

II

I reached Rome around six o'clock.

During the run I had looked out for the Renault, but I

hadn't seen it. Leaving the Lincoln in the parking lot, I walked up the private stairway that led directly to my apartment.

I unlocked the front door, carried my suitcase into my bedroom then, returning to the lounge, I mixed myself a whisky and soda and then sat down by the telephone. I put a call through to Carlotti.

After a little delay he came on the line.

'This is Dawson,' I said. 'I've just got back.'

'Yes? Il signor Chalmers has returned to New York?'

'That's right. The coroner seems satisfied it was an accident.'

'I wouldn't know about that,' Carlotti said. 'The inquest isn't until Monday.'

'Chalmers has talked to him. He has also talked to your boss', I said, staring at the opposite wall.

'I wouldn't know about that either,' Carlotti said.

There was a pause, but as he seemed determined to act cagey, I went on, 'There's something you can do for me if you will. I want information about the registration number of a car.'

'Certainly. Let me have the number and I will call you back.'

I gave him the number of the Renault.

'I won't keep you long.'

I hung up and settled myself more comfortably in my chair. I held my whisky and soda in my hand, while I stared down at the swirling traffic that made circles around the Forum.

I sat like that for ten minutes, not thinking, letting my mind remain a blank until the telephone bell rang.

'Are you sure you haven't made a mistake about that car number?' Carlotti asked.

That was one thing I was sure of.

'I don't think so . . . why?'

'There's no such number registered.'

I ran my fingers through my hair.

'I see.' I didn't want to raise his curiosity. 'I'm sorry about that, Lieutenant. Come to think of it, I could have made a mistake.'

'You have a reason for asking? It is something to do, perhaps, with la signorina Chalmers' death?'

I grinned without any humour.

'It was a guy who ran me pretty close. I thought of reporting him.'

There was a short pause, then Carlotti said, 'Never hesitate to ask for my help when you need it. It is what I am here for.'

I thanked him and hung up.

I lit a cigarette and continued to stare out of the window. This business was becoming complicated.

Although June Chalmers's argument that Chalmers could turn on me if I showed him the kind of daughter he had been doting on made sense, I knew that she wasn't thinking of me when she asked me to lay off an investigation: she was scared something that would effect her would come to light.

I knew too, that if I did lie down on the investigation, Chalmers would know. He would get rid of me and put someone else on the job.

I knew also that if Carlotti suspected that Helen had been murdered, no one, let alone Chalmers, would stop him hunting for the killer.

I levered myself out of my chair and went over to the telephone.

I called Maxwell.

The operator told me there was no answer from the office, so I asked her to put me through to Maxwell's hotel. The clerk told me Maxwell was out. I said I would call again and hung up.

I lit another cigarette and wondered what my next move was to be. It seemed to me that I had to go ahead with the investigation. I decided to go around to Helen's apartment. There might or might not be something there that would give me a lead on this set-up.

I locked the camera away in a drawer in my desk, and then went down to where I had left the Lincoln. Not bothering to get my car from the garage, I used the Lincoln. It took me twenty minutes to reach Helen's apartment block. I lugged her suitcases into the automatic elevator and then along with me to her front door.

As I took out the Yale key Chalmers had given me, I glanced at my watch. The time was twenty minutes to eight o'clock. I pushed open the front door and walked into the hall.

A very faint smell of her perfume gave me a spooky feeling as I crossed the hall and walked into the sitting-room. It seemed only a few hours ago that she and I were talking together about our planned stay in Sorrento: only a few hours since I had kissed her for the first and only time.

I stood in the doorway and looked across the room to the desk where the ten cartons of films had stood, but they weren't there. There had been a remote possibility that she had forgotten to have taken them to Sorrento. That they were not on the desk underlined the fact that someone had stolen them from the villa.

I moved into the room and looked around.

After a moment's hesitation I went over to the desk and sat down before it. I opened one drawer after the other. There were the usual things you expect to find in the drawers of a desk: notepaper, blotting-paper, ink, rubber bands and so on. I found all these, but I didn't find one personal paper, bill, letter or diary anywhere. It took me several moments to realize that someone must have been here before me, and had made a clean sweep of every used scrap of paper in the desk. Had it been the police or the same person who had stolen the films?

Uneasy in my mind, I went into the bedroom. It wasn't until I had looked into the various closets and into the drawers of the bureau that I saw what a tremendous stock of expensive clothes Helen had owned. Chalmers had told me to get rid of all her things, but looking at the dozens of dresses, coats, shoes, three drawers full of underwear and a drawer crammed with costume jewellery, I saw the job was too big for me to tackle alone. I decided I'd have to get Gina to help me.

I returned to the sitting-room and called her on the telephone. I was lucky to catch her. She told me she was just going out to supper.

'Could you come over here?' I gave her the address. 'I've a man-sized job for you to tackle. Take a taxi. When we're through I'll take you out to dinner.'

She said she would be right over.

As I hung up I noticed on the wall, near the telephone, a telephone number scribbled in pencil. I leaned forward to stare at it. It was scarcely visible, and it was only because I had switched on the table lamp that I had seen it. It was a Rome number.

It occurred to me that Helen wouldn't have scribbled it on the wall unless it had been important to her, and a number she had called frequently. I had looked for a list of telephone numbers when I had searched her desk, but hadn't found it. The fact there were no other numbers written on the wall seemed to me to be significant.

On the spur of the moment, I picked up the receiver and called the number. I regretted my impulse as soon as I heard the burr-burr on the line. For all I knew this might be X's number, and I didn't want him to suspect I was on to him so early in the game. I was about to replace the receiver when I heard a click on the line. My ear-drum was nearly shattered by a voice that bawled in Italian: 'WHAT DO YOU WANT?'

It was the most violent, undisciplined voice I had ever heard or ever want to hear over a telephone line.

I held the receiver away from my ear and listened. I could hear the faint sound of music: some throaty tenor was singing *E lucevan le stelle*, probably over the radio.

The man who had answered the telephone shouted, 'HELLO? WHO IS IT?'

His shattering voice was more than life-size.

I flicked my finger-nail against the mouthpiece of the receiver to hold his attention.

Then I heard a woman say, 'Who is it, Carlo? Must you shout so?' She spoke with a strong American accent.

'No one answers,' he returned in English and in a slightly lower tone of voice.

There was a violent click as he slammed down the receiver.

Very carefully I hung up. I stared out of the window. Carlo . . . and an American woman. It could mean something or nothing. Helen must have made a lot of friends during her stay in Rome. Carlo could have been just a friend, but the telephone number on the wall was puzzling. If he were just a friend, why the number on the wall? He might have given it to her, of course, over the telephone, and not having any scratch pad near, she had scribbled it on the wall. That could be the explanation, but somehow I didn't think so. If this had happened, she would surely have rubbed it out, after entering it in her telephone book.

I jotted down the number on the back of an envelope, then, as I was putting the envelope into my wallet, the front-door bell rang.

I let Gina into the apartment.

'Before we talk,' I said, 'come in here and look at all this stuff. Chalmers wants me to get rid of it. He said to sell it and give the money to some charity. It's going to be quite a job to handle. There's enough stuff here to stock a shop.'

I took her into the bedroom and stood back while she looked into the closets and drawers.

'This won't be difficult to get rid of, Ed,' she told me. 'I know a woman who specializes in good second-hand clothes. She'll make an offer for everything and take it all away.'

I sighed with relief.

'That's fine. I hoped you'd have the solution. I don't really care what she offers so long as she takes everything and we can get this apartment off our hands.'

'La signorina Chalmers must have spent a great deal of money,' Gina said, examining some of the dresses. 'Some of these have never been worn, and they were all bought at the most expensive houses in Rome.'

'Well, she didn't get the money from Chalmers,' I said 'I guess someone must have financed her.'

Gina lifted her shoulders and shut the closet door.

'She didn't get all these things for nothing,' she said. 'I don't envy her.'

'Come into the other room. I want to talk to you.'

She followed me into the lounge and dropped into a chair.

'Ed, why did she call herself Mrs. Douglas Sherrard ?' she asked.

If the walls of the room had suddenly fallen in on me I couldn't have been more shaken.

'What? What did you say? I asked, staring at her.

She looked at me.

'I asked you why she called herself Mrs. Douglas Sherrard. Obviously I shouldn't have asked that. I'm sorry.'

'How did you know she called herself that?'

'I recognized her voice when she called up just before you left on your vacation.'

I should have known that Gina would have recognized Helen's voice. She had spoken to Helen twice on the telephone when Helen had first come to Rome and she had an uncanny memory for voices.

I went over to the liquor cabinet.

'Have a drink, Gina?' I said, trying to keep my voice steady.

'I'd like a Campari, please.'

I took out a bottle of Campari and a bottle of Scotch. I

fixed myself a stiff drink, and a Campari and soda for Gina and brought the drinks over.

I had known Gina for four years. There had been a time when I had imagined I had been in love with her. Working with her day after day, most times alone together, had offered temptations to get intimate with her. It was because of this that I had been careful to keep our relations more or less on a business footing.

I had seen a number of newspaper men, working in Rome, who had got too friendly with their secretaries. Sooner or later, the girls either got out of hand or a visiting big-shot had spotted what was going on, and there had been trouble. So I had been strict with myself about Gina. I had never made a pass at her, and yet there was a bond between us, unspoken and unadvertised, that convinced me that, no matter what the emergency might be, I could completely rely on her.

I decided as I fixed the drink to tell her the whole story, not holding back a thing. I had a lot of faith in her opinions, and, knowing the mess I was in, I felt it was time to get an unbiased, outside opinion.

'Would it worry you if I made you my mother confessor, Gina?' I asked, sitting down opposite her. 'I have a lot on my mind that I'd like to share with someone.'

'If there's anything I can do . . .'

The sound of the front-door bell cut her short. For a long moment we stared at each other.

'Now, who can this be?' I said, getting to my feet.

'Perhaps it's the janitor wanting to find out who is in here,' Gina said.

'Yeah: could be.'

I crossed the room and went out into the hall. As I reached for the door knob, the bell rang again.

I opened the door.

Lieutenant Carlotti stood in the corridor. Behind him was another detective.

'Good evening,' Carlotti said. 'May I come in?'

III

Seeing him there made me understand for the first time what a criminal must feel like when he is suddenly confronted

95

by the police. For a second or so, I stood motionless, staring at him. My heart seemed to miss several beats, and then began to race so violently I had difficulty in breathing. Had he come to arrest me? Had he found out somehow that I was Sherrard?

Gina appeared in the sitting-room doorway.

'Good evening, Lieutenant,' she said. Her calm, quiet voice had a steadying effect on me.

Carlotti bowed to her.

I stood aside.

'Come in, Lieutenant.'

Carlotti moved forward.

'Sergeant Anoni,' he said, nodding to his companion who followed him into the hall.

I led the way into the lounge. By now I had got over the first shock of seeing Carlotti, but I was still pretty shaken.

'This is unexpected, Lieutenant,' I said. 'Did you know I was here?'

'I happened to be passing. I saw the lights were on. I was curious to see who could be here. It is fortunate. I wanted to talk to you.

Anoni, short, thick-set with a flat, expressionless face, leaned against the wall by the door. He seemed to be taking no interest in the proceedings.

'Well, sit down,' I said, waving Carlotti to a chair. 'We were just having a drink. Will you join us?'

'No, thank you.'

He moved around the room, his hands in his coat pockets. Going over to the window, he glanced out, then, turning, he came over to where I was standing and sat down near me. I sat down too. Gina perched herself on the arm of the settee.

'I understand you collected la signorina Chalmers's camera from Lieutenant Grandi this morning,' Carlotti said.

Surprised, I said, 'Yes, that's right. Grandi said you had finished with it.'

'So I had thought, but I've been thinking about that camera.' Carlotti took out a packet of cigarettes and lit one. He knew better than to offer Gina or myself this particular brand that he smoked. 'I feel I have been a little hasty in parting with the camera. You would have no objection to return it?'

'Why, no. I'll bring it to you to-morrow morning. Will that do?'

'It's not here?'

'It's at my apartment.'

'Perhaps it wouldn't inconvenience you if we collected it to-night?'

'Well, all right.' I lit a cigarette and took a pull at my glass. I needed the drink. 'Why the sudden interest in the camera, Lieutenant?'

'On reflection, it strikes me as odd that there was no film in it.'

'You've got around to that rather late in the day, haven't you?'

He lifted his shoulders.

'At first I thought it was possible la signorina had forgotten to put a film in the camera, but since then, I have talked with an expert. Bearing in mind that the footage indicator on the camera showed that twelve feet of film had been exposed, it would seem from that there had been a film in the camera, and that the film had been removed. I'm not familiar with cine cameras. I realize now that I shouldn't have parted with it quite so soon.'

'Well, there's no damage done. You'll have it to-night.'

'You have no idea who could have removed the film?'

'Not unless it was la signorina herself.'

'The film was removed apparently without the film gate being opened. That would mean the film would be exposed to the light as it was being taken out and therefore ruined. La signorina would scarcely do that, would she?'

'I suppose not.' I leaned back in my chair. 'I thought this business was all buttoned up, Lieutenant. Now you seem to have some doubts about it.'

'The doubts have been forced on me,' Carlotti said. 'La signorina bought ten cartons of film. They are missing. The film in the camera is also missing. I examined this apartment this morning. There are no private papers of any description here. Considering la signorina stayed here for nearly thirteen weeks, it seems odd that she apparently didn't receive or write a letter, never had any bills, kept no diary or telephone numbers: odd, unless, of course, someone has been in here and taken her personal papers away.'

'I noticed that myself,' I said, setting my glass down on the table. 'She could have had a tidy-up before she left, of course.'

'That is possible, but unlikely. You are here to close up the apartment?'

'Yes. Chalmers told me to get rid of all her things.'

Carlotti studied his immaculate finger-nails, then he looked directly at me.

'I am sorry to disturb your arrangements, but I must ask you to leave everything for the moment as it is. I intend to seal up the apartment until after the inquest.'

I had to challenge this, although I was pretty sure now what was going on in his mind.

'What's the idea, Lieutenant?'

'Let us say it is normal routine,' Carlotti said mildly. 'It is possible there may be an investigation after the inquest.'

'But, I understood from Chalmers that the coroner had agreed to record a verdict of accidental death.'

Carlotti smiled.

'I believe that was his intention, based on the present evidence, but as the inquest is not until Monday, it is possible further evidence may come to light that will alter the situation.'

'Chalmers won't be pleased.'

'That is unfortunate.'

It was obvious now that he was no longer in awe of Chalmers.

'You have spoken to your chief?' I said. 'I believe Chalmers has also had a word with him.'

Carlotti tapped ash from his cigarette into his hand and then dusted the ash on to the carpet.

'My chief agrees with me. It is still possible that la signorina's death was an accident, but the missing films, this American who was seen in Sorrento, the fact that this apartment has been stripped of all personal papers forces us to conclude there are grounds for an investigation.' He puffed lung-scorching smoke towards me. 'There is another point that puzzles me. I hear from la signorina's bank manager that she was made an allowance of sixty dollars a week. When she arrived in Rome she had with her a small trunk and a suitcase. You have probably seen the contents of the closets and drawers in the other room. I am wondering where the money came from to buy all these things.'

It was pretty obvious that he had already begun to dig into Helen's background, and I remembered June's look of fear when she begged me not to do this thing.

'I can see you have some problems on your mind,' I said as casually as I could.

'Perhaps we could go over to your apartment now and collect the camera,' Carlotti said, getting to his feet. 'Then I need not bother you again.'

'Okay.' I stood up. 'Come with us, Gina. We'll have dinner after I've given the camera to the Lieutenant.'

'Perhaps you would be kind enough to let me have the key to this apartment?' Carlotti said. 'I will return it to you within a few days.'

I gave him the key, which he handed to Anoni.

We moved out into the corridor. Anoni didn't come with us. He remained in the apartment.

As the three of us descended in the elevator, Carlotti said, 'That car number you were inquiring about. It had nothing to do with la signorina?'

'I told you: this guy nearly clipped me. He didn't stop. I thought I had got his number correct, but apparently I hadn't.'

I felt his eyes on my face. We didn't speak further until we got into my car, then he said. 'Can you give me the names of any of la signorina's friends?'

'I'm sorry, I can't. I think I told you already: I scarcely knew her.'

'But you have talked to her?'

The mildness of his tone put me on my guard.

'Of course, but she didn't tell me anything about her life in Rome. After all, she was my boss's daughter, and it didn't cross my mind to question her.'

'Did you take her out to dinner at the Trevi restaurant about four weeks ago?'

I felt as if someone had given me a punch under the heart. Just how much did he know? Someone must have seen us. I knew I didn't dare lie to him.

'I believe I did, come to think of it. I happened to run into her, and as I was going to dinner, I asked her along.'

There was a pause, then he said, 'I see.'

I swung the car into the street where I lived and pulled up outside my private entrance.

There was a pretty tense atmosphere in the car. My heart was bumping so heavily against my side that I was scared he would hear it.

'And that was the only time you took her out?'

99

My mind raced. We had gone to two movies; we had had at least two or three dinners together.

To gain time, I said, 'What was that?'

I opened the car door and got out. He followed me on to the sidewalk.

Patiently, and without much hope in his voice, he repeated the question.

'As far as I can remember.' I leaned into the car. 'I won't be a moment,' I said to Gina. 'Wait for me, then we'll have dinner together.'

Carlotti followed me up the spiral staircase. He was humming under his breath, and I could feel his eyes examining the back of my head.

I walked down the passage that led directly to my front door. I was half-way down the passage when I saw the front door was standing ajar. I came to an abrupt stop.

'Hello . . . that's funny,' I said.

'You shut it when you left?' Carlotti said, moving in front of me.

'Of course.'

We reached the door together.

'Oh, damn! Looks like burglars,' I said, and pointed to the smashed lock on the front door. I made a move into the hall, but Carlotti pulled me back.

'Please . . . let me go first,' he said curtly, and, moving silently, he stepped into the hall, crossed it with two quick strides and threw open the sitting-room door. I was right on his heels.

All the lights were on. We stood in the doorway and stared around the room that looked as if it had been struck by a hurricane.

Everything was in disorder. Cupboards stood open, a couple of chairs were overturned, all the drawers in the desk hung open, and all my papers were lying scattered on the floor.

Carlotti went swiftly into my bedroom. Then I heard him run down the passage to the bathroom.

I walked over to the desk. I looked in the bottom drawer in which I had locked the camera. The lock had been forced and, of course, the camera was gone.

PART VII

I

IT was ten minutes past eleven before I got rid of Carlotti and his mob of detectives who descended on my apartment, dusting everything for finger-prints, poking their noses in every nook and cranny, photographing the splintered door and generally raising all kinds of hell.

I had gone down to Gina, explained the situation and told her not to wait for me. She wanted to stay, but I wouldn't let her. I had too much on my mind to have her around as well as the police.

She said she would call me in the morning, gave me a worried look, and then went away in a taxi.

Carlotti listened to my explanation about the camera. I showed him where I had put it, and he examined the broken lock of the drawer.

I'm not sure if he believed what I was telling him. His face was expressionless, but I had an idea he was only maintaining his usual polite calmness by an effort.

'This is an odd coincidence, Signor Dawson,' he said. 'You have the camera for only a few hours, then a thief breaks in and steals it.'

'Yeah?' I said sarcastically. 'And he not only steals the camera, but also goes off with my goddamn clothes, my cigarettes, my booze and my spare cash. I don't call that a coincidence.

One of Carlotti's men came over and murmured there were no finger-prints to be found except mine.

Carlotti gave me a thoughtful stare, then shrugged his shoulders.

'I shall have to report this to my chief,' he said.

'Report it to the President if you want to,' I returned.

'Just as long as you get my clothes back.'

'The camera is a serious loss, signor.'

'I couldn't care less about the camera. That's your funeral. If you didn't realize until now that it was important to you, you can scarcely blame me that it's been stolen. Grandi gave me the camera, and I signed a receipt for it. He told me neither you nor he wanted it. So don't look at me as if I've cooked up this robbery just to get you into trouble.'

He said there was no need to get angry about such an unfortunate affair.

'Okay, so I'm not angry. Would you get your boys out of here so I can clear up and get some supper?'

It took them a further half-hour to satisfy themselves that there were positively no clues left by the burglar, then finally, and with the greatest reluctance, they went away.

Carlotti was the last to leave.

'This is an awkward situation,' he said as he paused in the doorway. 'You should never have been given the camera.'

'I know. I can see that. My heart bleeds for you, but I was given the camera and you've got my receipt. You can't blame me for what's happened. I'm sorry, but I'm not going to lose any sleep about it.'

He started to say something, changed his mind, shrugged his shoulders and went away.

I had an idea at the back of my mind that for a couple of dimes, he would have accused me of staging the burglary myself just so he couldn't lay his hands on the camera.

I wasn't kidding myself. I was quite sure that, although most of my clothes, cigarettes, three bottles of Scotch and a few thousand lire were missing, the thief had broken in only for one purpose: to get the camera.

I did a little thinking while I hastily cleared up the mess in my bedroom and sitting-room. At the back of my mind I had the picture of the broad-shouldered intruder I had seen creeping around the villa at Sorrento. I was willing to bet that he was the guy who had broken in here and had lifted the camera.

I had just finished tidying up my sitting-room when the front-door bell rang.

I went into the hall, thinking Carlotti had come back with a flock of new questions. I slid back the bolt and opened the front-door. Jack Maxwell stood outside.

'Hello,' he said. 'I hear you have had a burglar.'

'Yeah,' I said. 'Come on in.'

He looked at the broken lock on the front door with morbid interest, and then followed me into the sitting-room.

'Lost much?'

'Just the usual things. I'm insured . . . so what do I care?' I went over to the liquor cabinet. 'Have a drink?'

'I don't mind having a brandy.' He dropped into a chair. 'Was the old man pleased with the way I handled the write-up about Helen?'

'He seemed to be. Did you have much trouble?'

'One or two of the boys started to ask smart questions, but I told them they'd better talk to Chalmers. They said they'd rather kiss a smallpox case. That guy certainly is one of the best loved in this world.' He took the brandy I handed to him. 'Has he gone yet or is he staying on?'

'He left on the three-forty plane from Naples.' I made myself a highball. 'Hold everything for a moment. I want something to eat. I haven't had a thing since lunch.'

'Well, come out. I'll buy you something.'

'It's too late now.' I picked up the telephone receiver and called the hall porter. I told him to get me a chicken sandwich and bring it up pronto.

'Well, give us the dope,' Maxwell said, when I had hung up. 'Did you find what she was doing in that place all alone? How did she die?'

I was careful what I told him. I said it looked as if there was a man in the background, that the police weren't entirely satisfied that Helen's death had been accidental, and that Chalmers had told me to stick around and watch his interests. I didn't tell him what June had said, nor that Helen had been pregnant.

He sat listening, sipping his brandy.

'So you're not going home right away?'

'Not for a while.'

'I told you the old sonofabitch would want an investigation, didn't I? Well, thank my stars, I'm not involved.'

I said he was lucky.

'What's biting the police? Why aren't they satisfied?'

'Carlotti likes mysteries. He always turns molehills into mountains.'

'Does Chalmers think it was an accident?'

'He's keeping an open mind about it.'

103

'Do you?'

'I wouldn't know.'

'This girl was a ripe little bitch. You don't think her boy friend shoved her over the cliff, do you?'

'I hope not. Chalmers would love a set-up like that.'

'There's bound to be a man in this, Ed. She wouldn't have taken a villa in Sorrento if she hadn't a man to share it with. Any idea who he could be?'

'Not the vaguest, but never mind that, Jack. Tell me something: who's June Chalmers?'

He looked surprised, then grinned.

'She's a pippin, isn't she? But if you've got ideas about her, I'd forget them. You wouldn't get to first base.'

'Nothing like that. I want to know who she is. Where does she come from? Do you know anything about her?'

'Not much. She used to be a torch singer at one of Menotti's night spots.'

I stiffened. Menotti again.

'Is that how she and Helen met?'

'Could be: did they meet?'

'She told me she had known Helen for some years.'

'Did she now? I didn't know that. I heard Chalmers met her at a party, took one look at her and practically married her on the spot. It was lucky for her that he did. The night club she was working at closed down when Menotti was knocked off. Although she certainly has a shape, she can't sing for dimes.'

The night porter interrupted us by bringing my sandwich. Maxwell got to his feet.

'Well, here are your victuals. I'll be pushing along. When's the inquest?'

'Monday.'

'You'll go down, I suppose?'

'I guess so.'

'Rather you than me. Well, so long. Will you look in at the office to-morrow?'

'I might. I'm leaving you to handle that end. Officially, I'm still on vacation.'

'And having a wonderful time,' he said, grinned and went away.

I sat down and munched my sandwich. I did some heavy thinking at the same time. I had hoped to have found a list of telephone numbers or an address book among Helen's papers that might give me a lead on her friends. If she had kept such a list, then someone had taken it. The only clue I had so far was Carlo's telephone number. There was a girl I knew who worked on the Rome telephone exchange. She had once won a beauty competition, and I had given her a write-up. One thing had led to another, and for a couple of months we had been more than friendly. Then I lost sight of her. I decided I'd look her up in the morning and persuade her to get me Carlo's address.

Apart from Carlo, who else was there?

I dug down into my mind to recall anything that Helen had said during our various meetings that would give me a lead on her other friends. It wasn't until I was about to give up and go to bed that I suddenly remembered she had once mentioned Giuseppe Frenzi, who wrote a political column for *l'Italia del Popolo* and who was a good friend of mine.

When Frenzi wasn't writing his column, he was going around with women. He claimed that an association with a beautiful woman was the only true meaning of life. Knowing Frenzi, I was pretty sure that he and Helen had been a lot more than just friends. Frenzi had a technique of his own, and if I was to believe Maxwell, Helen wasn't the kind of girl to say no.

I thought Frenzi might be an important lead.

I looked at my watch. The time was twenty minutes to midnight: the beginning of a day for Frenzi, who never got up before eleven o'clock in the morning and never went to bed before four.

I picked up the telephone receiver and called his apartment. There was just a remote chance that he would be still there.

He answered immediately.

'Ed? Well, this is something,' he said. He prided himself on his American expressions. 'I was about to call you. I've only just read the news about Helen. Is it true? Is she really dead?'

'She's dead all right. I want to talk to you, Giuseppe. Can I come around?'

'Of course. I will wait for you.'

'I'll be right over,' I said, and hung up.

I left the apartment and ran down the staircase to where I had left the Lincoln.

It was raining, as it will do suddenly and unexpectedly in Rome. I ducked into the car, set the windscreen wipers in motion, started the engine and backed out of the parking space.

Frenzi had an apartment on Via Claudia in the shadow of the Colosseum. It wasn't more than a six-minute drive from my place to his.

There wasn't much traffic and, as I accelerated, I saw, out of the corner of my eye, a car that was parked nearby suddenly turn on its parking lights and, a moment later, it swung out into the road and came after me.

As it passed under the glare of a street light I saw it was the Renault.

ii

It isn't often that I lose my temper, but when I do, I have a field-day. The sight of the Renault gave me a rush of blood to my head.

I became determined to find out who the driver was, and what he was playing at. So long as the car was behind me, there wasn't much I could do about it. Somehow I had to get him in front of me, then I could crowd him into the kerb, force him to stop and get a look at him. If he wanted to play it rough, I was in the mood to hang one on his jaw.

I drove around the Colosseum with the Renault fifty yards in the rear. When I reached a dark patch in the road, I slammed on my brakes, swung the car to the kerb and pulled up.

Taken by surprise, the driver of the Renault had no chance to stop. The car shot past me. It was too dark to see whether the driver was a man or a woman. The moment the car had passed me, I let in my clutch and went after it, sending the Lincoln forward with my foot squeezing the gas pedal to the board.

The driver of the Renault must have guessed what I planned to do. His reaction was quicker than I expected. In his turn, he trod on the gas, and the Renault surged forward.

It went streaking down Via dei Fori Imperiali like a bullet from a gun.

For a moment I thought I was going to catch him. My front bumper was only a foot off his rear fender, and I was ready to swing the wheel over and hit him, but he began to pull away.

We were travelling now at around eighty miles an hour. I heard a shrill, indignant police whistle blasting somewhere in my rear. I saw beyond the speeding Renault the Piazza Venezia looming up. I saw the slow-moving traffic ahead, and my nerve faltered. I knew I couldn't roar into the piazza at this speed without hitting a car or killing someone. My foot went down on the brake pedal and I slowed.

The Renault leapt away from me. Its horn gave a long, warning blast, and then the car went screeching into the piazza, missing two cars by inches, and forcing another to skid to a standstill. Only slightly slackening its mad speed, the Renault, its horn blaring, stormed across the piazza, and disappeared into the darkness and towards the Tiber.

I heard the police whistle shrill again. Anxious not to have an argument with the law, and pretty certain I had been travelling too fast for any policeman in this light to have taken my number, I swung into the Via Cavour, slowed down to a respectable speed and took a long circular run back to the Colosseum.

I was rattled that the Renault had got away, but I would rather he escaped than for me to attempt to compete with his kind of driving. At least, I had the satisfaction of knowing I had given him a scare.

I arrived at Frenzi's ground-floor apartment, parked the Lincoln outside and went up the steps to the front door.

Frenzi answered my ring immediately.

'Come in,' he said. 'It is good to see you again.'

I followed him into his attractively furnished lounge.

'Will you have a drink?' he said.

'No, I don't think so, thanks.'

I sat on the arm of a lounging chair and looked at him.

Frenzi was slightly built, under medium height, dark, handsome with intelligent, shrewd eyes. His usually bright face was grave, and he wore a worried frown.

'You must have something to keep me company,' he said 'Join me in a brandy.

'Well, okay.'

While he was fixing the drinks, he went on, 'This is a very bad business, Ed. The account only says she fell off a cliff. Have you any details? What was she doing in Sorrento?'

'She was on vacation there.'

He brought the drinks over and, giving me mine, he began to move restlessly about the room.

'It's straightforward, isn't it?' he asked, without looking at me. 'I mean, it was an accident?'

This startled me.

'Confidentially, there is some doubt about it,' I said. 'Chalmers thinks she was murdered.'

He hunched his shoulders, his frown deepening.

'And the police—what do they think?'

'They're coming around to the same idea. Carlotti's handling the case. At first, he was sure it was an accident; now he's changing his mind.'

Frenzi looked at me.

'I'm willing to bet it was murder,' he said quietly.

I lit a cigarette and slid into the chair.

'What makes you say that, Giuseppe?'

'Sooner or later, someone was bound to get rid of her. She was asking for trouble.'

'What do you know about her then?'

He hesitated, then came over and sat opposite me.

'You and I are good friends, Ed. I need your advice. I was going to call you when you called me. Can we talk off the record?'

'Of course. Go ahead.'

'I met her at a party about five days after she had arrived in Rome. I was foolish enough to become friendly with her for four or five days—or rather nights.' He looked at me and lifted his shoulders. 'You know how it is with me. She seemed beautiful, exciting and everything a man could wish for. She was also alone. I made my offer and she accepted it, but . . .' He broke off and grimaced.

'But—what?'

'After we had spent four nights together, she asked me for money.'

I stared at him.

'You mean, she wanted to borrow money from you?'

'Well, no. She wanted money for services rendered: as sordid as that—quite a lot of money.'

'How much?'

'Four million lire.'

'For the love of mike! She must have been crazy! What did you do? Laugh at her?'

'She was serious. I had trouble in persuading her that I hadn't such a sum. There was a very disagreeable scene. She said if she told her father, he would ruin me. He would get me dismissed from my paper.'

I felt a sudden chill crawl up my spine.

'Wait a minute. Are you telling me she tried to blackmail you?'

'That's the technical name for it, I believe.'

'Well, what happened?'

'I compromised. I gave her a pair of diamond ear-rings.'

'You didn't submit to blackmail, Giuseppe?'

He shrugged.

'It is easy to criticize, but I was in a very difficult position. Chalmers is powerful enough to get me removed from my paper. I like my job. I'm not good at anything else. It was her word against mine. I haven't a very good reputation with women. I was pretty sure she was bluffing, but I couldn't afford to take the risk. The ear-rings cost me thirty-four thousand lire, so I suppose I got off fairly lightly: much lighter than one of your colleagues.'

I was sitting forward now, staring at him.

'What do you mean?'

'I wasn't the only one, of course. There was another newspaper man—an American—who she tricked in the same way. Never mind who he is. We compared notes together later. He parted with a diamond collar that cost him most of his savings. Apparently, she specialized in newspaper men. Her father's influence was more readily felt in that field.'

I felt suddenly sick. If what Frenzi had said was true, and I was sure it was true, then it was obvious that Helen had set a trap for me, and if she hadn't fallen over the cliff, I also would have been taken for a blackmail ride.

I saw then that if this story of Frenzi's got out, and the police discovered that I was the mysterious Mr. Sherrard, here was the obvious motive for her murder. They would say she had tried to blackmail me; I was unable to pay, and, to save my new job, I had pushed her off the cliff.

It was my turn now to wander around the room. Fortunately, Frenzi wasn't looking at me. He remained in his chair, staring up at the ceiling.

'You see now why I think she could have been murdered,' he went on. 'She might have tried this stunt once too often. I can't believe she went to Sorrento alone. I'm sure there was a man with her. If she was murdered, all the police will have to do is to find him.'

I didn't say anything.

'What do you think I should do? I've been trying to make up my mind ever since I read of her death. Should I go to the police and tell them how she had tried to blackmail me? If they really think she was murdered, it would give them the motive.'

By now I had got over my first shock. I returned to my chair and sat down.

'You'll have to be careful,' I said. 'If Carlotti passed on what you tell him to Chalmers, you'd still be in trouble.'

'Yes, I realize that.' He finished his brandy, got up and refilled his glass. 'But do you think I should do it?'

I shook my head.

'I don't. I think you should wait until the police are sure it is murder. You don't want to rush into this thing. You can't afford to. You must wait and see how it develops.'

'But suppose they find out she and I were lovers. Suppose they think, because I had a motive, that I killed her?'

'Oh, talk sense, Giuseppe! You can prove you were no-where near Sorrento when she died, can't you?'

'Well, yes. I was right here in Rome.'

'Then for the love of mike, don't be dramatic.'

He shrugged his shoulders.

'You are right. So you think I should say nothing to the police?'

'Not yet. Chalmers suspects there's a man involved. He's like a mad bull right now. If you came forward, he would jump to the conclusion that you were the man and he'd go for you. You may as well know the facts: Helen was pregnant.'

Frenzi's brandy glass slipped out of his fingers and dropped on to the floor. The brandy made a little pool on the carpet. He gaped at me, his eyes widening.

'Was she? I swear it wasn't me,' he said. 'My goodness! I'm damned glad I didn't go to the police before I talked to you.' He picked up his glass. 'Look what I've done!' He went into the kitchen to find a cloth. While he was gone, I had time to do some thinking. If Carlotti believed and could prove that Helen was murdered, I knew he would make every effort to trace the mythological Sherrard. Had I covered my tracks well enough to prevent him finding me?

Frenzi came back and mopped up the spilt brandy. Squatting on his heels, he practically voiced my thoughts by saying, 'Carlotti is very thorough. I've never known him to fail on a murder case. He could get on to me, Ed.'

He could get on to me, too.

'You have an alibi he can't upset, so relax,' I told him. 'Chalmers has given me the job of finding the man who might have killed her. Maybe you can help me. Could he have been this American newspaper man you were telling me about?'

Frenzi shook his head.

'Not a chance. I was talking to him on the afternoon she died.'

'Then who else is there? Any ideas?'

'No, I'm afraid not.'

'There is a man she knew whose first name is Carlo. Do you happen to know anyone of that name?'

He thought for a moment, then shook his head.

'I don't think so.'

'Did you ever see her with any man?'

He rubbed his jaw, looking steadily at me.

'I saw her with you.'

I sat very still.

'Did you? Where was that?'

'You were coming out of a movie together.'

'Chalmers wanted me to take her around,' I said. 'I did take her out once or twice. Apart from me, is there anyone else you can remember?'

I knew he was too shrewd to be fooled by my attempt at casualness, but he was also too good a friend to embarrass me more than he had already.

'I did see her with a big, dark fellow at Luigi's once. I don't know who he was.'

'How big?'

'He was impressively big: built like a prize-fighter.'

My mind jumped to the intruder I had seen in the villa. He too had been impressively big: he too had shoulders of a prize-fighter.

'Can you give me a description of him?'

'I'm pretty sure he was an Italian. I should say he was around twenty-five or six; dark, blunt featured, good looking in an animal kind of way, if you know what I mean. He had a scar on his right cheek: a white, zigzag mark that could have been an old knife wound.'

'And you have no idea who he is?'

'None at all, but he's easy to recognize if you ever see him.'

'Yes. No other ideas?'

He shrugged.

'This isn't even an idea, Ed. This fellow was the only man, apart from you, I ever saw her with, but you can be sure, she was always going around with men. I wish I could be more helpful, but I can't.'

I got to my feet.

'You have been helpful,' I said. 'Now look, relax, do nothing and say nothing. I'll try to find this guy. He may be the one I'm looking for. I'll keep you informed. If Carlotti does happen to get on to you, you have a cast-iron alibi. Remember that and stop worrying.'

Frenzi smiled.

'Yes, you're right. I rely on your judgment, Ed.'

I said it was the thing to do, shook hands with him and went down to where I parked the Lincoln.

As I drove back to my apartment, I felt I hadn't wasted my time. It seemed to me I had now found the reason why Helen had died at the foot of the cliff. It wasn't something I could explain to Chalmers, but at least, it gave me a clue: someone, as Frenzi had said, did not blackmail easily and Helen had died.

My next obvious move was to find Carlo.

III

It took me until four o'clock the following afternoon before I could contact my ex-girl-friend on the Rome exchange telephone.

She made the usual difficulties that a girl who has been dropped and now discovers you're interested in her again will make, and I had to exercise a lot of patience and tact before I could get around to what I wanted to ask her.

When she understood I wanted the name and address of a Rome telephone subscriber, she said promptly that it was strictly against regulations and by obliging me she could lose her job. After a lot of aimless talk which nearly drove me crazy, she finally suggested we might discuss the matter over a dinner.

I said I would meet her at Alfredo's at eight o'clock and hung up. I knew there would be more to it than a dinner, so I bought a powder compact for seventeen thousand lire that looked showy enough to have cost three times that price as a make-weight if she raised further difficulties.

I hadn't seen her for three years, and I didn't recognize her when she entered Alfredo's. I wondered how it had been possible for her ever to have won a prize in a beauty competition. Three years can make quite a dent in the shape and size of any Italian woman if she doesn't watch her diet, and this girl, apparently, hadn't watched anything since last I met her. She was really something to see.

After a lot of talk, hedging and wrangling, and not before I had slipped her the compact, she finally agreed to get me the name and address of the subscriber of the telephone number I had found scribbled on Helen's lounge wall.

She promised to call me the following morning.

I had to wait until half-past eleven o'clock before the call came through. By then I was fit to strangle her.

There was a waspish note in her voice when she told me that the subscriber was a woman.

'Okay, so it's a woman,' I said. 'You don't have to get worked up. It had to be either a man or a woman, hadn't it? You wouldn't expect it to be a dog, would you?'

'You don't have to shout at me,' she said. 'I have no business to give you this information.'

I counted up to five mentally before I could trust myself to speak, then I said, 'Look, let's have it. This is strictly business. How many times do I have to tell you?'

She said the subscriber lived at villa Palestra, viale Paolo Veronese, and her name was Myra Setti.

I wrote down the name and address.

'Thanks a lot,' I said, staring at the scribble on the pad. 'Setti? S-e-t-t-i? Is that right?'

She said it was.

Then the nickle dropped.

Setti!

I remembered the New York police had believed that Frank Setti, Menotti's gangster rival, had been responsible for Menotti's death. Was Myra Setti connected in some way with him—his wife, his sister or even his daughter? Was there some hook up between this woman, Menotti's murder, Frank Setti and Helen?

I became aware that my late girl-friend was talking. Her high-pitched voice slammed against my ear-drum, but I couldn't be bothered to listen to what she was saying.

I dropped the receiver back on to its cradle, my heart bumping with excitement.

Setti!

This might be the clue I had been looking for. I remembered Maxwell had said that Helen was thought to be mixed up in the Menotti killing, and that was the reason why she had come to Rome.

If Setti had really engineered the killing . . .

I decided it might pay off to take a look at the villa Palestra.

The telephone bell rang. My late girl-friend was possibly wanting to know why I had hung up on her.

I settled further down in my chair and let the telephone bell ring.

PART VIII

I

I was pretty busy for the next two hours.

I knew by now Chalmers would be back in his New York office and would be waiting impatiently to hear from me. I would have to get some sort of report to him during the day.

I called the International Investigating Agency and told them to send their best operator around. I said the job was confidential and urgent. They said they would send their Signor Sarti. Then I put a call through to Jim Matthews of the Associated Press. Matthews had been in Rome for fifteen years. He knew everyone who was likely to make news and a few who wouldn't.

I said I'd like to have a word with him when he was free.

'For you, Ed, I'm always free,' he said. 'Suppose you buy me a large and expensive lunch and let us talk?'

I looked at my watch. The time was just after twelve.

'I'll meet you at Harry's bar at one-thirty,' I said.

'Fine. I'll be seeing you.'

I then made a few notes on a pad and did a little thinking, trying to make up my mind how much to tell Chalmers. His wife's warning bothered me. I could see if I gave him the whole story he wasn't likely to react favourably to me, and yet, it wasn't going to be easy to keep much back. I was still brooding on what I was going to tell him when the front-door bell rang.

I opened the door to find a short, fat elderly Italian, dressed in a shabby grey suit, standing on my doormat. He introduced himself as Bruno Sarti from the agency.

At first glance Bruno Sarti wasn't particularly impressive. He hadn't shaved this morning; his linen was grubby and he had the beginning of a boil under his right eye. He also carried with him a devastating smell of garlic that poisoned the atmosphere in my room.

I asked him in. He removed his shabby velour hat to show a balding head and a scurfy scalp and came in.

He sat on the edge of a straight-backed chair while I went over to the open window and sat on the sill. I felt in need of a circulation of fresh air.

'I want some information and I want it fast,' I told him. 'The cost doesn't matter. I'd be glad if your agency would put on as many men as they think necessary.'

His black, blood-shot eyes opened a trifle and he showed me several gold-capped teeth in what he imagined was a smile. It looked to me like the kind of spasm you see on someone's face when they have a sudden stomach cramp.

'The information I want and the fact I am your client must be regarded as strictly confidential,' I went on. 'You may as well know the police are also investigating the affair and you'll have to watch out that you don't tread on their toes.'

His so-called smile faded and his eyelids narrowed.

'We are good friends of the police,' he said. 'We wouldn't want to do anything to annoy them.'

'You won't do that,' I assured him. 'This is what I want you to do: I want you to find out who were the men friends of an American girl who stayed in Rome for the past fourteen weeks. Her name is Helen Chalmers. I can give you some photographs of her. She stayed at the Excelsior hotel for four days and then moved to an apartment.' I handed him a number of photographs I had got Gina to send over from our files, as well as the address of Helen's apartment. 'She had a number of men friends. I want all their names and where I can find them. I also want to know what she did with herself during the time she was in Rome.'

'La signorina died accidentally at Sorrento, I believe?' Sarti asked, looking at me. 'She is the daughter of il Signor Sherwin Chalmers, the American newspaper owner?'

In spite of his unimpressive looks, at least he appeared to keep abreast with the news.

'Yes,' I said.

The gold teeth flashed. Obviously he now realized he was in with the big money and that pleased him. He produced a notebook and a stub of pencil and made a few notes.

'I will begin immediately, signor,' he said.

'That's the first job. I also want to find out who owns a dark green Renault with this registration number.'

I handed him a slip of paper on which I had jotted down the Renault's number.

'The police tell me there is no such number registered. Your only hope is to watch out for the car and if you spot it either to follow it or get a look at the driver.'

He made more notes and then closed his notebook. He looked up and asked, 'The death of la signorina was not perhaps accidental, signor?'

'We don't know. You needn't bother your brains about that. Get me this information fast and leave the other angle to the police to handle.' I stood up. 'Call me here as soon as you have anything. Don't wait to give me a written report. I want this job cleared up in a hurry.'

He said he would do his best, suggested I might like to pay the usual retaining fee of seventeen thousand lire, took my cheque, assured me that he would have something for me before long, and bowed himself out of the apartment.

I opened another window, and then left the apartment myself to keep my date with Matthews.

I found him drinking Scotch and crushed ice at Harry's bar: a tall thin, hard-faced man with grey, steady eyes, a hooked nose and a jutting jaw.

We had a couple of drinks, and then went into the restaurant. We began our meal with *bottarga*, which is a kind of caviar made of mullet roes, followed by *polo in padella* or chicken cut up and cooked with ham, garlic, marjoram, tomatoes and wine. We talked of this and that and enjoyed the meal. It wasn't until we were eating the famous Roman cheese, *ricotta*, sprinkled with cinnamon, that I got down to business.

'I want some information from you, Jim,' I said.

He grinned at me.

'I'm not such a mug as to think you bought this meal for me because you love me,' he returned. 'Go ahead— what is it?'

'Does the name of Myra Setti mean anything to you?'

His reaction was immediate. The pleased, relaxed expression on his face slipped away. His eyes became intent.

'Hello, hello' he said. 'Now this could be interesting. What makes you ask that?'

117

'Sorry, Jim, I'm not giving reasons. Who is she?'

'Frank Setti's daughter, of course. You should know that.'

'The gangster?'

'Oh, come on, you're not all that wet behind the ears.'

'Don't be superior. I know something about Setti, but not much. Where is he right now?'

'That's something I'd like to know myself. He's somewhere in Italy, but just where he's holed up I don't know and the police don't know either. He left New York about three months ago. He arrived by boat at Naples, and registered with the police, giving the hotel Vesuvius as an address. Then he vanished, and the police haven't been able to trace him since. All we know is that he hasn't left Italy, but just where he's got to, no one knows.'

'Not even his daughter?'

'She probably does, but she isn't talking. I've had a word with her. She's lived in Rome for the past five years, and she says her father hasn't made contact with her; not even written to her.'

'Tell me something about Setti, Jim.'

Matthews leaned back in his chair.

'You wouldn't like to buy me a brandy, would you? Seems a pity not to finish such a good meal correctly.'

I signalled to the waiter, ordered two large Stocks, and when they arrived, I offered Matthews a cigar I had been keeping on ice for such an occasion.

He examined it dubiously, bit off the end and set light to it. We both watched it burn a little anxiously. When he had satisfied himself that I hadn't sold him a pup, he said, 'There's not much I know that you don't know about Setti. He was boss of the Bakers' and Waiters' Union. He's a tough and dangerous thug who stops at nothing to get his own way. He and Menotti were sworn enemies, both of them wanting to be the head man. You probably know that Menotti had a load of heroin planted in Setti's apartment. He then tipped off the Narcotic Squad, who moved in, grabbed the load and arrested Setti. But it was a clumsy job, and Setti's attorney didn't have much trouble in shooting holes in the D.A.'s case. Setti was found not guilty, but there was such a yell from the press, who were gunning for him, that he was later charged as an undesirable alien and deported. He had always kept his Italian nationality, so the Italian authorities couldn't stop him from landing here. They were busy trying to find some excuse to get rid of him when he vanished.'

'I hear the police think he engineered Menotti's killing.'

'That's more or less certain. Before he left, he warned Menotti he would fix him. Two months later, Menotti was killed. You can bet your last buck that Setti arranged it.'

'How did it happen? Didn't Menotti take the threat seriously?'

'He certainly did. He never moved a yard without a bunch of gunmen surrounding him, but Setti's killer got him in the end. Menotti made a fatal mistake. He used to go to an apartment once a week regularly to spend the night with his girl-friend. He thought he was safe there. His boys took him there; they searched the apartment. They waited until the girl arrived, then, after Menotti had bolted himself in, they went home. In the morning, they arrived outside the door, identified themselves and escorted Menotti back to his home. On this particular night, they went through the usual routine, but when they came to collect Menotti the following morning, they found the door open and Menotti dead.'

'What about the girl? Who was she?'

Matthews shrugged.

'No one seems to know. There was no sign of her when they found Menotti and no one has seen her since. She didn't live at the apartment. She was there waiting for Menotti when he and his boys arrived. None of them ever got a look at her. She would stand looking out of the window while they searched the apartment. All they can say is that she was a blonde with a good shape. The police couldn't trace her. They thought she must have let the killer in, because the door wasn't forced. I think it's pretty certain she sold Menotti out.'

I brooded over this for a moment, then asked, 'Do you know a big, broad-shouldered Italian, with a white zigzag scar on his face whose first name is Carlo?'

Matthews shook his head.

'He's a new one to me. Where does he fit in?'

'I don't know, but I want to find out. If you ever get a line on him, Jim, will you let me know?'

'Oh, sure,' He tapped the ash off his cigar. 'Look, tell me, what is all this sudden interest in Setti about?'

119

'I can't go into that right now, but if I turn up anything that you can use, I'll let you know. Sorry, but that's as far as I can go at this stage.'

He pulled a face.

'I hate a guy going secretive on me,' he said, then shrugged. 'Well, okay, after all, the lunch wasn't so bad.' He pushed back his chair. 'If you haven't any work to do this afternoon, I have. Anything else you want to know before I get back to the treadmill?'

'I don't think so, but if I do think of anything, I'll call you.'

'That's the idea. Don't be scared to pick my brains.' He got to his feet. 'You don't happen to know where Setti's hiding, do you?'

'If I did, I'd tell you.'

He shook his head sadly.

'Yeah, I know: like I'd tell my wife my secretary has a chest like Jane Russell. Well, so long handsome. If I don't see you before then, I'll be at your funeral.'

I watched him go, then for the next ten minutes, I turned over in my mind what he had told me. I hadn't learned a great deal, but what there was of it had been worth the money I had paid out on the lunch.

II

By the time I had got back to my apartment, I had mapped out in my mind what I was going to tell Chalmers. My best plan, I told myself, anyway for the moment, was to be as non-committal as I could: There were angles to this business that had to be investigated before I could even think of giving Chalmers a glimmer of the truth.

I left the Lincoln outside the building and hastily climbed the private staircase to my apartment. As I was walking down the passage, I saw the figure of a man loitering outside my front door.

My heart skipped a beat when I recognized the short, broad-shouldered form of Lieutenant Carlotti.

He turned at the sound of my footfalls and gave me a long, steady stare that was meant to be disconcerting and succeeded in being disconcerting.

120

'Hello, Lieutenant, you haven't been waiting long, have you?' I said, trying to sound breezy.

'I have only just arrived,' he said. 'There was something I wanted to ask you.'

I fetched out my latchkey, opened the front door and stood aside.

'Come on in.'

He walked into the lounge the way an undertaker walks into the room where the body is laid out. He placed himself with his back to the window so that, if I faced him, the full light from the window would fall on my face.

I wasn't willing to give him this advantage, so I went over to my desk that stood in a corner out of the light and sat on it, making him turn to face me.'

'What's bothering you, Lieutenant?' I asked, lighting a cigarette and trying to keep calm.

He looked around, found a chair that would put him in line with me and sat down.

'I regret it is now no longer possible to advise the Naples coroner that la Signorina Chalmers's death was accidental,' he said. 'There are several points that are suspicious. We intend to make a full investigation.'

I kept my face expressionless.

'And so ... ?' I said, meeting his cold, searching stare.

'La signorina had a number of men friends,' he said. 'We find she has been free and easy with her favours.'

'That's very tactfully put, Lieutenant. You're telling me she led an immoral life?'

He nodded.

'I am afraid so.'

'That is something Chalmers won't welcome. You're sure of your facts?'

He made an impatient movement.

'Of course. We think it is more than possible that one of her men friends killed her. This is now a murder investigation. I have already collected the names of a number of men she knew. Your name is among them.'

'Are you suggesting I had immoral relations with her?' I said, forcing myself to meet his eyes. 'Because if you are, I'll take a lot of pleasure in suing you.'

'I am making no suggestions, signor. You knew her. I am trying to clarify the position. We feel satisfied that a man she knew killed her. Perhaps you would be kind enough to help me. Can you please tell me where you were on the day of her death?'

This was a question I had been waiting to be asked for what seemed a long, long time.

'Do you think I killed her?' I asked in a voice I scarcely recognized as my own.

'No, I don't think so. I am making a list of all the names of the men who knew her. Against each name, I am putting the whereabouts of this man at the time of her death. In this way, I shall save a considerable amount of time. I need only investigate those men who can't account for their movements at that time.'

'I see.' I drew in a long, slow breath. 'You want to know where I was four days ago?'

'If you please.'

'That won't be difficult. It was the day I began my vacation. I had intended to go to Venice. I forgot to book a room and, finding I had left it too late, I stayed here, working on my novel. The following morning . . .'

'I'm not interested in what happened on the following morning,' Carlotti said. 'I just want to know what happened on the 29th.'

'Okay. I was right here working on my novel. I worked all the afternoon and evening up to three o'clock the following morning. I didn't move out of here.'

He looked down at his highly polished shoes.

'Perhaps someone called on you?' he asked hopefully.

'No one came near me, because I was thought to be in Venice.'

'Perhaps someone telephoned you?'

'No one did, for the same reason.'

'I see.'

There was a long, awkward pause while he stared at his shoes, then he suddenly looked up. Meeting his eyes was like having a blow-lamp across my face.

'Well, thank you, signor,' he said, and got to his feet. 'This is a complicated business. It is only by making inquiries and asking questions that we shall eventually arrive at the truth. I am sorry if I have taken up too much of your time.'

'That's okay,' I said, aware that my hands were clammy and my mouth was dry.

'If there is anything that I think you can help me with,

122

I'll be in touch with you again.' He moved to the door. Then he paused to look at me. 'Is there anything you would wish to add? Anything that may have slipped your mind that might help me?'

'My mind's not all that slippery.'

He stared at me.

'I don't think you should treat this matter flippantly, signor. It is, after all, a murder investigation. Perhaps you will think about it. Some idea may occur to you.'

'Sure. If it does, I'll call you.'

'I'd be glad if you would.'

He nodded and, opening the door, he went into the hall. I was feeling so shaken I didn't trust myself to escort him to the front door. He found his own way out. When I heard the front door shut behind him, I stubbed out my cigarette and, getting to my feet, I walked over to the window.

I watched the traffic swirling around the Forum. There were a few dark clouds creeping up behind the stark outline of the Colosseum: a sure sign that it was going to be a wet night. I saw Carlotti get into the police car and drive away.

* * * * *

I remained motionless, my mind crawling with alarm. I might have known Carlotti wouldn't have missed the significance of the missing films. This was something I couldn't keep from Chalmers.

I had a sudden feeling of urgency. I had to find this mysterious X before Carlotti found me. I didn't underrate him. Already he was getting too close to me for comfort.

The telephone snapped me out of my mood. I picked up the receiver. It was Gina.

'You said you would call me yesterday,' she said. 'I've been waiting. What is happening, Ed?'

I did some quick thinking. I couldn't confide my troubles to her now Carlotti had told me this was a murder case. She might get hooked in as an accessory if she knew I was Douglas Sherrard.

'I'm right up to my ears at the moment,' I said. 'I'm on my way out. Give me a couple of days, and you'll hear from me.' ..

'But, Ed ... what was it you were going to tell me? Can't we meet to-night?'

'I'm sorry, Gina, but not to-night. I can't stop now. I'll call you in a couple of days. So long for now,' and I hung up.

I waited a moment, then put a call through to New York. The operator said there was a two-hour delay.

There was nothing for me to do but to sit down and mull over the information I had got from Matthews and to consider the threat that was beginning to develop from Carlotti. After a while I got tired of frightening myself and turned on the radio. Maria Meneghini Callas was giving a recital of Puccini's songs. Her dark, exciting voice carried me out of my troubles for the next hour. She was in the middle of *Sola perduta, Abbandonata*, and making my hair stand on end, when the telephone bell rang and I had to cut her short.

Chalmers came on the line after only a two-minute delay.

'What have you got?'

Even at that distance I could hear the iron in his voice.

'I've just had Carlotti here,' I said. 'He's now decided it looks like murder, and he'll tell the coroner so.'

There was a pause, then Chalmers said, 'How did he get on to it.'

I told him about the camera and the missing films. I told him how I had taken the camera, had found the scrap of film in it and how the camera had been stolen before I could hand it back to the police.

The news seemed to stun him, for he was hesitant when he began to talk again.

'What are you going to do, Dawson?'

'I'm trying to get a list of Helen's men friends,' I said, and told him I had got an inquiry agency on the job. 'Carlotti's working on the same angle. He seems to think your daughter had a number of men friends.'

'If he tries to stir up a scandal about the girl, I'll break him!' Chalmers snarled. 'Keep in touch with me. I want to know what you're doing . . . understand?'

I said I understood.

'And talk to this coroner fella. He promised me he'd fix this pregnancy business. I don't want that to come out. Get tough with him, Dawson. Throw a scare into him!'

'If this turns out to be a murder case, Mr. Chalmers,' I said, 'there's nothing we can do about the verdict.'

'Don't tell me what we can't do!' he bawled. 'Talk to this punk. Call me back to-morrow at this time.'

I said I would, and hung up.

I put a call through to coroner Maletti. When he came on the line I told him I had been talking to Chalmers, who was anxious to be assured that the arrangements he had made would stand. Maletti was full of oil and soft soap. Unless further evidence came to light, he said, il Signor Chalmers need not disturb himself about the verdict.

'You'll be the one who's disturbed if the verdict's the wrong one,' I said, and slammed down the receiver.

By now it was dark and rain showed on the windows.

It was time, I decided as I went into my bedroom to get my raincoat, to pay a visit to the villa Palestra.

iii

I left my car in the parking lot at the Stadium and walked up via le Paolo Veronese until I came to double wrought-iron gates, set in an eight-foot high stone wall that surrounded the acre or so of garden in which the villa Palestra stood.

By now it was raining hard, and the long street was deserted. I pushed open one of the gates, moved into a dark driveway, screened by cypress trees and flowering shrubs.

Moving silently, I walked up the drive, hunching my shoulders against the rain. Fifty yards of driveway brought me to a bend, and around the bend I caught sight of the villa, a small, two-storey affair with a Florentine overhanging roof, white stucca walls and big windows.

There was a light on in one of the lower rooms, but the rest of the villa was in darkness.

The neatly kept lawns that surrounded the villa offered no cover. I moved around its edge, keeping close to the shrubs until I was facing the window of the lighted room. The curtains hadn't been drawn, and I could look into the room, which was only about thirty yards from where I stood.

The furnishing was modern: the room was large. I could see a girl standing by a table, occupied in looking through a black evening bag.

I assumed she was Myra Setti and looked closely at her. She was quite something to see. Around twenty-five or six, tallish with chestnut-coloured hair that reached to her shoulders, she was in a white evening dress that fitted her like a second skin, and then flared out just below her hips into a waterfall of tulle and glittering sequins.

After she had rearranged her bag, she picked up a mink stole and slung it carelessly over her shoulders. Then, pausing to light a cigarette, she crossed the room, flicked off the lights and left me looking at an expanse of black glass that reflected the swiftly moving rainclouds and pointed cypress trees.

I waited.

After a minute or so, I saw the front door open and she came out, sheltering under a large umbrella.

She ran down the path to the garage. A light sprang up as she pushed open the double doors. I could see a white and bottle-green Cadillac in the garage, about the size of a trolley car. She got into the car, leaving the umbrella against the wall. I heard the engine start up, and she drove out, passing within ten yards of where I was crouching. The headlights of the car made a white glare of rain, grass and shrubs.

I remained where I was, listening. I heard the car stop at the end of the drive, there was a long pause while she opened the gates, then the sound of the car door slamming, and the sound of the engine accelerating told me she had gone.

I remained where I was, looking towards the dark villa. I stayed motionless for several minutes. No light showed. I decided it was safe to explore. Turning up my collar against the rain. I walked around the villa. There were no lights to be seen in any of the rooms. I found a window unlatched on the ground floor. I eased it open, took out the flashlight I had brought with me and inspected a small, luxury kitchen beyond. I slid over the double sink and dropped noiselessly on to the tiled floor. Closing the window, I made my way silently out of the kitchen, along a passage and into the hall.

A curved stairway on my left led to the upper rooms. I went up the stairs to a landing and inspected the four doors that faced me.

Turning the handle of the door that lay to the far right, I pushed the door open and looked in. This was obviously Myra's room. There was a divan bed with a blood-red cover. The walls were of quilted grey satin. The furniture was silver. The carpet blood red. It was quite a room.

I nosed around without finding anything to interest me. There was a jewel box on the dressing-table. The contents would have made the most hardened burglar's mouth water, but it left me cold. But it did tell me that she had plenty of money to burn or else she had a host of besotted admirers who were showering these baubles on her.

It wasn't until I reached the last room, which appeared to be a spare bedroom, that I found what I had vaguely wondered I might find.

Against the wall were two suitcases. One of them lay on its side, open. In it were three of my best suits, three bottles of my favourite brand of whisky and my silver cigarette box. For a long moment I stood staring down at the suitcase, the beam of my flashlight unsteady. Then I knelt down and opened the second case. That too was full of the things that had been stolen from my apartment: everything was there except Helen's camera.

Before I had time to consider the significance of this discovery, I heard a sound downstairs that made me practically jump out of my skin.

It was the kind of sound a hunter in the wilds of an African jungle who has been stalking some comparatively harmless animal hears that warns him a rogue elephant has arrived on the scene.

The disturbance in this still, dark villa was of the violence of an earthquake.

There was a crash: someone had unlocked the front door and flung it open so that door smashed against the wall.

Then a man's voice bawled 'MYRA!'

When I was a kid, and back home, I had been taken to a hog-calling contest. I had been tremendously impressed by the colossal volume of sound that had come from the leathery lungs of the hog callers. This sound that came up the stairs and reverberated around the dark, still room was as violent. It froze me, making the hairs on the nape of my neck stand up and making my heart skip a beat.

There was another crash that shook the house as the man below slammed the front door shut. Then the horrible, undisciplined voice yelled again: 'MYRA!'

I recognized that voice. I had heard it on the telephone. Carlo had arrived!

Moving silently, I slid out of the bedroom. The lights were on in the hall. I went to the banister head and cautiously looked over. I couldn't see anyone, but there were lights now on in the lounge.

Then the raucous voice began to sing.

It was the voice of a hooligan: a tuneless, obscenely loud, ruthlessly vulgar sound. You couldn't call it a song: it was something out of the jungle: a sound that made me sweat.

I waited there, with the sound of this rough, brutal bawling. So long as Carlo was there, I wasn't taking any chances of showing myself. But then there was a sudden silence, and the silence was almost as bad as the noise.

I remained in the shadows, a foot away from the banisters where I couldn't be seen. It was as well, for I suddenly saw the figure of a man standing in the lighted doorway of the lounge.

I edged back into the deeper shadows. It was the same broad-shouldered figure I had seen creeping around in the villa at Sorrento. I was sure of it.

There was a long, nerve-racking pause while Carlo remained motionless, his head cocked on one side as if he were listening.

I held my breath, my heart slamming against my ribs and I waited.

He moved slowly into the middle of the hall. Then he stopped, his hands on his hips, his long legs apart, facing the stairs.

The light from the overhead lamp fell fully on him. He was as Frenzi had described him: a bull-necked, blunt-featured, handsome animal. He was wearing a black turtle neck sweater, black trousers, the ends of which were tucked into a pair of highly polished Mexican boots. He had a small gold ring in the lobe of his right ear, and he looked as big and as strong as a fighting bull.

For a long moment he stared up at the exact spot where I was standing. I was sure he couldn't see me. I didn't dare move in case the movement drew his attention to me.

Then suddenly he bawled, 'Come on down or I'll come up and fetch yah down!'

PART IX

I

I CAME down.

There was nothing else I could do. There was no room up on the landing if it came to a fight and, besides, the only way out of the villa was down the stairs and out through the front door or one of the ground-floor windows.

I came down slowly.

I'm not exactly a pigmy, but I didn't kid myself that I had much chance against this bull of a man. By the way he had moved from the lounge to the centre of the hall I knew he could be as fast as a streak of lightning once he got going.

When I reached half-way down the stairs I came into the full glare of the hall light, and I stopped so he could take a look at me.

He grinned, showing big, white even teeth.

'Hello, Mac,' he said. 'Don't think this is a surprise. I was right behind you all the way from your joint to this. Come on down. I've been waiting to have a talk with you.'

He took four paces back so he wouldn't be too close to me when I reached the hall. I came down. If he went for me, I'd try to handle him, but I wasn't starting anything—anyway, not just yet.

'Go in there and sit down,' he went on, jerking his thumb towards the lounge.

I went in there, chose a comfortable chair that faced the door and sat down. By now I had control of my nerves. I wondered what he was going to do. I doubted if he would call the police. I had only to show them my things upstairs for him to be in a worse jam than I.

He followed me into the lounge and sat on the arm of a big leather chair, facing me. He was still grinning. The zigzag scar on his face looked sharply white against the deep tan of his skin.

'Find your stuff up there?' he asked, taking out a pack of American cigarettes. He flicked one out, pasted it on his thick lower lip and set fire to it with a match he scratched alight with the thumb-nail. He looked like a shot from a Hollywood gangster movie when he did that.

'I found it,' I said. 'What have you done with the camera?'

He blew smoke towards me.

'I'll do the talking, Mac,' he said. 'You listen and answer. How did you get on to this place?'

'A girl wrote the telephone number on her wall. It wasn't difficult to get the address,' I said.

'Helen?'

'That's right.'

He pulled a face.

'The dumb cluck.' He leaned forward. 'What did the copper want with you this afternoon?'

I suddenly wasn't scared of him any more. I told myself the hell with him. I wasn't going to sit there and answer his questions.

'Why don't you ask him?' I said.

'I'm asking you.' His smile went away. There was a sudden vicious look in his eyes. 'Let's get this straight. You don't want me to get tough with you, do you?' He laid his hands on his knees so I could see them and slowly closed them into fists. They were sharp-knuckled, big fists that looked as if they had been carved out of a hunk of mahogany. 'I'll tell you something: I like to hit a guy. When I hit him, he stays hit. Right now I want to talk to you, so don't make me hit you. What did the copper say?'

I braced myself.

'Go ahead and ask him.'

I was half-way out of the chair by the time he reached me. I had been a mug to have sat in such a low chair. If I had sat on the arm as he had done I would have been more ready for his rush. He came across the space between us so fast I hadn't a chance. He threw a left-hand punch towards my stomach that I managed to knock aside, but he was only making an opening for his right. I didn't see it coming. I had a brief glimpse of his brown, snarling face and his gleaming teeth when something that felt like a club hammer slammed against the side of my jaw. The room exploded into a blinding flash of white light. I was only vaguely aware that I was falling, then black oblivion wiped out everything.

I came to the surface in about five or six minutes. I found myself spread out in the lounging chair with a sore jaw and a head that pulsated like the breathing bag of a dentist's gas equipment.

Carlo was sitting close to me. He kept slamming his balled-up fist into the palm of his hand as if he were itching to hang another bone crusher to my jaw.

I struggled into an upright position and looked at him, trying to get him into focus. That punch had taken a lot of steam out of me.

'Okay, Mac, don't say I didn't warn you. Now, let's start again. The next time I hit you, I'll bust your jaw. What did the copper want?'

I tested my teeth with the tip of my tongue. None of them seemed loose. I felt cold, and there was a rage growing in me that made me want to get to close quarters with this thug and maim him. But I wasn't all that crazy in the head. Maybe I am big and fairly tough, but I know when I am out of my class. I wouldn't mix things with Rocky Marciano: not because I'd be scared to, but because I know I wouldn't stand a chance. I knew if it came to a fight, this bull of a man was too strong and much, much too fast for me.

The way to take him was to surprise him. There was no other way, and I'd have to have a club in my hand to slow him down first.

'He wanted the names of Helen's men friends,' I said thickly. It hurt to speak.

Carlo scratched the end of his nose.

'Why?'

'Because he's hunting for her killer.'

I hoped that would faze him, but it didn't. Instead, his grin switched on again, and he left off pounding his fist into his palm.

'Is that right? He thinks she was knocked off?'

'He's sure of it.'

'Well, well.' He continued to grin. 'I didn't think he'd be that smart.' He lit a cigarette. 'Here, Mac, have one. You look as if you could use a smoke.'

I took the cigarette and the box of matches he flicked into

131

my lap. I lit the cigarette and dragged down a lungful of smoke.

'Why is he so sure she was knocked off?' he asked.

'You ripped the film out of the camera and stole all her spares. That was a pretty dumb thing to have done.'

'Think so? I think it was smart, pally. Has he got on to you yet?'

I tried to control my start, but I wasn't successful.

'What do you mean?'

Carlo's grin widened.

'Don't feed me that crap: you know what I mean. You're an open and shut case for the job. Why, I even took the trouble to alter her watch so the cops would think you were up there when she took her dive, and believe me, Mac, that was quite a climb to get to her. I nearly broke my neck.'

I stared at him.

'So you did kill her.'

He shook his head.

'The record says you did it. You were up there when she fell. You're the guy named Douglas Sherrard.' He leaned forward and pointed a thick finger at me. Emphasizing each word, he went on, '*And you're the sucker who left a note for her telling her to meet you on the cliff head.* You forgot that little item, didn't you? I found it where you had left it on the table, and I've got it.'

II

I felt as if the bottom of my world had fallen out. It was only at this moment, hearing this, that I remembered the note I had left for Helen in the villa.

'I've got it right here,' Carlo went on, tapping his hip-pocket. 'It's a beaut. That and the watch could fix you, Mac. You wouldn't stand a chance.'

He was right. If Carlotti ever got hold of that note, I'd be finished. In my mind, I saw the note now as plainly as if it lay before me.

Helen (I had written), *meet me on the path beyond the garden gate if we miss each other. Ed.*

132

I had even put the time and the date on the note and I had written it on the villa's headed notepaper. The shock of finding Helen had completely driven the note out of my head until now.

'When the cops find your bags left in a luggage office, they'll also find the camera and some of the films,' Carlo continued. 'They'll also find a letter from Helen to you that will clinch the case if it needs clinching. She wrote it before she took her dive.'

I made an effort and pulled myself together. I couldn't be in a worse jam, and because it was so bad, it made me angry. The only way to get out of this situation was to get the note and destroy it. He said he had it on him. I had to surprise him, knock him cold and get the note.

'She never wrote to me,' I said.

'Oh, yes, she did. I persuaded her to. It's quite a letter. In it she tells you how she's hired the villa and how you two are going to stay there as Mr. and Mrs. Sherrard. It's a complete give away, Mac. Don't make any mistake about that. I've got you sewn up tight.'

But he was too glib. I was sure he was lying. There was no letter; not that it mattered. The note I had written to Helen would be enough to fix me.

'Okay, so you've got me sewn up tight,' I said. 'What are you going to do about it?'

He got to his feet and began to wander around the room. He didn't come near me while he wandered.

'I've been hoping to find a guy like you for months,' he said. 'When Helen told me she was making a play for you and who you were, I knew you were the boy I wanted. I've got a job for you. You're going to take a parcel across the French frontier for me. It'll be a cinch for you. You'll sail through. With your background and job, they won't even bother to look in your bags, let alone examine your car. I've been hoarding the stuff up for months for just such a chance as this.'

'What stuff?' I asked, watching him.

He grinned.

'You needn't know that. All you have to do is to drive from here to Nice. You'll spend the night at a certain hotel, leaving your car in the hotel garage. I'll have planted the parcel in your car before you leave, and my contact in Nice will collect it during the night. It's as simple as that.'

'And if I don't do it, Carlotti gets my note to Helen, is that the idea?'

'You cotton on fast.'

'And if I do do it, what happens then?'

He shrugged.

'You have a nice vacation and come back. Then maybe in about six months' time, you'll find you'll have to make another trip to Nice. A newspaper man is expected to travel. You're custom-made for the job. That's why I picked on you.'

'So long as I know,' I said. 'Did Helen have anything to do with the picking?'

'Oh, sure, but she was strictly small-time.' He grimaced. 'She wanted to put the bite on you for a thousand bucks, but I talked her out of that. I showed her you'd be far more useful as a carrier.'

I suddenly realized what this was all about.

'She was a drug addict, wasn't she?' I said. 'That's why she had to have money and didn't care how she got it, so long as she got it. And it's a parcel of dope you want me to take to Nice, isn't it?'

'You don't think it's face powder, do you, Mac?' he returned, grinning.

'And you supplied her with the drugs?'

'That's it, pally. I'm always willing to help a girl if she's got dough to spend.'

'Was it your idea or hers we should go to the villa?'

'Why should you care?'

'It was your idea, wasn't it? It was a convenient villa, and there was a convenient cliff to fall off. You knew I wouldn't play unless you really got a stranglehold on me. You laid the trap, threw her off the cliff and I walked into it.'

He laughed.

'You've certainly got a great imagination. Anyway, that's a yarn you can't prove, Mac, but I can prove mine.'

'Did she take you on her cine when you two were up there? Is that why you were so anxious to get rid of the film?'

'Nothing like that, pally. Don't worry about the cine. That was a plant to make the cops think it was murder.' He lit another cigarette. 'Now let's get down to business. Are you going to Nice or do I send the note to Carlotti?'

'Doesn't look as if I have much choice, does it?'

I glanced aimlessly around the room, looking for a likely weapon. There was nothing I could see substantial enough to hit him with. I knew I wasn't going to stop him with my bare fists.

Near the door was a small occasional table, and on the table stood a large vase full of carnations. By the vase was a large photograph in a silver frame of Myra Setti. She was in a white swimsuit, lying on a lounging chair and sheltered by a big sun umbrella. There was something vaguely familiar about this photograph, but I only half-glanced at it. My eyes shifted to a solid glass paper-weight that stood by the photograph. That, I told myself, might do.

'So you'll do it,' he said, watching me.

'I guess I'll have to.'

'That's the boy.' He grinned. 'I knew you'd play. Okay, this is what you do. Leave your car in your garage on Thursday night. Don't lock the garage. I'll be along during the night to plant the parcel. Get off early on Friday morning. Stay the night at Geneva, then, on Saturday, you drive to Nice. You want to time it so that you cross the frontier around seven in the evening. That's when they'll be thinking of their suppers and they'll be glad to push you through quickly. You go to the Soleil d'Or hotel. It's one of the swank joints on the Promenade des Anglais. Maybe you'd better book a room there. Leave your car in the hotel garage and forget about it. Got all that?'

I said I had got it.

'And no funny business, Mac. I have a little fortune tied up in that stuff, and I'll fix you for sure if you try a double-cross.' His eyes hardened as he stared at me. 'You're on the hook, so don't forget it. You're on it for keeps.'

'What happens if Carlotti finds out I was at the villa when Helen died?'

'Let him prove it,' Carlotti said. 'If he gets too tough, I'll fix an alibi for you. I've got ways of fixing alibis. You've got nothing to worry about so long as you play with me. You and I can work this racket for years. There's the Swiss run you can handle too.'

'Looks like I've got myself a new career.'

'That's the idea.' He stubbed out his cigarette. 'Well, Mac, I've got things to do. You be set to leave on Friday. Okay?'

I got slowly to my feet.

'I guess so.'

He moved around me, keeping his distance and watching me.

I paused by the table and looked at the framed photograph. 'Is this your girl-friend?' I asked.

He moved a little closer, but he was still out of reach.

'Never mind who she is . . . beat it, Mac. I've got things to do.'

I lifted the frame.

'Some dish. Is she on drugs too?'

With a snarl, he stepped up to me and snatched the frame out of my hand. That put his right hand out of action. I gave the vase of carnations a swipe with my left hand and grabbed the paper-weight with my right hand.

The vase, water and carnations exploded against Carlo's knees. For a split-second he looked down, cursing.

I had the paper-weight balled in my fist. I hit him on the side of the head with everything I had got packed behind the punch.

He went down on his knees. I saw his eyes roll back. I clubbed him on the top of his head and he slid forward, stretching out at my feet.

I dropped the paper-weight and knelt beside him. That was a mistake. He was unbelievably tough. His right hand groped upwards towards my throat and he very nearly had me. I knocked his arm aside as he levered himself upwards. His eyes were blank. He was practically out, but he was still dangerous. I set myself, and as he lifted his head, I hung a punch on his jaw that jarred me from my fist to my elbow. His head slammed back on the floor and he went limp.

Breathing hard, I caught hold of him and rolled him over on his face. I slid my hand into his hip pocket and my fingers closed over a leather wallet.

As I was pulling the wallet out, the door jerked open and Myra Setti came in.

She held a ·38 automatic in her hand and she pointed it at me.

III

For a long moment we looked at each other. There was a look in her eyes that told me she would shoot if I gave her

136

the slightest encouragement, so I remained motionless, my hand half in Carlo's pocket.

'Take your hand away!' she said.

Slowly I withdrew my hand from Carlo's pocket. He stirred, half-turned over and made a growling sound in his throat.

'Get away from him!' she said sharply.

I stood up and backed away.

Carlo pushed himself on to his hands and knees, shook his head and then staggered to his feet. For a moment he stood swaying backwards and forwards, his legs rubbery, then he got his balance, shook his head again and looked over at me. I expected to see a vicious, furious expression on his face, but, instead, he grinned.

'You've got more guts than I thought you had, Mac,' he said, and ruefully rubbed the side of his head. 'I haven't been hit so hard for years. You didn't really think I'd be such a sucker as to carry that note around, did you?'

'It was worth a try,' I said.

'What is all this?' Myra demanded impatiently. 'Who's your playmate?' She didn't lower the gun nor did she take her eyes off me.

'This is Dawson—the guy I was telling you about. He's taking the stuff to Nice on Friday,' Carlo said. He touched his head again and grimaced.

'Look at the mess you two apes have made. Get out of here!' she said. 'Go on, clear out, both of you!'

'Aw, skip it!' Carlo said. 'You're always beefing about something. I want to talk to you.' He turned to me. 'Go on, Mac, scram. Don't try that dodge again. Next time I'll get tough too.'

I looked dejected again.

'I'm on my way,' I said, and slouched towards the door.

Myra gave me a contemptuous look and turned her back on me. As I passed her, I grabbed the gun out of her hand, gave her a shove with my shoulder that sent her reeling into one of the lounging chairs, spun around and covered Carlo.

'Okay,' I said. 'Let's have that wallet!'

For a long moment he stood transfixed, then he threw back his head and gave a burst of raucous laughter that rattled the windows.

'Gee! You'll kill me!' he bellowed, slapping his thigh. 'Talk about crust!'

'Give me that wallet!' I said, and there was something in my voice that made him stiffen.

'Listen, dope, it's not on me,' he said, his face hardening.

'If you don't want a slug in the leg, you'll chuck the wallet right here!'

We stared at each other. He saw I wasn't fooling. He suddenly grinned, took the wallet from his hip-pocket and tossed it at my feet.

I kept him covered, bent, picked it up, backed against the wall and went through the wallet. It was stuffed with ten thousand lire notes, but there was no other paper in it.

Myra was glaring at me, her eyes smouldering.

'Some kid, isn't he?' Carlo said to her. 'Nearly as tough as I am. But we've got him hamstrung. He's got to do what he's told. Haven't you, pally?'

I tossed him the wallet.

'Looks like it,' I said. 'But watch out: it won't be all that easy.'

I put the gun on the table and walked out.

Carlo's loud explosive laughter followed me.

It was still raining as I walked down the steps to the drive. Near the front door was the dark green Renault. Behind it stood the Cadillac.

I broke into a run, reached the street, and kept on running until I reached my car. I drove fast to my apartment, left the car outside, bolted up the stairs into my lounge. Without taking off my soaked raincoat I called the International Investigating Agency and asked for Sarti. I hadn't much hope of finding him in as it was now getting on for half-past ten, but he came on the line almost at once.

'The Renault I was talking about is standing in the drive of the villa Palestra on viale Paolo Veronese,' I said. 'Get some men to cover it right away. I want to know where the driver goes when he leaves. Watch out: he'll probably be on the look-out for a tail.'

Sarti said he would take care of it at once. I heard him speaking to someone, giving instructions to get men out to Myra's villa.

When he was through, I asked, 'Any news for me?'

'I will have something for you by to-morrow morning, signor.'

'I don't want you to come here.' The fact that Carlo had known that Carlotti had been to see me that afternoon

138

warned me that my apartment was being watched. I told him to meet me at ten o'clock at the Press Club. He said he would do that.

I stripped off my raincoat, took it into the bathroom, then I came back to the lounge and poured myself a big shot of whisky. I sat down. My jaw ached and I was feeling pretty sick with myself. I was in a jam, and there was no one to get me out of it except myself.

To-morrow was Sunday. On Monday I would have to fly down to Naples to attend the inquest. Friday morning I would have to leave for Nice unless I could pin Helen's killing on to Carlo. It didn't leave me a lot of time.

I was sure he had killed her, but I couldn't think why he had done it.

I couldn't believe he had killed her to get a hold on me. That idea had come after he had killed her, and probably after he had found the note I had left for her.

Then why had he killed her?

She was spending money with him. He had her where he wanted her. A drug pedlar always has his victims where he wants them ... unless, of course, the victim happens to find out something about the pedlar that gives her a bigger hold on him than he has on her.

Helen was a blackmailer. Had she been crazy enough to try to blackmail Carlo? She wouldn't have attempted it unless what she had found out was sheer dynamite: something, she must have been sure, that was so dangerous to Carlo that he would have to toe the line. Had she found some evidence that really put Carlo on the spot? If she had, she would have lodged it somewhere under lock and key before she dared to put the squeeze on Carlo.

The fact that he had killed her either proved that he had found the evidence and destroyed it, or else she hadn't had the time to tell him she had it hidden. As soon as she began her blackmail threat, he had swept her off the cliff.

Was that what had happened?

It was a long shot, but a likely one. If I could get my hands on this evidence, I could draw Carlo's teeth. If it existed, where had she hidden it? In her apartment? In her bank? In a safe deposit?

There was nothing I could do about her apartment. Carlotti had a police guard there. There was not much I could do about finding out if she had a safe deposit, but I could call on her bank before I flew down to Naples on Monday.

I might be wasting time, but I had to think of every angle. This one seemed to be promising.

I was still thinking about it when, half an hour later, the telephone bell rang. As I picked up the receiver, I glanced at the clock on my desk. It was just after eleven-ten.

'I have traced the Renault, Signor Dawson,' Sarti told me. 'The owner is Carlo Manchini. He has an apartment on via Brentini. It is over a wine-shop.'

'Is he there now?'

'He went in to change. He left five minutes ago, wearing evening clothes.'

'Okay. Stick where you are. I'm coming over,' I said, and hung up.

I pulled on my soaking raincoat, left the apartment and went down to the car. It took me twenty minutes to reach via Brentini. I left my car at the corner of the street and walked quickly down until I spotted Sarti's fat figure sheltering from the rain in a dark shop doorway. I stepped out of the rain beside him.

'He hasn't returned?'

'No.'

'I'm going in there to have a look around.'

Sarti pulled a little face.

'It is illegal, signor,' he said without any hope.

'Thanks for telling me. Any idea how I can get in?'

I was looking at the wine-shop opposite. There was a side entrance that obviously led to the apartment over the shop.

'The lock isn't complicated,' Sarti said, fumbled in his pocket and pressed into my hand a bunch of skeleton keys.

'These are strictly illegal too,' I said and grinned at him. He looked depressed.

'Yes, signor. Not everyone would want my job.'

I crossed the road, paused to look up and down the deserted street, took out my flashlight and examined the lock. As Sarti had said, it didn't look complicated. I tried three of the keys before I turned the lock. I pushed open the door. Moving into darkness, I closed the door, once more turned on my flashlight and went quickly up the steep, narrow stairs that faced me.

There was stale smell of wine and sweat on the landing, also the smell of cigar smoke. Three doors invited inspection.

I opened one and glanced into a small, dirty kitchen. In the sink was an accumulation of dirty pots and two frying pans around which flies buzzed busily. The remains of a meal of bread and salami lay on a greasy paper on the table.

I moved down the passage, looked into a small bedroom that contained a double bed, unmade and with grimy sheets and a greasy pillow. Clothes were scattered on the floor. A dirty shirt hung from an electric light bracket. The floor was spotted with tobacco ash and the smell in the room nearly choked me.

I backed out and entered the sitting-room. This too looked as if a pig had lived in it for some time. There was a big settee under the window and two lounging chairs by the fireplace. All three pieces looked grimy and dark with grease. On a small table stood six bottles of wine, three of them empty. A vase of dead carnations stood on the dusty overmantel. There were grease marks on the walls, and the floor was spotted with tobacco ash.

On one of the arms of the chairs was a big ash-tray loaded with cigarette butts and three cheroot butts. I picked up one of these butts and examined it. It seemed to me to be the exact fellow of the butt I had found on top of the cliff head. I put it in my pocket, leaving the other two.

Against one of the walls stood a battered desk on which were piled old, yellowish newspapers, movie magazines and pictures of pin-up girls.

I opened the desk drawers, one after the other. Most of them were crammed with junk that a man will accumulate who has never had a clear out, but in one of the lower drawers I found a new T.W.A. travelling bag that is given to passengers to keep their overnight kit in. I took it from the drawer, zipped it open and looked inside.

It was empty except for a screwed-up ball of paper. I smoothed this out and found it to be the duplicate of a return ticket from Rome to New York, dated four months ago and made out in Carlo Manchini's name.

I stood looking at the ticket for several seconds, my mind busy.

Here was proof that Carlo had been in New York before Helen had left for Rome. Did it mean anything? Had they met in New York?

I slipped the paper in my wallet, then returned the bag to the drawer.

Although I spent another half-hour in the apartment, I found nothing else to interest me, nor did I find my note to Helen.

I was glad to get out into the rain and the fresh air once more.

Sarti was very uneasy when I joined him.

'I was getting nervous,' he said. 'You stayed there too long.'

I had too much on my mind to bother about his nerves. I told him I'd be at the Press Club at ten the following morning and left him.

When I got back to my apartment I sent the following cable to Jack Martin, *Western Telegram's* New York crime reporter:

Supply all dope you can find on Carlo Manchini: dark, blunt-featured, broad, tall with white zigzag scar on chin. Will telephone Sunday. Urgent. Dawson.

Martin was an expert at his job. If there was an angle to Carlo's visit to New York, he would know it.

PART X

I

At ten the following morning, I entered the Press Club and asked the steward if there was anyone waiting for me.

The steward said there was a gentleman in the coffee bar. From the tone of his voice he indicated that he was using the word 'gentleman' as a matter of courtesy.

I found Sarti sitting in a corner, twiddling his hat and staring blankly at the opposite wall.

I took him over to a more comfortable chair and sat him down. He was clutching a leather portfolio which he rested on his fat knees. The garlic on his breath was enough to strip the barnacles off a ship's keel.

'Well? What have you got?' I said.

'Following your instructions, signor,' he said, undoing the straps on his case, 'I have set ten of my best men to work on la Signorina Chalmers' background. I am still waiting for their reports, but in the meantime I have been able to gain a considerable amount of information from another source.' He scratched the tip of his ear, wriggling uncomfortably in his chair, then went on, 'It is always possible that in making such a searching investigation that unpleasant facts may come to light. I suggest that to prepare you for what is in my report, I should give you a brief résumé of what I have discovered.'

From what I had already found out about Helen's background, I wasn't surprised that he and his men had made similar discoveries.

'Go ahead,' I said. 'I know more or less what you are going to tell me. I warned you this was a confidential business. La signorina was the daughter of a very powerful man, and we've got to be careful.'

'I am aware of that, signor.' Sarti looked even more miserable. 'You must realize Lieutenant Carlotti is also working along the same lines as we, and it will not be long before he will have the same information as I have here.' He tapped his portfolio. 'To be more exact, he will have the information in three days' time.'

I stared at him.

'How do you know that?'

'Perhaps you know that la signorina was a drug addict?' Sarti said. 'Her father made her a very small allowance. She needed considerable sums of money to buy drugs. I regret to tell you, signor, that to raise the money she blackmailed a number of men with whom she had been intimate.'

I suddenly wondered if he had found out that I had been a prospective victim of hers.

'I had more or less gathered that,' I said. 'You didn't answer my question. How do you know Carlotti . . . ?'

'If you will excuse me signor,' Sarti broke in. 'I will come to that in a moment. In this folder I have a list of names and addresses of the men from whom la signorina obtained money. I will leave the list for you to study.' He gave me a long, slow stare that brought me out into a sudden sweat. I was sure now that my name was on the list.

'How did you get hold of this information?' I asked, bringing out my packet of cigarettes and offering it to him.

'No, thank you. I don't care for American cigarettes.' Sarti said, bowing. 'If I may be allowed . . .'

He fished out the usual Italian cigarette and lit it.

'I obtained the list from il Signor Veroni, a private detective who once worked for the police. He only undertakes special cases and is very expensive. I have been able to help him from time to time with my much larger organization. Knowing you wanted information urgently, I approached him. He immediately produced all this information I have here from his files.'

'How did he get it?' I asked, leaning forward and staring at Sarti.

'He had been instructed to watch la signorina on her arrival in Rome. He and two of his men, taking it in turns, never let her out of their sight during the time she was in Rome.'

That really shook me.

'Did they follow her to Sorrento?' I asked.

'No. They had no instructions to do that. Veroni was told only to watch her while she was in Rome.'

'Who instructed him to watch her?'

Sarti smiled sadly.

'That I am unable to tell you, signor. You will understand that what I have already told you is strictly confidential. It is only because Veroni is my very good friend, and also because I gave my sacred word that I would not pass on the information, that he agreed to help me.'

'As you've broken your sacred word already,' I said impatiently, 'what's to stop you telling me who instructed him?'

Sarti lifted his shoulders.

'Nothing, signor, except that he didn't tell me.'

I sat back.

'You said Carlotti would have this information in three days' time. How do you know this?'

'Veroni is giving the information to the Lieutenant. It was I who persuaded him not to do so until this period has elapsed.'

'But why should he give Carlotti this information?'

'Because he suspects la signorina was murdered,' Sarti said mournfully, 'and he feels that it is his duty to give the Lieutenant the information. It is only when investigators help the police that the police in their turn will help them.'

'Why have you told him to hold up the information for three days?'

He moved uncomfortably.

'If you will kindly read through the report I have prepared, you will see the reason, signor. You are my client. There may be things you wish to do. Let us say I have gained a little time for you.'

I tried to meet his eyes, but I didn't make it. I stubbed out my cigarette and lit another. I was feeling pretty bad.

'My name is on the list, is that it?' I said, trying to make it sound casual.

Sarti inclined his head.

'Yes, signor. It is known that you went to Naples on the afternoon she died. It is known you visited her apartment twice during the night. It is also known that she telephoned you at your office and asked you to bring a piece of photographic equipment with you when you went to join her at

145

Sorrento, and that she used, while speaking to you, the name of Mrs. Douglas Sherrard. Veroni took the precaution to tap your telephone line.'

I sat for a moment, motionless.

'And Veroni is going to turn this information over to Carlotti?'

Sarti looked as if he were going to cry.

'He feels it is his duty, signor; besides, he knows he could get into serious trouble by withholding evidence in a murder case. He could be charged as an accessory.'

'But in spite of that he is still willing to give me three days' grace?'

I have persuaded him to do so, signor.'

I looked at him, feeling like a rabbit who has seen a ferret in its burrow. This was it. This was something I just couldn't lie myself out of. If Carlotti knew I was Douglas Sherrard, he wouldn't even need the note that I had left for Helen. He had only to hammer away at me, and sooner or later I would crack. I wasn't kidding myself that I could get out of this spot once Carlotti had Veroni's report in his hands.

'Perhaps you would care to study the report, signor?' Sarti said. He was careful not to look at me. He managed to exude the sympathetic, mournful air of an undertaker. 'Then perhaps we might talk again. You may have instructions for me.'

I had an idea that there was something sinister behind this remark, but I couldn't put my finger on it.

'Let me have it,' I said. 'If you're not in a hurry, you might wait here. Give me half an hour, will you?'

'Certainly, signor,' he said, and pulled a sheaf of papers from his portfolio. He handed them to me. 'I am in no hurry.'

I took the papers and, leaving him, I walked down the corridor to the cocktail bar. At this hour and the fact that it was Sunday, I had the place to myself.

The bar steward appeared. He conveyed to me by his hurt look that this was no time to disturb him.

I ordered a double whisky, carried the drink to a corner table and sat down. I took the whisky neat. It did something to blot out my trapped feeling, but it didn't take away my fear.

I read the twenty-odd pages of carefully typed script. It

146

contained a list of fifteen names: most of them were familiar to me. Giuseppe Frenzi's name headed the list. Mine came half-way down. There were dates when Helen spent the night with Frenzi, when he called on her at her apartment, when she spent nights with other men. These I skipped through. I studied the details concerning my own activities with Helen. Sarti hadn't been lying when he had told me that Veroni and his men had never let Helen out of their sight. Every meeting I had had with her was carefully logged. Every word that she and I had ever said to each other on the telephone was there to read. There were details of other telephone conversations between her and other men, and it was so obvious now, after reading the report, that I was just another of her prospective blackmail victims.

Three days!

Could I possibly pin Helen's murder on Carlo before then? Would it be wiser to go to Carlotti and tell him the whole truth and let him get after Carlo? But why should he? He had only to listen to my story to be convinced that I had killed Helen. No ... that wasn't the way to handle it.

Then a sudden thought struck me. There was not one mention of Carlo or Myra Setti in Veroni's report. Helen must have telephoned either one or the other at least once. The fact that Myra's telephone number had been scribbled on Helen's wall proved that. Then why wasn't Carlo or Myra in the report?

There was a chance that Veroni had only noted down the conversations Helen had had with her blackmail victims, but surely she must have said something to Carlo or Myra over the telephone at one time that was worth recording in the report?

I sat thinking about this for several minutes. Then I asked the bar steward to get me the Rome telephone book. He handed it to me as if he were doing me a favour and asked if I would like another drink. I said not at this moment.

I flicked through the pages of the book, looking for Veroni's name, but it didn't show. This didn't mean much. He probably ran his agency under a fancy name.

I crossed over to the telephone booth near the bar and called Jim Matthews.

It took me a little time to wake him up and get him out of bed.

'For the love of mike!' he exclaimed when he came on the line. 'Don't you know it's Sunday, you crazy lug? I didn't get to bed until four this morning.'

'Quit beefing,' I said. 'I want some information. Have you ever heard of Veroni, a private detective who handles special cases and is very expensive?'

'No, I haven't,' Matthews said. 'You've got the name wrong. I know all the private dicks in this city. Veroni isn't one of them.'

'He couldn't be someone you've missed?'

'I'm damn sure he isn't. You've got the name wrong.'

'Thanks, Jim. Sorry to have got you out of bed,' I said, and before he could start cursing me, I hung up.

I told the bar steward that I had changed my mind about a drink, carried the whisky back to my table and went through the report again.

Out of the fifteen men whom Helen had blackmailed, I was the only one, according to the report, who not only had the motive, but the opportunity of killing her.

I spent another five minutes turning the set-up over in my mind, then I finished my drink, and, feeling a little high, I went back to the coffee bar.

Sarti still sat where I had left him, twiddling his hat and looking sad. He rose to his feet as I came across to join him and sat down when I did.

'Thanks for letting me read this,' I said, and offered him the sheaf of papers.

He recoiled from it as if I had waved a black mamba in his face.

'It is for you, signor. I wouldn't wish to keep it.'

'Yes of course. I wasn't thinking.' I folded the papers and put them in my inside pocket. 'Il Signor Veroni has copies of these papers?'

The corners of Sarti's mouth turned down.

'Unfortunately, yes.'

I lit a cigarette and stretched my legs. I wasn't feeling scared any more. I now had the idea what was behind this set-up.

'Is il Signor Veroni wealthy?' I asked.

Sarti raised his black, bloodshot eyes and looked inquiringly at me.

'A private detective is never wealthy, signor,' he said. 'For a month you work, then for three months, perhaps, you wait. I wouldn't say il Signor Veroni is well off.'

'Do you think we might make a deal with him?'

Sarti appeared to consider this. He scratched the top of his scurfy head and frowned down at the bronze ashtray that stood on the table by him.

'In what way—a deal, signor?'

'Suppose I offered to buy these reports from him,' I said. 'You must have read them.'

'Yes, signor. I have read them.'

'If Carlotti got hold of them, he might jump to the conclusion that I was responsible for la signorina's death.'

Sarti looked as if he were going to burst into tears.

'That was the unfortunate impression that I got, signor. That was the only reason why I begged il Signor Veroni not to do anything for three days.'

'Do you imagine Veroni's high sense of duty would prevent him from making a deal with me?'

Sarti shrugged his fat shoulders.

'In my work, signor, one always looks ahead. It is a good thing to be prepared for every contingency. I thought it was possible that you would wish to keep these reports from Lieutenant Carlotti. I mentioned the fact to il Signor Veroni. He is a difficult man: his sense of duty is over-developed, but I have been friends with him for a long time and it is possible for me to put my cards on the table. I know his ambition is to buy a vineyard in Tuscany. It is possible that he could be persuaded.'

'Would you undertake to persuade him?'

Sarti appeared to hesitate.

'You are my client, signor. When I accept a client, I give him my whole support. It is how I built up my business. This is difficult and dangerous. I could be prosecuted, but, nevertheless, if you wish it, I would be prepared to take the risk to give satisfaction.'

'Your motives are as impressive as il Signor Veroni's,' I said.

He smiled mournfully.

'I am here to serve, signor,' he said.

'What do you imagine a vineyard in Tuscany would cost?' I asked looking directly at him. 'Did you think to ask him?'

He met my eyes without any effort.

'I did touch on the subject. Il Signor Veroni isn't entirely without means signor. It would seem he is lacking half the required sum: ten million lire.'

Ten million lire!

That would clean me right out. During my fifteen years as a newspaper man I had managed to save just that amount.

'And for that sum he would be prepared to hand over all the copies of this report and say nothing to the police?'

'I don't know, signor, but I could ask him. I believe I might be able to persuade him.'

'Would you need any encouragement to do that? I mean, would there be a fee for the work?' I asked. 'Frankly, ten million lire would leave me flat. If there was to be a rake-off for you, you would have to get it from Veroni.'

'That could be arranged if it were necessary, signor,' Sarti said simply. 'After all, I shall be paid for my work on this case by il Signor Chalmers. I think you mentioned that the fee would be a substantial one. I wish to be of service to you. It is by being useful to one's clients that one keeps them.'

'That is a sterling thought,' I said. 'Then you will see what you can arrange?'

'Immediately, signor. I should have news for you in a few hours. Will you be at your apartment at one o'clock?'

I said I would.

'Then I will be able to tell you if I have been successful or not.'

He got to his feet, gave me a mournful bow and waddled across the room and out of my sight.

I had no doubt that il Signor Veroni didn't exist and that Sarti had been hired by someone to watch Helen. Nor had I any doubt that, if I were going to pay up, then ten million lire would go directly into Sarti's pocket.

There wasn't much I could see that I could do about this. There might be a way out, given a little time to think of one. It depended if I could gain time.

I returned to my apartment and waited.

Sarti didn't telephone until two o'clock. By then I was pacing the room and sweating.

'The arrangement we spoke about has been successfully concluded, signor,' he said when I answered the telephone.

'Would Wednesday morning be convenient for you to settle the conditions?'

'I can't do it before Thursday,' I said. 'It will mean selling . . .'

'Not over the telephone, signor,' Sarti said, sudden agony in his voice. 'It is always unwise to discuss anything of this nature over an open line. Thursday would do. Our associate has asked me to deal with you. I will call on you at mid-day on Thursday.'

I said I would be expecting him and hung up.

II

I spent the next hour chain smoking and viewing the whole set-up from every angle.

I couldn't be in a bigger mess if I had deliberately set out to look for trouble. I was not only heading to be arrested for murder, with enough evidence against me to make a conviction certain, but I was also being blackmailed by two unscrupulous thugs.

With this hanging over me, I made a discovery. I found I no longer cared whether I had the foreign desk at *Western Telegram* or not, nor did I care two hoots how Chalmers would react if he learned I was the man with whom his daughter had planned to spend a month at Sorrento.

Thinking about the way I had handled this thing, I realized what a fool I had been not to have called the police when I had found Helen's body. If I had done so, Carlo wouldn't have had time to alter Helen's watch or rig the rest of the evidence against me. If I had gone back to the villa to call the police I would have found the note I had left for Helen before Carlo had got there.

I told myself it was up to me to get out of this mess. I had been fool enough to get into it, now I had to be smart enough to beat these two thugs at their own game.

I didn't have much time. I had to hand over every cent of my savings to Sarti on Thursday unless I had thought of some way to fix him. I would have to take the consignment of dope to Nice on Friday unless I could pin Helen's murder on Carlo.

151

I thought about Carlo. I had very little evidence against him. I had two cheroot butts; one that I had found on the top of the cliff head, the other I had found in his room. That wouldn't be enough to convict him of murder. What else was there? I had proof from the telephone number scribbled on the wall that Helen knew Myra Setti, and it could follow from that that she also knew Carlo, but that wasn't strong enough to convince a jury. Frenzi would swear he had seen Helen and Carlo together, but as she went around with a number of other men while she was in Rome, that didn't amount to much either.

I took out of my wallet the T.W.A. air ticket that I had found in Carlo's desk and examined it. Was this of any value to me? Carlo had been in New York three days before Helen had left Rome. Maxwell had hinted that Helen had left for Rome because she was involved in Menotti's murder.

I suddenly sat bolt upright. Both Maxwell and Matthews, who should know, had said it was practically certain that Setti had ordered Menotti's death. Had Carlo been sent to New York to do the job? Was he Setti's gunman? Menotti had been killed on the night of June 29th. According to the air ticket, Carlo had arrived in New York on the 26th and had left for Rome on the 30th. The dates fitted. What was more, Helen had also left on the 30th, and within four days she was apparently friendly with Carlo. It had puzzled me how she could have got to know him so quickly, unless she had met him in New York.

Was that the hold Helen had on Carlo, always assuming that she had been blackmailing him? Maxwell and Matthews had mentioned a mysterious woman who had sold Menotti out. Maxwell had said it was believed that woman had been Helen. Again this made sense. Suppose Carlo had known Helen was a drug addict, and on his arrival in New York had contacted her. He might have offered her a sum of money or a free supply of drugs to sell Menotti out. She would have let him into the apartment. Later, thinking about it, she may have realized how easy it would be to put pressure on him for more money or more drugs. What better hold could she have had to blackmail him than the threat of the electric chair?

I got to my feet and began to pace up and down. I felt I was at last getting somewhere.

I went over in my mind the conversation I had had with Carlo. He had admitted that he was in Sorrento at the time Helen died. Why had he been there? I couldn't believe he had gone there deliberately to kill Helen. If he had wanted to kill her he could have done it in Rome instead of going all the way to Sorrento.

With my mind working like a buzz-saw, I continued to pace up and down. It was several minutes before I remembered the photograph I had seen in Myra's lounge of her in a white swimsuit and which had looked vaguely familiar to me. It was then that I remembered the lone, inaccessible villa built into the cliff face I had seen when I had been looking for Helen. I remembered I had seen a girl, half-hidden by a sun umbrella, who had been sitting on the terrace of the villa. I was sure now that the girl had been Myra Setti.

If Myra owned the villa, Carlo would probably go down there quite often, and that would probably account for the fact that he had been there when Helen had arrived.

I told myself I'd take another look at this villa, after I had attended the inquest.

Feeling I had got as far as I could with Carlo, I turned my attention to Sarti. There was only one way to make him hold off, and that was to throw a scare into him, but I didn't kid myself I could do it. If anyone could throw a scare into him, Carlo could, and I suddenly grinned. It seemed to me to be a good idea to play Carlo off against Sarti. It was in Carlo's interest for me to keep clear of the police.

Without hesitation, I dialled Myra's number. Carlo answered the call himself.

'This is Dawson,' I said. 'I want to talk to you in a hurry. Where can we meet?'

'What's it all about?' he demanded, his voice suspicious.

'Our arrangement for Friday can blow up,' I said. 'I can't talk over an open line. We've got competition.'

'Yeah?' There was a snarl in his voice that I wished Sarti could hear. 'Okay. Meet me at the Pasquale Club in half an hour.'

I said I would be there and hung up.

I looked out of the window. It was raining again, and as I put on my raincoat the telephone bell rang.

'There's a call for you from New York,' the operator told me. 'Will you hold on?'

I guessed it was Chalmers and I was right.

'What the hell's happening?' he demanded when he came on the line. 'Why haven't you called me?'

I was in no mood to take anything from him right at this moment. It was because he hadn't bothered to keep any kind of control over his rotten little daughter that I was in this jam.

'I haven't time to keep calling you,' I snapped back. 'But now you're on the line, you may as well know that we're heading for a scandal and a stink that even you won't be able to keep off the front pages of every paper except your own.'

I heard him draw in his breath sharply. I could imagine his face turning purple.

'Do you know what you're saying?' he demanded. 'What the devil . . . ?'

'Listen: I've got a date and I'm in a hurry,' I broke in. 'I have indisputable proof that your daughter was a drug addict and a blackmailer. She went round with degenerates and criminals, and she was Menotti's mistress. It's common talk that it was she who put the finger on him, and she was probably murdered because she was fool enough to try to blackmail his killer.'

'My God! You'll be sorry for this,' Chalmers bellowed. 'You must be drunk or insane to talk this way to me. How dare you tell such lies! My daughter was a good, decent girl . . .'

'Yeah, I've heard that one before,' I broke in impatiently. 'But wait until you see the evidence. I have a list of names of fifteen men with whom she was intimate and whom she blackmailed because she had to have money to buy drugs. This isn't something I've dreamed up. Carlotti knows. There's a private dick who has been shadowing her ever since she arrived in Rome, and he has pages of evidence with dates and details that you can't shout off.'

There was a sudden silence at the other end of the line and, for a moment, I thought we had been cut off but, listening carefully, I could hear his heavy breathing.

'I'd better come out,' he said at last, and in a much milder tone. 'I'm sorry I bawled at you, Dawson. I should have known you wouldn't say anything against my daughter without proof. This is a shock to me. Perhaps it's not so bad as it sounds.'

'This isn't the time to kid yourself,' I said. 'This is a mess and we've got to face it.'

'I'm tied up until Thursday,' he said, all the iron out of his voice by now. 'I'll be in Naples on Friday. Will you meet me?'

'If I can I will, but things are happening so fast, I can't look that far ahead.'

'Can't you talk to Carlotti? Can't we get an adjournment at the inquest? I've got to have time to study this thing.'

'It's a murder case,' I said. 'There's nothing either of us can do.'

'Well, try. I'm relying on you, Dawson.'

I grinned mirthlessly at the opposite wall. I wondered how much longer he would rely on me. I wondered what he would say and do if I told him I was one of the fifteen men who had fooled around with his precious daughter.

'I'll talk to him,' I said, 'but I don't think he'll listen.'

'Who killed her, Dawson?'

'A guy called Carlo Manchini. I can't prove it yet, but I'm going to have a try. It's my bet he killed Menotti and your daughter sold Menotti to him.'

'This is fantastic.' He really sounded as if he had taken a knock. 'Anything I can do at this end?'

'Well, if you can get the boys to dig into Menotti's background,' I said, 'they might turn up something useful. See if they can get anything on Manchini and Setti. I want a hook-up between those two. See if they can get any dope on what Helen was up to and if she did go to Menotti's apartment.'

'I can't do that!' His voice rose to a shout. 'I don't want anyone to know about this thing! This has got to be hushed up, Dawson!'

I laughed.

'You have as much hope of hushing this up as you've got in keeping an H-bomb explosion quiet,' I said, and dropped the receiver back on its cradle.

I waited a brief moment, then put a call through to police headquarters. I asked if Lieutenant Carlotti was on duty. The desk sergeant said he thought he was in his office. He told me to hold on. After about a minute wait, Carlotti came on the line.

'Yes, Signor Dawson?' He sounded smooth and unexcited. 'Is there anything I can do for you?'

'I'm just checking on the inquest. It's at eleven-thirty. That right?' I said.

'That is right. I am flying down to-night. Do you wish to come with me?'

'Not to-night. I'll catch the early morning plane. How's the investigation going?'

'Satisfactory.'

'No arrest yet?'

'Not yet, but these things take time.'

'Yeah.' I wondered if I should tell him that Chalmers was yelling for an adjournment, but I decided it wouldn't do any good. 'How about la Signorina Chalmers's apartment? are you through there yet?'

'Yes. I was going to tell you. The key is with the porter. I took the police guard off this morning.'

'Okay, then I'll get busy and have the place cleared. Did you notice the telephone number scribbled on the wall in her lounge?'

'Oh, yes,' Carlotti said. He didn't sound very interested. 'We checked it. It is the number of la Signorina Setti, a friend of la Signorina Chalmers.'

'Did you know that Myra Setti is the daughter of Frank Setti, whom you boys are supposed to be looking for?'

There was a pause, then he said coldly, 'I was aware of that.'

'I just thought it might have slipped your mind,' I said, and hung up.

III

Carlo was waiting for me in the Pasquale Club. He was drinking wine and smoking a cheroot. He waved to me as I crossed the empty lounge to join him.

'What's biting you?' he said. 'Have a drink?'

I shook my head.

'You said if I played with you, you'd play with me,' I said. 'Okay, here's your chance.'

He tilted back his chair, blew smoke towards the ceiling and listened with half-closed eyes as I explained about Sarti.

'Old man Chalmers told me to put a private eye to work, digging into his daughter's background,' I said. 'I didn't imagine Sarti would dig so deep. He's dug me up.'

Carlo looked at me, his face expressionless.

156

'So what?'

'So he's blackmailing me for ten million lire. If I don't pay, he's handing the information he's collected over to the police.'

'How bad is the information?' Carlo asked, tilting his chair further back and scratching his jaw with a dirty finger-nail.

'As bad as it can be. If the police get this information from him, I'm cooked. I haven't ten million lire—nothing like it. If you want me to do this run to Nice for you, you've got to do something fast.'

'Such as what?'

'That's up to you. I don't suppose you want to spring ten million lire, do you?'

He threw back his head and sounded off with his raucous laugh.

'You kidding?' He let his chair come to earth with a crash that shook the room, stood up and hunched his shoulders. 'Come on, pally. Let's go and see this bum. I'll fix him.'

'He's probably out.' I wasn't anxious to get mixed up in this. 'Why don't you call around at his office to-morrow? I'd come with you, but I have to be in Naples to-morrow to attend the inquest.'

He put his enormous hand on my arm. His fingers dug into my muscles.

'He'll be in. This is feeding time. Come on, pally. This is your mess. You and me will fix him together.'

He led me out of the bar, across the sidewalk to where the Renault was parked. We got in, and he sent the car shooting away from the kerb.

'The office will be shut,' I said, flinching as Carlo narrowly missed a man and woman who were crossing the street.

Carlo leaned out of the car window to curse them, then pulled in his head and gave me his wide, animal grin.

'I know where the punk lives,' he said. 'He and I have done a couple of jobs together. He loves me. There's nothing he wouldn't do for me.'

I gave up, and for the rest of the reckless drive I said nothing.

We pulled up outside an apartment block off via Flaminia Nuova. Carlo got out, crossed the sidewalk, pushed open the entrance door and walked up the stairs, three at a time. He paused outside a shabby door on which was tacked one of Sarti's business cards. He dug his thumb into the bell-push and kept it there.

There was a six seconds' pause, then the door opened cautiously. I had a glimpse of Sarti's fat, unshaven face before he tried to slam the door shut.

Carlo was ready for his move. His knee came up and smashed into the door panel, slamming the door into Sarti who went over with a little yelp of fear and pain. He sat down on the floor of the hall. Carlo walked in, let me pass then kicked the door shut.

He reached out and hauled Sarti to his feet by his necktie. The tie tightened around Sarti's fat throat and his face turned purple. He hit Carlo feebly in the face, his small fat hands making as much impression on Carlo as a rubber hammer would make on a lump of rock.

Carlo suddenly let go of the tie and gave Sarti a violent shove. Sarti went reeling back through a door into a small sitting-room. He cannoned into a table set for a meal, and he and the table went over on the floor.

I stood aside and watched.

Carlo wandered into the room, his hands in his trousers pockets, whistling under his breath.

Sarti sat in the wreckage of his lunch, his face the colour of a ripe Camembert cheese, his bloodshot eyes bolting out of his head.

Carlo wandered over to the window and sat on the sill. He smiled at Sarti.

'Listen, fatso, this guy's my pal.' He jerked his thumb at me. 'If anyone is going to put the bite on him, it'll be me. I won't tell you a second time. Do you get it?'

Sarti nodded. He licked his lips, tried to say something, but he couldn't get the words out.

'You've got a lot of written stuff about him, haven't you?' Carlo went on. 'Bring it around to my place to-morrow morning: all of it. Get it?'

Again Sarti nodded.

'If any of it gets in the hands of the cops, then someone will tip them off about that little job you did in Florence. Get that?' Carlo went on.

Sarti nodded. Sweat began to run down his face.

Carlo looked at me.

158

'Is that okay, pally? This bum won't worry you again. I guarantee it.

I said it was okay with me.

Carlo grinned.

'Fine. Anything for a pal. You play with me and I'll play with you. You get off and enjoy yourself. Me and fatso are going to have a little session together.'

Sarti's eyes bulged until I thought they were going to drop out of his head. He waved his fat, dirty hands at me.

'Don't leave me, signor,' he implored in a voice that chilled me. 'Don't leave me alone with him.'

I had no pity for him.

'So long,' I said to Carlo. 'I'll be seeing you.'

As I went down the stairs I heard a sound like the scream of a frightened rabbit.

I was sweating by the time I reached the street.

PART XI

I

It was only as I was driving back to my apartment I realized I still didn't know the name of Sarti's client who had hired him to watch Helen. This was something I had to know.

I wondered if I should go back to Sarti's apartment and get Carlo to squeeze the information out of him, but I decided against this. There was no point in giving Carlo any more information than I could help.

I happened to be near the offices of the International Investigation Agency. I wondered if I should risk trying to get the information for myself. It would mean breaking into the place. At least at this hour of three o'clock on a Sunday afternoon it should be fairly safe. I decided to do it.

I left my car down a side street, took from the boot a tyre lever and screw driver and, concealing them in the pocket of my raincoat, I walked quickly to the block of offices where the agency was housed.

The front entrance was shut and locked. I went around to the back of the building to the janitor's entrance and found the door open. I walked into a lobby full of dustbins and empty milk bottles, paused to listen, then, hearing nothing, I made my way quietly up the stairs to the first floor.

I found the International Investigation Agency at the far end of a corridor. It consisted of six rooms, and no light showed through the frosted panels of the doors. I went from door to door, rapping on each and waiting, but no one answered my knock.

With a heavily beating heart I took out my tyre lever, inserted it in between one of the doors and the doorpost and put a little pressure on it. The lock broke without any alarming noise and the door swung open. I entered an empty office, closed the door and looked around.

This office belonged to one of the executives. I went through the communicating door into the second office. It wasn't until I reached the fourth office that I found what I was looking for. Along the wall was a row of filing cabinets. I selected the file marked 'C', and with the aid of my screw driver and tyre lever I managed to force the lock and get the file open.

I spent ten minutes going through the mass of folders in the file, but I didn't find one with Helen's name on it. I stood back, foxed. There were so many files in the drawers that it would have been an impossible task to have gone through them all. It then occurred to me that there was a chance that Sarti had kept Helen's file away from the rest. I went into the fifth office.

There were three desks in this room: one of them was Sarti's. I knew that by the notes in the In-tray addressed to him.

I sat down at the desk and went through the drawers. The third one down on the right was locked. I made short work of it with my tyre lever, pulled it open and felt a surge of relief run through me. The only thing in the drawer was the file I was looking for.

I took it from the drawer and laid it on the desk and opened it. For about a minute I examined it, then I shoved back the chair, reached for a cigarette and lit it. I knew now who had instructed Sarti to watch Helen, and I was completely taken out of my stride.

Sarti's file began:

Acting on the instructions of la Signorina June Chalmers, I have to-day arranged with Finetti and Molinari to keep a twenty-four hour watch on la Signorina Helen Chalmers . . .

June Chalmers!

So she was at the back of this! I flicked through the reports until I came to one headed with my name. There were ten pages given up to my association with Helen. At the top of the page was the following:

Copy of report sent to la Signorina Chalmers, Ritz Hotel, Paris, August 24th.

The report contained all the details of Helen's plan to rent a villa in Sorrento, of her suggestion to me that we should go there as Mr. and Mrs. Sherrard, that she should arrive at Sorrento on the 28th and I would join her on the 29th.

I sat back, feeling sweat on my forehead. It was obvious that at some time Sarti had planted a microphone in Helen's apartment to have learned all these details. It was obvious too that June Chalmers had known I had gone to Sorrento to be Helen's lover when I first met her at the Naples airport. Then why hadn't she told Chalmers?

I hurriedly folded the file and put it away in my pocket. I couldn't remain here any longer. There was always the chance that the janitor might take a walk around the office block and catch me here.

I put my tools in my pocket, then after peering cautiously down the long corridor I made my way quickly down the stairs and out into the street.

I drove back to my apartment. Stripping off my raincoat, I sat down and again went through the file.

It was far more comprehensive and complete than Sarti had led me to believe. Not only were the telephone conversations recorded, but also my conversations with Helen while I had been with her. There were conversations between her and other men also recorded that made hair-raising reading: the file was bulging with evidence that proved beyond doubt the kind of immoral life Helen had lived. Every one of these reports had been sent to June Chalmers, either to New York or to Paris.

Why hadn't she used this information? I kept asking myself. Why hadn't she given me away to Chalmers? Why hadn't she warned him of the life his daughter was leading?

I had no answer to these questions and, finally, I locked the file away in my desk.

The time was now after five o'clock. I put a personal call through to Jack Martin, and was told there was a half-hour wait for New York. I booked the call, and went over to the window and stared down at the fast-moving Sunday traffic until the call through.

'Is that you, Ed?' Martin asked as I came on the line. 'For the love of mike! Who's paying for this call?'

'Never mind that. What have you got for me? Have you managed to dig up anything on Manchini yet?'

'Not a thing. I've never heard of him,' Martin returned. 'Are you sure you've got the name right? You don't mean Toni Amando, do you?'

163

'My guy calls himself Carlo Manchini. Where does Amando come in?'

'Your description fits him. He's big, tough and dark, and he's got a zigzag scar on his chin.'

'That sounds like him. My man's got a voice like a hog caller and he wears a gold ear-ring in his right ear.'

'That's the fella!' Martin said excitedly. 'That's Amando! There can't be two of them.'

'What do you know about him, Jack?'

'He's not here any longer, I'm glad to say. He was a trouble-maker and as dangerous as a rattlesnake. He's somewhere in your territory, I believe. He left with Frank Setti when they ran Setti out of this country.'

'Setti?' My voice shot up.

'That's right. Amando was Setti's gunman and lieutenant.'

This was the first really constructive piece of news I had had up to now.

Setti's gunman!

Now, at long last, some of the pieces of this jigsaw puzzle were falling into place.

Martin was speaking again. 'Have you run into him in Italy?'

'Yes. I think he's hooked up in a dope-smuggling racket. I wanted to get a check on him.'

'Setti ran dope here before he was kicked out. He's in Italy, too, isn't he?'

'So I hear. Look, Jack, I can prove Amando flew from Rome to New York two days before Menotti was knocked off, and he returned to Rome the day after.'

'Well, that's something. I'll pass the information to Captain Collier. He may be able to use it. That may be the link he's looking for. He was so sure either Setti or Amando knocked off Menotti, but both of them had cast-iron alibis at the time Menotti died. They had a flock of witnesses that put them in a gambling joint in Naples.'

'Amando boasts that he is red-hot at manufacturing alibis. Talk to Collier, Jack, and thanks for the information.'

I began to pace the room while I turned over this new information. It looked as if my theory that Carlo had killed Menotti and that Helen had tried to blackmail him was right. But I hadn't as yet a shred of evidence that would convince a jury. It was all theory, but I was moving in the right direction.

I was tempted to go to Carlotti and tell him the whole story. With his organization, there was a chance that he might get at the truth with this theory as a lead.

I resisted the temptation. The moment Carlo learned that I had been to Carlotti, he would produce his mass of evidence against me and that would cook me.

It wasn't the time yet to tell Carlotti the truth. I had to have some real concrete evidence.

I spent the rest of the evening going through Sarti's report again and racking my brain for angles. My hope now, I decided, was to concentrate on Carlo. When I got to Naples, I would go out to Myra's villa and see if I could turn up anything there.

II

Before I caught the first plane out to Naples on Monday morning, I called Gina at her apartment.

'Hello, Ed,' she said. 'I've been waiting to hear from you. What is happening?'

'Plenty. I can't talk now. I'm in a rush. I'm flying down to Naples in five minutes to attend the inquest. We'll get together when I get back.'

'But you keep saying that. I'm sure there is something wrong. I'm worried about you, Ed. Why do you keep avoiding me?'

'I'm not avoiding you! I'm busy! Skip it, will you? I've only got a couple of minutes. Here's what I want you to do. The police have taken the guard off Helen's apartment. The key is with the janitor. Will you get the apartment cleared for me?'

'Yes, of course.'

'I'll be back sometime to-morrow and I promise to call you. Can you do something about the apartment to-day?'

'I'll try.'

'Tell Maxwell the old man wants it done. He won't raise objections.

'And you will call me when you get back?'

'Yes, of course. So long for now.'

I had to run across the tarmac to catch the plane.

I reached Naples soon after ten-thirty. I booked a room for the night at the Vesuvius, had a wash, then took a taxi to the coroner's court.

I was surprised to find I was the only witness to be called. Grandi and Carlotti were there. Grandi gave me a long, gloomy stare and then looked away. Carlotti nodded, but he didn't come over.

Guiseppe Maletti, the coroner, a bald-headed little man with a sharp, beaky nose, avoided meeting my eyes. He kept looking in my direction, but always managed to focus on a spot just above my head at the last moment.

I was called upon to identify Helen's body and to explain why she had been in Sorrento.

The three newspaper men who attended were obviously bored by the proceedings, and their expressions became gloomier as I explained that, as far as I knew, Helen had rented the villa for a month's vacation. There was nothing said about her renting it in the name of Mrs. Sherrard.

As if for something to say, Maletti asked me if I knew if Helen had had a bad head for heights. I was tempted to say she had, but, catching Grandi's sardonic eyes at this moment, I decided it was safer to say I didn't know.

After a few more stock questions that got no one anywhere Maletti indicated that I could step down. He then called Carlotti.

Carlotti's evidence electrified the three newspaper men and the odd stragglers who had come in to pass an hour out of the heat.

He said he wasn't satisfied Helen's death was accidental. He and the Naples police were pursuing certain investigations that would probably prove that Helen had met with foul play. He said their investigations should be successfully concluded by the following Monday, and he would like the inquest adjourned until then.

Maletti looked as if he had been stricken with a sudden attack of toothache. He said he hoped the Lieutenant had substantial reasons for asking for an adjournment, and Carlotti said mildly that he had. After a long hesitation, Maletti granted the adjournment, and scuttled away as if he were scared someone would question his authority for such an action.

The three newspaper men cornered Carlotti, but he had nothing to tell them. As they made a bee-line for the door, I blocked their way.

'Remember me?' I said and smiled at them.

'This is something you can't talk us out of,' the reporter for *L'Italia del Popolo* said. 'This is news, and we print.'

'Just so long as you print facts and not opinions,' I said. 'Don't say I haven't warned you.'

They shoved past me and ran for their cars.

'Signor Dawson . . .'

I turned.

Grandi was standing at my side. There was a bleak expression in his eyes.

'Hello there,' I said.

'Signor Dawson, I hope for your co-operation. We are looking now for the American who was at Sorrento on the day la signorina died. We have found a man who answers to the description we have obtained from witnesses. We are arranging an identity parade. You happen to be of the same height as this man. Would you very kindly consent to be a member of the parade?'

I felt a cold, sinking feeling inside me.

'I've got a cable to get off. . . .'

'It will only take a few minutes, signor,' Grandi said. 'Please come with me.'

Two uniformed policemen moved forward, smiling at me. I went with them.

There were ten men already standing in a line: two of them were Americans, one was a German, the rest were Italians. They were all shapes and sizes. The two Americans were about my height.

'Merely a matter of a few seconds,' Grandi said with the air of a dentist who is about to extract a molar.

A door opened and a thick-set Italian came in. He stood looking along the line, his unshaven face embarrassed. I didn't recognize him, but by his worn overcoat and the leather gauntlet gloves he carried I guessed he was the taxi-driver who had driven me from Sorrento to Naples on the mad rush to catch the Rome train.

He looked down the line and his eyes rested on me. I found I was beginning to sweat. He stared at me for about three seconds. They felt like an eternity, then he turned around and went out, slapping his thigh with his gloves.

I wanted to wipe my face, but I didn't dare. Grandi was looking at me and when I met his eyes, he gave me a sour smile.

Another Italian was brought in. I knew who he was: he was the attendant at the left luggage office at Sorrento station where I had left my suitcase before walking out to the villa. His eyes swept down the line until they reached me. We stared at each other, then after looking at the other two Americans he went out.

Two more men and a woman then came in. I had no idea who they were. They too glanced down the line, their eyes passing over me. They concentrated on one of the Americans at the far end of the line. They stared at him and he stared back, grinning. I envied him his lack of a guilty conscience. I was glad they didn't stare at me as they had at him. I saw Grandi was scowling. Finally, they went away.

Grandi indicated that the parade was over.

The ten men drifted away.

'Thank you, signor,' Grandi said to me as I moved after them. 'I am sorry to have detained you.'

'I'll survive,' I said. I saw he didn't look too pleased and I guessed the last three witnesses could have upset his hopes. 'Did you find the man you are after?'

He looked fixedly at me.

'I'm not prepared to answer that question at the moment,' he said and, nodding curtly, he went away.

I left the coroner's court and drove back to the hotel. Going up to my room, I put a call through to my Rome office.

Gina told me that she had arranged with the woman who specialized in second-hand clothes to inspect the contents of Helen's apartment that afternoon.

'It should be cleared by to-morrow,' she told me.

'That's fine. Is Maxwell there?'

'Yes.'

'Put him on the line, will you?'

'Ed, you should know this: Lieutenant Carlotti has been asking questions about you here,' Gina said.

I stiffened.

'What sort of questions?'

'He asked me if you knew Helen Chalmers. He wanted to know if the name of Mrs. Douglas Sherrard meant anything to me.'

'Did he? What did you say?' I found I was gripping the receiver unnecessarily hard.

'I told him Mrs. Douglas Sherrard meant nothing to me, and that you did know Helen Chalmers.'

'Thanks, Gina.'

There was an awkward pause, then she said, 'He also wanted to know where you were on the 29th. I said you were at your apartment, working on your novel.'

'That's what I was doing.'

'Yes.'

There was another awkward pause, then she said, 'I'll put you through to Mr. Maxwell.'

'Thanks, Gina.'

After a moment or so, Maxwell came on the line.

I told him the coroner had adjourned the inquest until Monday.

'What's biting him then?' Maxwell asked.

'The police think it's murder.'

He whistled.

'That's pretty. What makes them think that?'

'They didn't say. Cable head office and tell them the facts, and ask for guidance. It's up to the old man whether they print or not. The other papers are certain to cover it.'

'Well, what are the facts?'

'The inquest is adjourned until next Monday as the police want more time to make further inquiries. They have evidence that points to foul play.'

'Okay. Nothing more?'

'That's all.'

'I'll handle it. By the way, Ed, you didn't by any chance bump the girl off, did you?'

I felt like a boxer who has taken a low punch.

'What's that?'

'Oh, skip it. I was only fooling. That lynx-eyed cop was asking me questions about you and Helen. He seemed to think you knew her better than most.'

'He's crazy.'

'I guess you must be right. I've always thought cops were crazy. Well, so long as you've got an easy conscience, why should you care?'

'That's right. Get that cable off, Jack.'

Maxwell said he'd get it off right away.

'So long,' he said. 'Try and keep out of trouble.'
I said I would.

III

Soon after nine o'clock, I left the Vesuvius hotel and drove
the car I had hired out to Sorrento. I arrived at the harbour
a little after nine-thirty. Leaving the car parked under the
trees, I walked down to the harbour.

There were still three or four boatmen lounging outside the
steamer station, and I went over to them. I asked one of
them if I could hire a rowing-boat. I said I wanted to have
a couple of hours' exercise, and I wanted to row myself.

The boatman stared at me as if he thought I was crazy,
but when he realized I was willing to pay him for his boat,
he got down to business. I haggled with him for ten minutes,
and finally got it for five thousand lire for three hours. I
gave him the money, and he took me down to the boat and
shoved me off.

It was a fine, dark, star-lit night, and the sea was as smooth
as a pond. I rowed until I was out of sight of land; then
I shipped oars and stripped off my clothes. I had put on
a pair of bathing trunks before I left the hotel, and, thus
clad, I again started rowing, heading towards Myra Setti's
villa.

It took me about an hour of steady rowing before I saw in
the distance a red light on the harbour wall.

I paused, letting the boat drift. Above the harbour I could
see the outlines of the villa. There was a light on in one
of the ground-floor rooms.

I began to row again, and finally reached the rocks only
a few hundred yards from where Helen had been found. Just
around the cliff, another three hundred yards further on,
would be Myra's villa.

I beached the boat, pulling it up on the soft sand, making
sure that the tide wouldn't drift it off. Then I waded out
into the sea and began to swim towards the villa.

The sea was warm and I made good progress, being careful
to make no noise. I swam silently into the harbour, keeping
away from the circle of red light that reflected down on the
still water.

There were two powerful motor-boats moored in the harbour and a small rowing-boat. I headed towards the steps that led up to the villa. I swam cautiously, looking along the wall of the harbour, my ears pricked for any suspicious sound. It was as well that I was on the alert, for I suddenly saw a little red spark make a circle in the air, and then drop into the sea and go out with a hissing splutter. Someone out of sight in the shadows had just tossed away a cigarette butt.

I trod water, making no sound. By now I was close up against the harbour wall. I saw a mooring ring just above my head and, cautiously, I reached up and caught hold of it. I hung on to it, looking in the direction from where the cigarette butt had come.

After a minute or so I made out the dim figure of a man, sitting on a bollard. He appeared to be looking out to sea. He was on the other arm of the harbour, a hundred feet or so from where I was some thirty yards from the steps. I waited. After about five minutes, he got to his feet and walked slowly along the harbour arm to the far end.

He came under the red light and I could see him clearly. He was tall and powerfully built. He was wearing a white singlet, black trousers, and a yachting cap on the back of his head. He lolled over the wall, his back to me, and I saw him light another cigarette.

I lowered myself into the water again and, using a breast stroke, I swam silently to the steps. With my hand on the lowest one, I looked over my shoulder. The man was still staring across at the lights of Sorrento, his back turned to me. I pulled myself out of the water and moved silently up the steps, keeping in the shadows of the overhanging trees. I looked back, but the man was still motionless, looking away from me.

I went up the steps until I reached a terrace that overlooked the harbour. There I paused, and stared up at the villa, fifty feet above me.

I could see a big, lighted window, uncurtained. There was no sign of life up there, but I could hear the faint sound of dance music coming either from a radio or a record.

Keeping to the shadows, I moved silently and slowly up another flight of steps that brought me on to the second terrace.

There was a patch of dark shadow, made by an orange tree, opposite the lighted window. I kept in the shadow, sure that no one could see me, and looked into a large luxuriously furnished lounge.

There were four men around a table in the centre of the room. They were playing poker. Beyond them, lying on a settee, was Myra Setti. She was reading a magazine and smoking; by her was a radiogram from which came the soft sound of dance music.

I looked at the men at the table. Three of them were the rough types you can see any day in a Warner Bros. movie. Their clothes were flashy, their neckties dazzling, their faces, burned brown by the sun, were hard, thin and vicious. It was the fourth man who held my attention. He was a man of about fifty; big, grossly fat and dark-skinned. I had seen too many pictures of him in the papers in the past not to recognize him. I felt a little surge of triumph run through me. I had succeeded where the whole of the Italian police force had failed! I should have guessed before now that this inaccessible villa could be Frank Setti's hide-out but, somehow, I hadn't thought of him being here.

The four men were intent on their game of poker. It was easy to see who was winning. Six tall stacks of counters stood before Setti. The other three had scarcely a counter between them. As I watched them, a tall, thin rat of a man threw down his cards with a gesture of disgust. He said something to Setti, who grinned wolfishly at him, shoved back his chair and stood up. The other two also threw in their hands and relaxed back in their chairs, scowling.

Setti looked over at Myra and said something to her. She glanced up, her face heavy with boredom, nodded, then returned her attention to her magazine.

The tall man came over to the window and threw it open. I crouched down against the low wall. The sound of dance music came out through the open window loudly now.

'Jerry's late,' the tall man said, speaking over his shoulder to Setti.

Setti got up from the table, stretched his massive limbs and came to the window.

'He'll be here,' he said. 'Jerry's a good boy. He has a long way to come.' He looked over at Myra. 'Turn that damn thing off. I can't hear myself speak.'

Without looking up from her magazine, Myra reached out and turned off the radiogram.

172

Setti and the tall man stood by the window, listening. I listened too. I thought I could hear the faint throb of a motor-boat engine somewhere out at sea.

'Here he comes now,' the tall man said. 'Harry's down there, isn't he?'

'He damn well better be,' Setti growled. He moved away from the window and walked out of the room. A moment later, he came out on to the terrace.

I began to sweat. I knew if I was found here my life wouldn't be worth a dime. They'd cut my throat and bury me at sea. My hiding-place wasn't any too safe. If any one of them came over to the orange tree they couldn't fail to see me. It was too late to move now. I lay flat, holding my breath and squeezing myself against the terrace wall.

Setti sat down at one of the tables, about fifty feet from me. The tall man came out and stood looking out to sea.

'Here he comes,' he said.

Myra came out and joined him. He pointed out into the darkness.

'Do you see him?'

'I see him,' she said. She put her hands on the top of the wall and leaned forward. She was so close to me I could smell her perfume.

The red harbour light flicked off and then came on again. There was a long pause. Setti lit a cigar. Myra and the tall man continued to stare down at the harbour. I lay so still that a lizard, mistaking me for part of the scenery, ran lightly across my bare back.

Then I heard the sounds of someone running up the steps. A man appeared, wearing a red singlet, black trousers and rope-soled shoes. He was youngish, good-looking in a flashy, tough way, and he grinned widely at Myra as he came on to the terrace.

'Hi, there,' he said.

Myra's boredom vanished. She gave him a dazzling smile. 'Hi, Jerry!'

He crossed over to where Setti was sitting and dumped on the table an oilskin-wrapped parcel.

'Hi, boss. Here it is.'

Setti leaned back and smiled at him.

'Fine. Sit down, kid. Here, Jake, get him a drink.'

Jake went into the lounge. Myra came over and Jerry took her hand.

'May I kiss your daughter, boss?' he asked, grinning at Setti.

'Go ahead,' Setti said, shrugging his shoulders. 'If she wants it, why should I worry? Have any trouble coming over?'

'Not a thing.'

Myra and he kissed, then he pulled her on to his lap and put his arms around her.

'This is a good place for a run,' he went on, 'but how are you going to get the stuff into Nice, boss?'

'Carlo's fixed that,' Setti said. 'Now, there's a smart boy.'

Jerry's face hardened.

'He could be too smart.' He looked at Myra. 'Have you been seeing anything of him lately, babe?'

Myra's eyes opened wide, innocently.

'Carlo? Don't be crazy! Why should I want an ape like him around when I've got you?'

'I guess that's right,' Jerry said, frowning. He didn't seem convinced. 'Well, watch out, baby. You keep clear of him.'

Setti sat back, smiling and listening.

'You're jealous,' Myra said, and touched Jerry's face. 'You don't have to be.'

Jerry patted her flank, then looked over at Setti.

'What's Carlo fixed then?'

'He's got a newspaper man to run the stuff into Nice: Ed Dawson of the *Western Telegram*,' Setti said, grinning from ear to ear.

'Dawson!' Jerry sat forward. 'I know that punk! I've seen him around in Rome. Is he doing it?'

'That's the idea. Carlo's got him where he wants him. We can't go wrong with a guy like Dawson acting as carrier. Smartest thing Carlo's ever done.'

'Well, for the love of mike! Yeah, that sure is smart.'

Jake came out with a whisky and soda and gave it to Jerry.

'Come on in, kid. I've got the dough for you,' Setti said, getting to his feet. 'Are you going to stay for a while?'

'I don't have to get back until to-morrow night.'

Myra got off Jerry's lap and slid her arm through his.

'Never mind about the money now, honey,' she said. 'Let's go to my room. I want to talk to you.'

Jerry looked over at Setti.

'Is that okay with you, boss?'

174

Setti smiled.

'Sure. Myra's a big girl now. She does what she likes. The dough's all ready for you when you want it. When's the next run?'

'Three weeks from to-night. It's all fixed.'

Carrying his drink, Jerry followed Myra into the villa. Jake stared after them, frowning.

'Carlo's going to stick a knife into that guy one of these days,' he said.

Setti laughed.

'Forget it! Let Myra have her fun. If she wants two boy friends, let her have them.' He tossed what remained of his cigar over the terrace. 'Put the stuff in the safe, Jake. Carlo doesn't want it until Thursday. You take it to Rome on Wednesday night . . . understand?'

Jake grunted. He picked up the oilskin package and the two men went into the villa.

As soon as they were out of sight, I got to my feet. Here was the way out for me. If the package failed to get into Carlo's hands by Thursday, then I wouldn't have to take it to Nice. There was only one way to handle this. I had to get back to Sorrento fast and alert Grandi.

I went down the steps towards the harbour, being careful to move silently. I reached the last few steps. I could see the red light on the harbour wall, and I paused in the shadows, looking for the man they had called Harry.

There was no sign of him. I hesitated. Where was he? I didn't dare slide into the water until I knew just where he was. My eyes searched the dark shadows. I looked along both arms of the harbour. There was still no sign of him.

Then suddenly I became aware of soft breathing behind me. A cold creepy chill snaked up my back. I half-turned when a muscular, hairy arm hooked under my chin and slammed against my throat, and a hard, bony knee drove into my spine.

PART XII

I

IN the brief second before the arm tightened on my throat, cutting the air from my lungs, I realized this man, probably the one who they called Harry, was as strong, if not stronger, than I was. Already I was fighting for breath, and my lungs felt as if they were bursting. I couldn't get at him, for he was bending me back, his knee grinding into my spine. There was only one way out of a hold like this: I let myself go limp. My legs buckled and I collapsed on my knees. As I did so I managed to arch my back and bring him forward.

I heard him give a muffled curse, and his grip on my throat tightened viciously. I made a desperate effort to heave him over my head, but he was too heavy. Instead, my heave unbalanced us both. My feet slipped on the wet steps and together we rolled into the sea.

The shock of landing in the water loosened his hold. I caught hold of his wrist and peeled his arm off my throat, then I twisted around so that I faced him and drove my hand under his chin, sending him over on his back. I broke free of him and rose to the surface, gasping.

My one fear was that he would shout for help. Whatever happened, those in the villa mustn't know I had been up there.

He bobbed up within three yards of me. I saw him before he could shake the water out of his eyes. I dived under him, caught hold of one of his feet and dragged him down.

He kicked so violently that I had to let go of him. We both came to the surface together. I could just see his staring eyes and snarling mouth. He came at me and lifted his right hand out of the water. I saw a flash of steel. I threw myself sideways. The knife blade missed me by inches. I dived, came around in a tight circle, spotted the dark form of his body within reach and grabbed him around his waist, pulling him under the water. My left hand groped and found his right wrist.

He fought like a madman, and it was as much as I could do to hold him. I held him down as long as I could, then, when my own lungs were at bursting point, I let go of him and kicked my way up to the surface. He took four or five seconds longer to break surface, and when he did come up, I could see by his feeble strokes that he was on his last legs.

He had lost the knife, and as he tried desperately to get away from me, he gave a croaking shout.

I sprinted after him and, putting my hand between his shoulders, I shoved him under again. I dived after him, but now he was offering practically no resistence, and when we came to the surface once more he was done. He would have sunk if I hadn't grabbed him by his collar and held him up. His head lolled on his shoulders and I couldn't hear him breathe.

I was only a few yards from the moored rowing-boat. I towed him over to it, and heaved him in, nearly upsetting the boat as I did so. I got in after him and knelt beside him. As he seemed in a bad way, I rolled him over on his face so the water he had swallowed could drain out of him, then I untied the mooring line, got the oars out and began to row as hard and as fast as I could towards Sorrento

I must have got about half-way—I had lost the lights of the villa—when Harry stirred and started to mumble. I wasn't going to give him a chance to recover. I didn't fancy a fight with him in this small boat. I hurriedly shipped oars, then, scrambling over the other rowing seat, I reached him as he slowly hauled himself into a sitting position.

He lifted his head and his chin made a perfect target. I hung a right on the point of his jaw that took the skin off my knuckles. He went over backwards as if he had been shot, and then, as his head cracked on the bottom of the boat, he went limp.

I scrambled back to the oars and began to row again. He didn't begin to move until I reached Sorrento harbour.

My boatman was waiting for me, and his eyes bugged out when he saw I wasn't in his boat. He nearly dropped in his tracks as I caught hold of Harry and heaved him on to the beach. The movement brought Harry around, and he slowly hauled himself upright. I stepped up to him and, brushing his feeble left lead aside, I hung another bone bender on his jaw, sending him flat on his back at the boatman's feet.

'Get a policeman!' I said. 'Never mind about your boat. Get a policeman, quick!'

A policeman, who must have been standing in the shadows of the car-park, came up. I was lucky that he didn't argue as they usually do. He listened to what I told him. Frank Setti's name seemed to mean something to him. He turned to the boatman and told him to hold his tongue, put hand-cuffs on Harry, requisitioned a car and drove Harry and I to the police station.

I was lucky too that Grandi was still on duty. He stared blankly at me as I came into his office, naked, except for a pair of swimming trunks. When I told him I had found Frank Setti and had got one of Setti's men, he came alive.

I told him there was a consignment of dope at the villa, and if he moved fast he would have all the evidence he needed for an arrest. He got on the telephone to Rome headquarters and had a quick talk with the head of the Narcotic Squad. He got orders to go ahead and raid the villa.

As he made for the door, I said, 'Watch out. There're five men out there, and they're tough and dangerous.'

He gave me a sour smile.

'I can be tough and dangerous too.'

He went out and I heard him shouting orders. A little later a policeman came in and showed me where I could have a hot shower. He also gave me a pair of flannel slacks and a sweater.

By the time I was dressed, Grandi had gone down to the beach where he was to await reinforcements from Naples. I decided I would have time to telephone Maxwell before the raid began.

I got Maxwell on the line. I told him that within an hour Frank Setti would be arrested, and warned him to stand by for details. I said I was going down right away to the beach where the police were embarking for Setti's villa.

Maxwell said he would warn New York what was coming, and would wait for me to call back.

I then took a taxi down to the harbour.

179

Grandi with thirty carabiniere, armed to the teeth, were piling into three motor-boats. When I suggested I should go with them, Grandi waved me away.

They went roaring off into the darkness, leaving me with my boatman who, by now, was tearing his hair and yelling for his boat.

I said I would show him where I had left it if he could find a motor-boat to take us there. After some argument, he persuaded one of his friends to take us, and we set off.

By the time we had picked up the rowing-boat from the beach where I had left it, Grandi and his men had landed at Setti's villa. I kept my ears pricked for the sound of shooting, but I heard nothing.

I managed to persuade the boatman to hang around just outside Setti's harbour. The moon had now come up, and I could see the three police boats in the harbour.

After a twenty-minute wait, I saw a bunch of men come along the harbour wall and get into the boats. There was a girl with them and I guessed it was Myra.

I told the boatman to get back to Sorrento, and was waiting on the beach when Grandi and his men and prisoners landed. He had got them all.

While they were being hustled into the waiting police van, I crossed over to where Grandi was standing.

'Did you get the consignment of drugs?'

'Yes, I got it all right.'

'No trouble?'

He shook his head.

'I didn't give them a chance to make trouble.'

'I want to be kept out of this. I've got to get back to Rome right away. You won't need me, will you?'

'No. But you will be down next Monday for the inquest?'

'I'll be down.'

Leaving him, I got into my car and drove back to the hotel. I called Maxwell and gave him the details of Setti's arrest. I told him to let Matthews of the Associated Press have the story too. He said he would get a cable off to New York right away and then call Matthews.

'I'm coming back to-night,' I said. 'I'll see you in the morning.'

He asked if I didn't think I should stay on in Naples and cover the case when Setti come up in court.

He was right, of course, but I had Carlo on my mind. I

didn't know how Carlo was going to react when he heard Setti had been arrested and the consignment of drugs he was waiting for had been seized. I had to convince him I had nothing to do with it or he would fix me.

'He won't come before a court for a couple of days. I've things to do in Rome.'

'Well, okay, please yourself. I'll be seeing you.'

I said I would be seeing him.

II

Back in Rome, around nine o'clock the following morning, and still in bed, I called Maxwell again.

He said he had had a call from New York for more details of Setti's life in Italy, and could I do anything about it?

I said it might be an idea if he went to Naples instead of me.

'Yeah, I want to,' he said, 'but Gina's not in to-day. She's fooling around with the stuff at Helen's apartment. I can't leave the office without someone to handle the telephone calls.'

'Isn't she there now?'

'She wanted the day off. She will be at Helen's apartment around ten o'clock. She said the old man wanted the place cleared.'

'That's what he does want. Okay. I'll go over there and send her back. Then you can get off.'

'I should have thought you would have wanted to have handled this yourself,' Maxwell said. 'It's the biggest story in years.'

'As you're taking over the Rome office,' I said, 'this is now your story. I'll get Gina back to you by half-past eleven. There's a plane to Naples at two o'clock. You'd better get yourself a reservation.'

He said he would do that.

I got out of bed, took a shower, shaved and dressed, then went down to the garage. I got to Helen's apartment and rang the bell. Gina opened the door.

'Why, hello, Ed,' she said. Her smile was a little uncertain.

'Hello there,' I said, and, following her into the lounge, I went on, 'How are you getting on here?'

'I'm packing. There's so much to clear. I'll be through in about half an hour.'

'Have you got rid of it all?'

'Yes.' She sat on the arm of a chair and looked at me. 'What's been happening, Ed?'

I dropped into an easy-chair.

'Plenty.' I went on to tell her about the capture of Setti. 'Maxwell wants to get down to Naples. He's waiting now for you to relieve him. You'd better get off, Gina. I can handle what you haven't finished here.'

'He'll have to catch the two o'clock plane, so there's plenty of time,' Gina said firmly. 'Ed, how did you know that Setti was in this villa?'

I looked at her.

'Why should you worry how I knew?'

'I'm asking you, Ed,' she said. 'It's too good to be true. You must see that. Every policeman in Italy has been looking for Setti. Then you find him. How did you know he was there? If I don't ask you, someone else will.'

I could see the sense in that. Now she had put the question, I was surprised that Grandi hadn't asked me.

'I guess you're right,' I said. 'Well, it's a long story.'

'I want to hear it. You have deliberately kept away from me. Please, don't deny it. You have. You're involved somehow in this business, aren't you? You knew she was calling herself Mrs. Douglas Sherrard. There's something wrong somewhere. I'm worried. You must tell me.'

'You've got to keep clear of it,' I said. 'Don't ask questions. Helen was murdered. I didn't kill her, but the police have an idea that I did. You must see I can't tell you anything without getting you involved.'

Her small hands turned to fists.

'Do you think I care about that?' she said. 'I want to know, Ed, please. What kind of trouble are you in?'

'I'm in a lot of trouble. But I can't tell you the details. You've got to keep clear of it, Gina.'

'Did that girl mean anything to you?'

I hesitated.

'At one time I think she did, but not when I found out what she really was. I guess I was acting like a . . .'

'Don't say it. I know how it was. Tell me what happened, Ed.'

'Forget it!' I got to my feet and wandered over to the

182

window. 'I stuck my neck out, and now I've got to take what's coming.'

'Are you scared il Signor Chalmers will find out?'

'I've got beyond that. He's offered me the foreign desk. When he knows what I've been up to, I won't get it. The foreign desk is important to me, Gina.'

'You'll leave Rome?'

'That was the idea, but it looks now as if I won't have a job at all.'

There was such a sharp silence that I turned and looked at her. She had lost colour and her eyes were full of unshed tears.

'Don't look like that, Gina. The end of the world hasn't come.'

'Not to you perhaps.'

I realized for the first time since I had known her what she really meant to me. I went over to her. Putting my hands on her hips, I pulled her to me.

'Okay, I admit it. I'm in a hell of a mess. It's my own stupid fault. You've got to keep clear of it. If you know too much, they could hang an accessory rap on you.'

'For heaven's sake, Ed' she said, beginning to cry. 'Do you think I care? It's you I care about.'

My hands slid around her back. She raised her face, glistening with tears, and my lips came down on hers. We stood like that for a long moment, then I pushed her back.

'This isn't the way,' I said. 'I guess I must have been crazy to have chased after that little tramp. Now I've got to take what's coming to me. Keep clear of me, Gina. You must keep clear of me.'

Her fingers moved up into my hair and she smiled at me.

'I can help you. I know I can. Do you want me to?'

'I want you to keep clear of it.'

'Ed, do you love me a little? Do I mean anything to you?'

'I guess you do. I've taken a long time to find that out, haven't I?' I pulled her to me. 'But that's beside the point, Gina. I'll need a lot of luck to beat this rap. Carlotti is more or less convinced that I'm the guy he's looking for.'

'Won't you tell me what really happened? Right from the beginning?'

I sat down and told her. I gave her the whole story. I didn't hold a thing back.

She sat listening, her face pale, her lips parted, and when I had finished, she drew in a long, slow breath.

'Oh, darling, it's been dreadful for you!'

'It's been bad, but I asked for it. If I could only pin Helen's death on Carlo I would be in the clear. I just can't see how I'm going to do it.'

'You must tell Carlotti the whole story just as you've told it to me. It rings true. He'll understand. You must tell him.'

I shook my head.

'There's too much evidence against me. I should have told him before. He'll only think my nerve's cracked and I'm trying to get out of it. He'll arrest me, and then I won't be able to get after Carlo. I've got to fix Carlo myself if that's possible.'

'No, please, Ed. You must tell him. I am sure it's the only thing to do.'

'Well, I'll think about it. I'm not going to tell him yet.'

'Ed! I've suddenly thought of something,' Gina said, jumping to her feet. 'Yesterday while I was here the postman brought a carton of film addressed to Helen.'

I stared at her.

'A carton of film!'

'Yes. She must have sent it to be processed.'

I was aware that my heart was beginning to thump painfully.

'Have you got it?'

She opened her handbag and took out a yellow carton.

'It may be a film she took in Sorrento,' she said, and held out the carton to me.

As I reached for it, the door swung open. We both turned quickly.

Carlo stood in the doorway, his thick lips parted in a grin.

'I'll have that,' he said. 'I've been waiting days for that damn thing to turn up. Give it here!'

III

Gina's reflexes worked a lot faster than mine. She must have recognized Carlo from my description the moment she

184

saw him. She whipped the carton into her bag and was on her feet by the time Carlo was half-way across the lounge.

She spun on her heels and made a dash for the bedroom door.

Snarling, Carlo jumped forward, his thick fingers reaching for her. As he passed me, I shot out my foot and hooked his legs from under him. He sprawled headlong, his fingers closing on Gina's blouse. She gave a frantic twist of her body. The thin material tore from her shoulder and she broke free. She didn't attempt to take the longer way around the room to the front door. She dashed into the bedroom, slammed the door, and I heard the key turn.

The apartment was on the fourth floor. There was no escape from the bedroom, but at least the door was solid. Carlo would have to break it down.

All this flashed through my mind as I heaved myself out of the chair I was sitting in.

Carlo was still sprawled on the floor, cursing. I didn't make the mistake of tangling with him. I jumped across the room to the fireplace and snatched up a heavy steel poker. He was on his feet as I turned.

We faced each other.

He crouched, his big hands held out before him, his thick fingers hooked. There was an expression on his face that made him look like something out of the jungle.

'Okay, you dirty double-crosser,' he said softly. 'Now you're really going to get it.'

I waited for him.

He began to move slowly forward, circling a little to my left, his black eyes vicious and intent. I turned slightly, set for his rush, the poker in readiness. I knew I could stop him if I landed one good smash on his head.

But I underestimated his speed. I knew he was fast, but I didn't realize just how fast he could be until he suddenly dived for my knees.

His shoulder crashed against my thighs as I brought down the poker which landed across his shoulders, missing his head. I felt as if a house had fallen on me. We went down together with a thump that rocked the room.

I let go of the poker and drove my fist into his face. I couldn't get much weight behind the punch, but it sent his head back. I aimed another punch at his throat, but my fist sailed past his head as he twisted aside. He caught me on the side of my neck with a clubbing punch that dazed me.

I got my hand under his chin and heaved him off me. He swung a punch at my head. I blocked it with my right arm, kicked him in the chest and sent him crashing against the settee that shot across the room, mowing down an occasional table and a standard lamp.

I was on my feet in time to meet his rush. We collided like a couple of fighting bulls. I hung a jolting right on the side of his jaw and took a thump in the ribs that turned me sick.

He backed away; his face was contorted with savage rage. He showed his teeth in a snarling grimace. I steadied myself and waited for him. As he came in, I shoved my left into his face, jolting his head back. I jumped away as he countered with a punch that swished past my jaw, bringing him forward. I hooked him on the side of his head, catching him too high up to damage him. He crowded me, bashing my ribs with four short-arm jolts that thumped the breath out of me. I broke away from him, jumped behind an armchair, and as he came at me, I shoved the chair at him, spoiling his rush.

Punch for punch, I knew he was too good for me. He hit with the force of a steam hammer, and every time he caught me, I weakened.

I began to back away. He moved forward, blood trickling down his chin from a cut lip. As he came within reach, I shot out my left. My fist caught him on the nose, but it didn't stop him. He swung at me. His fist came over my shoulder and exploded against my ear. It was a hell of a punch, and I felt my knees sag. I threw up my hands to protect my jaw and took another punch to the body. I went down.

I expected him to finish me, but he was too anxious to get at Gina. He left me and charged across the room. He took a flying kick at the bedroom door; his foot landing against the lock. The door split, but the lock held.

From inside the room I heard the crash of breaking glass and then the sound of Gina's screaming out of the broken window at the top of her voice.

Somehow I got to my feet. My legs felt like rubber sticks. I reeled forward as he set himself for another kick at the lock. I flung my arm around his neck and dragged him over backwards. I got a lock on his throat. But it was like holding on to a wild cat. He was much too strong for me.

He dragged my arm from his throat, drove his elbow into my body, turned, and his fingers closed around my throat. I got my hand under his chin and exerted pressure. For a long moment we remained motionless; his fingers digging into my throat; my hand slowly wedging his head back. My hold hurt him more than his hurt me and he let go, heaved backwards, scrambled to his feet as I got up on to my knees.

He set himself and swung a punch. I saw it coming, but I was too far gone to get out of its way. Lights exploded before my eyes and I went down.

I remained out for maybe three or four seconds. The sound of the bedroom door crashing open brought me round. I heard a wild scream and I knew he had got to Gina.

I staggered up. Near me, on the floor, was the poker. My fingers closed around it. I staggered across the room and into the bedroom.

Carlo had Gina flat on her back across the bed. One of his big hands gripped her throat. He knelt over her. He was shouting: 'Where is it? Come on! Give it to me!'

I swung the poker. He half-turned, but he was a shade too late. The poker came down on top of his head. His hand slid off Gina's throat. He slipped sideways. I hit him again. He spread out on the floor.

I dropped the poker, stepped over him and leaned over Gina.

'Did he hurt you?'

She looked up at me, her face white. She tried to smile.

'He didn't get it, Ed,' she gasped, then, turning her head, she began to cry.

'What's going on here?' a voice demanded at the door.

I looked over my shoulder. Two policemen stood in the doorway; one of them had a pistol in his hand.

'Not much right now,' I said, making an effort to keep upright. 'This guy broke in here and we had a free-for-all. I'm Ed Dawson of the *Western Telegram*. Lieutenant Carlotti knows me.

At Carlotti's name, the policemen's faces brightened.

'Do you want to charge this man?'

'You bet I do. Get him out of here, will you? I'll have a clean up and then I'll come down to the station.'

One of the policemen bent over Carlo. He caught hold of his collar and dragged him upright.

I had already learned the danger of getting close to Carlo and I started to shout a warning.

Carlo came to life. His right fist shot out and connected with the policeman's jaw, sending him crashing into the other policeman.

Carlo came to his feet. He gave me a back-hand slap across the face that flattened me on the bed, then he dived out of the room.

The policeman with the gun in his hand recovered his balance, swung around, lifted his gun and fired.

I saw Carlo stagger, but he reached the front door as the policeman fired again.

Carlo dropped on hands and knees. He turned his head, his face a savage mask of pain and fury. Somehow, he hauled himself to his feet and took three tottering steps out on to the landing and stood swaying at the head of the stairs.

The policeman moved slowly towards him.

Carlo looked past him at me. His face twisted into a ghastly attempt at a grin, then his eyes rolled back and his knees buckled. He toppled backwards down the stairs, and landed on the floor below with a crash that shook the building.

IV

Forty minutes later, I was back in my apartment, fixing my bruises. I had dropped Gina off at her apartment and had telephoned Maxwell to hold everything until I had time to contact him again. The police had told me that Carlo was still alive, but there was no hope for him. They said he would die within an hour or so. They had rushed him to hospital.

I had just finished putting a strip of plaster over a cut above my eye when the front-door bell rang. It was Carlotti.

'Manchini is asking for you,' he said. 'He's going fast. I have a car outside. Will you come?'

I followed him down to where the police car was waiting. While we were driving to the hospital, Carlotti said, 'You seem to be having some excitement. Grandi telephoned me that it was you who put him on to Setti's hide-out.'

'I've had too much excitement.'

He gave me a thoughtful stare.

'After you have talked with Manchini, I want to have a talk with you.'

Here it comes, I thought, and told him that I was at his disposal. Nothing more was said until we reached the hospital. Then Carlotti said, 'I hope he's still alive. He was in a bad way when I left him.'

We were taken immediately to a private ward where Carlo lay, guarded by two detectives. He was still alive, and as we came into the room he opened his eyes and gave me a twisted grin.

'Hello, pally,' he said in hoarse whisper. 'I've been waiting for you.'

'What is it?' I asked, standing over him.

'Get those coppers out of here. I want to talk to you alone.'

'You talk in front of me or not at all,' Carlotti said.

Carlo looked at him.

'Don't be a sucker, copper. If you want to know how Helen Chalmers died, you'll get out of here and take these two flat-feet with you. I want to talk to my pal first. Then I'll have something for you.'

Carlotti hesitated, then shrugged.

'I'll give you five minutes,' he said and, beckoning to the two detectives, he went out. They followed him and closed the door.

Carlo looked at me.

'You've got guts, pally. I like the way you fight. I'm going to put you in the clear. I'm going to tell them it was me who killed Helen. They can't do anything to me now. I'm not going to last much longer. If I tell them I did it, will you do me a favour?'

'If I can.'

'Get rid of that film, pally.' A spasm of pain ran through him and he shut his eyes. Then, opening his eyes, he grinned savagely. 'I'm getting to be a sissy, aren't I?' he said. 'Will you give me your word you won't show that film to anyone? It's important to me, pally.'

'I don't think I can do that,' I said. 'The police must see it if it is anything to do with Helen's death.'

'I'm going to tell them I killed her. The case will be closed,' Carlo said. Every word made him sweat. 'Look at

189

the film yourself. You'll see what I mean after you've looked at it. It's not evidence. When you've seen it, destroy it. Will you do that?'

'Okay. If I'm satisfied that it isn't evidence, I'll destroy it.'

'You'll give me your word?'

'Yes, but I must be sure it isn't evidence.'

He managed to grin.

'Okay, shoot them in. I'll give them a confession—the full treatment.'

'So long, Carlo,' I said and gripped his hand.

'So long, pally. I was a sucker to involve you in this. I didn't think you had so much on the ball. Get them in here and hurry.'

I went out and told Carlotti Manchini wanted him. He and the two detectives went into the room and closed the door. I walked down the passage to the entrance hall. I waited there for Carlotti.

Twenty minutes later, he came into the hall.

'He's gone,' he said soberly. 'Suppose we go to your apartment? I want to talk to you.'

Well, at least, he wasn't taking me to the police station. We drove in silence to my apartment.

'You might like a drink?' I said as soon as we were in my lounge.

'I'll have a campari,' Carlotti said.

As I knew he never drank on duty, I felt easier in my mind. I fixed a campari and a whisky and soda for myself and we sat down.

'Well, now,' he said. 'Manchini has given me a signed confession that he killed la Signora Chalmers. I have reason to believe that you were also at the villa at the time of her death. You have been identified by two witnesses. I should like your explanation.'

I didn't hesitate. I gave him the whole story without holding a thing back. The only thing I didn't tell him was that June Chalmers had hired Sarti to watch Helen. I said I thought Sarti's client had been Chalmers himself.

Carlotti listened without interrupting me. When I had finally finished, he stared at me for a long moment before saying, 'I think you have behaved very foolishly, signor.'

It was such an anticlimax that I grinned at him.

'I guess I have, but if you had been in my place, I think

190

you would have done the same. As it is, I've lost my new job. All this is bound to come out at the inquest.'

Carlotti stroked his nose.

'Not necessarily,' he said. 'Manchini said that he was the man la signorina planned to spend a month with at the villa. I see no reason why I shouldn't accept that story. After all, you gave us the information about Setti and you have always been helpful in the past. I am satisfied that your story is true. I don't see why you should be penalized. Manchini said he caught la signorina taking a film of Setti's villa. Apparently, Setti was on the terrace. Manchini realized that this film could be used as a blackmail weapon against Setti. He got the camera from la signorina and ripped out the film. To teach her a lesson, so he said, he slapped her. She jumped back and fell over the cliff. This explanation will satisfy the coroner if I tell him we are satisfied. I don't think you should suffer for a woman of that kind. My advice to you is to say nothing that will involve yourself with il Signor Chalmers.'

'It's not as easy as that,' I said. 'Now Manchini is dead, there is nothing to stop Sarti trying to blackmail me again. He could tell Chalmers.'

Carlotti gave a wintry smile.

'You don't have to worry about Sarti. Manchini gave me enough evidence to put Sarti away for years. He has already been arrested.'

I suddenly realized that I was in the clear. I was out of the jam I thought was impossible ever to get out of.

'Thank you, Lieutenant,' I said. 'All right. I won't say anything to Chalmers. You won't be worried with me for much longer. If I have any luck I'll be going to New York.'

He got to his feet.

'You don't worry me, signor. There are times when it is good to be able to help one's friends.'

When he had gone I took from my pocket the carton of film and turned it over in my hand. What did it contain? I wondered. Why had Carlo been so anxious to make a deal with me? I stood thinking for a long moment. Then, remembering that Guiseppe Frenzi had a 16 mm. projector, I called him and asked him if he would give me the loan of it for an hour.

'It's all set up in my apartment, Ed,' he said. 'Go around there and help yourself. The janitor will let you in. I'm up to my eyes in work and can't get away until late or I'd come around and show you how it works.'

'I can manage it,' I said. 'Thanks, Guiseppe,' and I hung up.

A half an hour later, I was in Frenzi's apartment with Helen's film threaded into the projector. I turned off the lights and started the film.

She certainly knew how to take photographs. The scenes of Sorrento that flashed on the screen were first class. From the busy piazza, the scene changed to the villa, and then to the view from the cliff head. I was sitting forward, my heart thumping, watching the screen fixedly. Then suddenly there was a long shot of Setti's villa. I could just make out two men on the terrace. Then the scene switched to a close-up by Helen's powerful telephoto lens. There was Setti, easily recognizable, talking to Carlo, and, a moment later, Myra joined them. So Carlo had told Carlotti the truth. He must have spotted Helen up the cliff as she took this shot, come up after her, snatched the camera out of her hand and given her a back-hand slap that had sent her off the cliff. Then why had he been so anxious that I shouldn't show this film to anyone since he had already told Carlotti what had happened?

I got the answer in the next shot. From the terrace the scene changed once more to the cliff head. Carlo was standing with his back to the camera, looking out to sea. He suddenly turned and his dark, blunt-featured face lit up. The camera moved away from him to the direction where he was looking.

A girl was coming along the path. She waved to Carlo. He went to meet her and, putting his arms around her, he pulled her to him and kissed her.

The shot lasted about twenty seconds. I was standing up, staring at the screen, scarcely believing my eyes.

The girl in Carlo's arms was June Chalmers!

V

Sherwin Chalmers and his wife arrived at the Vesuvius hotel on the afternoon of the Friday before the inquest.

He and I had a two-hour session together. I told him the

story of Helen's past and her life in Rome. I let him read some of Sarti's reports, having taken the report concerning myself out of the file. I told him Carlo Manchini was the man known as Douglas Sherrard.

Chalmers listened and read the reports, a cigar between his teeth, his face expressionless. When I was through, he tossed Sarti's file on the table, got to his feet and walked over to the window.

'You've done a good job, Dawson,' he said. 'This has been a shock to me, as you can imagine. I had no idea I had a daughter who could behave like this. She got what was coming to her. The thing to do now is to try to keep it out of the papers.'

I knew how hopeless that was, but I didn't tell him so.

'I'll go along and talk to this coroner fella,' Chalmers went on. 'He can play it down. I'll also talk to the chief of police. Burn those reports. You've done your job here. Will you be ready to come to New York with me after the inquest?'

'I'll have a few things to tidy up first, Mr. Chalmers,' I said. 'I can be in New York by Monday week.'

'Do that.' He came away from the window. 'I'm pleased with you, Dawson. It's better for the punk to have died. I'm going to see this coroner fella now.'

I didn't offer to go with him. I went downstairs with him to where the Rolls was waiting and saw him drive off, then I crossed over to the reception desk and asked the clerk to send my name up to Mrs. Chalmers. He made the call and told me to go on up.

June Chalmers was sitting by the window, looking out over the harbour. She turned her head as I entered the small sitting-room and her eyes looked steadily at me.

'Mr. Chalmers has just told me he is pleased with me,' I said, closing the door and moving over to join her at the window. 'He wants me back in New York as quickly as possible to take the foreign desk.'

'My congratulations, Mr. Dawson,' she said. 'But why tell me?'

'Because I need your approval.'

She raised her eyebrows.

'Why should I approve?'

'For the obvious reason that, if you don't approve, you could prevent me taking the job.'

193

She looked away, opened her bag, took out a cigarette and before I could get out my lighter she had flicked her own alight.

'I don't understand, Mr. Dawson. I don't have anything to do with my husband's business affairs.'

'Since you know I am the man called Douglas Sherrard, I'm anxious to know if you intend to tell your husband.'

I saw her hands turn into fists.

'I mind my own business, Mr. Dawson. Helen meant nothing to me. I have no interest in her lovers.'

'I wasn't her lover. Does that mean you are not going to tell him?'

'Yes.'

I took the carton of film out of my pocket.

'You will want to destroy this.'

She turned quickly. Her face drained of colour.

'What do you mean? Why should I want to destroy it?'

'If you don't, then I will. Carlo asked me to get rid of it, but I thought it would be more satisfactory to you if you did it yourself.'

She drew in a deep breath.

'So the little devil did take another film.' She got to her feet and began to move around the room. 'Have you seen what is on it?'

'Yes. Carlo told me to look at it.'

She turned, her face the colour of old ivory, but she managed to smile.

'So we now know something about each other, Mr. Dawson. I'm not going to give you away. What are you going to do about me?'

I again offered her the film.

'You'll have trouble in destroying it. It doesn't burn easily. I'd cut it in pieces and flush it down a drain.'

She took the carton.

'Thank you. I'm very grateful to you.' She sat down. 'My husband tells me Carlo confessed to killing Helen.'

'That's right.'

'No one killed her. He only said that to keep the police from investigating further. I suppose you have guessed that we were lovers?' She looked at me. 'I want you to know about this. I believe I was the only person in the world that he treated decently. We knew each other in New York when I was a singer at the Palm Grove Club. I had known him

194

long before I met my husband. I know he was crude, brutal and dangerous, but he did have his decent side. He meant a lot to me. I was crazy about him. I wrote him stupid letters which he kept. You remember Menotti got rid of Setti? Carlo told me he would have to go back to Rome with Setti. I didn't think I would ever see him again. Sherwin Chalmers fell in love with me. I married him because I was sick of singing in a cheap night club and of always being short of money. I've regretted it ever since, but that's my affair, and it doesn't come into this.' She smiled bitterly. 'As they say, "the job's rotten, but the pay's good". I'm one of those weak, wretched people who can't be happy without a lot of money, so at the moment my husband is important to me.' She paused, then asked, 'I hope this doesn't make you feel sick? It does me often.'

I didn't say anything.

'You know Helen was Menotti's mistress,' she went on. 'Carlo found out she was on drugs. He told Setti that he could get at Menotti through Helen. Setti sent him back to New York. Foolishly, I couldn't keep away from him. Helen saw us together. When Carlo approached her to sell Menotti out, she agreed. She went to Carlo's apartment while she was negotiating her price. I don't know how she did it, but she got hold of four of my letters to him. We only found this out much later. For two thousand dollars she let Carlo into Menotti's apartment. I want you to believe that I didn't know anything about this until I met Carlo weeks later on the cliff head where Helen died. It was she who told me.'

'You don't have to go into all this, Mrs. Chalmers,' I said 'All I want to know is how Helen died.'

'It doesn't make sense without the dirty details,' she returned. 'Helen began to blackmail me. She told me she had four of my letters to Carlo, and if I didn't give her a hundred dollars a week, she would hand them to her father. I could afford a hundred dollars a week, so I paid up. I was sure Helen was leading a rotten life, and it occurred to me that if I could get something on her, I could force her to return the letters to me. When she went to Rome, I instructed an inquiry agency to watch her and report back to me. When I learned that she had taken a villa in the name of Mrs. Douglas Sherrard, and was going to live there with some man, I decided this was my chance. I planned to go there, confront her and threaten to tell her father if she didn't give me my letters. I told my husband I wanted to do some shopping in Paris. He loathes shopping and, besides, he was very busy. He said he would join me later. I went to Paris, then on to Sorrento. I went to the villa, but Helen wasn't there. While I waited for her, I took a walk along the cliff head and I ran into Carlo. Helen must have been up there too, out of sight, with her camera. She must have taken pictures of our meeting. Is that what this film contains?'

'There's a twenty seconds' shot of you two meeting,' I said. 'As this shot is on the last few feet of film, it's my guess she went back to the villa, put in a new film, dropped the completed film into the mail box that is outside the villa, then returned to the cliff head in the hope of getting more shots of you.'

'Yes, that is what must have happened. Carlo heard the motor of the camera running. He caught Helen. There was a dreadful scene. She told me that Carlo had shot Menotti. She threatened to tell the police. She said she had taken pictures of Setti on the terrace of the villa below, and he would have to pay for the film if he didn't want her to hand it to the police. She seemed half out of her mind, screaming and raving. Carlo slapped her face. He was trying to stop her screams. She dropped the camera. She turned and ran. It was horrible. She kept running until she went over the cliff. She didn't kill herself. She didn't see where she was going. She was half out her mind. Carlo didn't kill her. You must believe that.'

I ran my fingers through my hair.

'Yes, I believe it. Carlo took the film out of the camera but he didn't think to look in the mail box?'

'We didn't think of the mail box. When I got back to Naples I kept thinking about the possibility of her having more films of us elsewhere. When Carlo called me on the telephone later in the evening. I told him to go to the villa and destroy all the films he could find just in case she had taken others. I believe that was when you were there. He also went to her apartment. He found the four letters she had taken—the letters I had written to him—and he destroyed them. I want you to believe I had no idea he was trying to incriminate you, Mr. Dawson. I want you to believe that. He was always good to me, but I do know he had a rotten

196

streak in him. There was nothing I could do about that. It was my bad luck that I loved him.'

She stopped speaking and stared out of the window. There was a long pause.

'Thank you for telling me all this,' I said. 'I can understand the jam you were in. I know how you must have felt. She got me in a jam too.' I got to my feet. 'Get rid of that film. I don't know what will come out at the inquest. Your husband is trying to fix it. Knowing him, he'll probably succeed. As far as I'm concerned, you have nothing to worry about.'

Chalmers did fix it. The verdict was wilful murder against Toni Amando, known as Carlo Manchini, with insufficient evidence to show motive. The pressmen had been tipped off not to be too inquiring. Carlotti was bland and non-committal. The whole affair evaporated into a puff of illusive smoke.

I didn't see June Chalmers while she was in Naples. She and Chalmers left as soon as the inquest was over and I returned to Rome.

I went right away to the office. Gina was there on her own.

'It's over and I'm in the clear,' I told her. 'I fly to New York on Sunday.'

She struggled to smile.

'It's what you want, isn't it?' she said.

'It's what I want, providing I don't go alone,' I said. 'I want to take something of Rome with me.'

Her eyes began to sparkle.

'What sort of thing?' she asked.

'Something that is young and lovely and smart,' I said. 'Will you come with me?'

She jumped to her feet.

'Oh, yes, darling! Yes—yes—yes!'

She was in my arms and I was kissing her when Maxwell came in.

'Now I wonder why I never thought of doing that,' he said, sourly.

I waved him towards his office.

'Can't you see we're busy?' I said, and pulled Gina closer.

THE END

LAY HER AMONG THE LILIES BY JAMES HADLEY CHASE

It was odd that a healthy young heiress like Janet Crosby should die of heart failure. Odder still, that on the day she died she sent a note and $500 to Vic Malloy, private investigator, asking him to trace the person who was blackmailing her sister.

Intrigued by the note, Malloy tried to see Maureen Crosby but only got as far as her nurse – a curvaceous blonde with an engaging bedside manner. Next he tried to see Janet's personal maid, but found that somebody else had reached her first and made sure that she wouldn't talk to anyone – ever again . . .

552 09551 6   35p

I WOULD RATHER STAY POOR BY JAMES HADLEY CHASE

Like most bank managers, Dave Calvin had acquired an irresistible charm that he could switch on whenever he felt the necessity. Underneath it he was cold, calculating, brutal – a perfect murderer . . .

For years he waited – watching an endless stream of money pass through his hands – knowing that a risk was only worth taking if the reward was justified. And a three hundred thousand dollar payroll was justification enough – even for murder . . .

552 09491 9   35p

CALL FOR THE BARON BY JOHN CREASEY, writing as
Anthony Morton, creator of The Baron

A series of minor thefts at Vere House prompts Martin and
Diana Vere to call in their old friend John Mannering to
investigate. But while Mannering is doing so, the jewels and the
famous Deverall necklace belonging to Lady Usk, a guest of the
Vere's are stolen. Reluctantly, the police are brought in and
much to Mannering's disquiet, Scotland Yard send their top man,
Chief Inspector Bristow, one of the few who suspect Mannering
to be the Baron – the cleverest jewel thief in the country.

And Mannering realizes it is even more imperative that he
prove his innocence when he discovers someone has planted the
stolen Deverall necklace in his room . . .

552 09297 5   30p

DEATH IN HIGH PLACES BY JOHN CREASEY, writing as
Gordon Ashe

Capt. Patrick Dawlish is on manoeuvres in the wilds of Salisbury
downs when he receives a cryptic message from Colonel Cranton
to meet him next day in Salisbury. Once there, he finds his old
friends Tim Jeremy, Ted Beresford and his fiancee Felicity, have
also been summoned – but no-one knows why.

Then, just as Colonel Cranton arrives, his car is involved in a
strange accident that Dawlish realizes was deliberate and in
which the Colonel has been seriously injured. Leaping into
another car he sets off on a dangerous chase that is to lead him
through a maze of murder, espionage and blackmail before he is
able to crack the riddle of Colonel Cranton's message – and the
organization behind it all . . .

552 09384 X   30p

A SELECTED LIST OF CRIME STORIES FOR YOUR READING PLEASURE

All these books are available at your bookshop or newsagent: or can be ordered direct from the publisher. Just tick the titles you want and fill in the form below.

CORGI BOOKS, Cash Sales Department, P.O. Box 11, Falmouth, Cornwall.

Please send cheque or postal order, no currency, and allow 10p to cover the cost of postage and packing (plus 5p each for additional copies).

NAME..

ADDRESS ....

(SEPT 74) ....

While every effort is made to keep prices low, it is sometimes necessary to increase prices at short notice. CORGI Books reserve the right to show new retail prices on covers which may differ from those previously advertised in the text or elsewhere.